Most everything about this man threw her.

His very presence in the Grande Prairie courthouse had sent her, dry-mouthed and shaking, into the women's washroom to regain her composure. On top of the heartache of the past few days, he had walked in and proposed to take away the one good thing that had come from her brother's sudden, recent death.

He had applied for guardianship of her four-year-old niece, Sadie Garin. Technically, *their* niece. The judge at the courthouse had cleared both of their applications and turned it over to them to come up with a workable solution.

"Too bad we can't hear from Sadie what she'd like," Brock said. "I'd like to know her thoughts, and take them into consideration."

Sadie would choose Brock. He was typical cowboy handsome—tall and broad-shouldered, lean jaw. Not that Sadie would register his good looks, but she would pick up on Brock's way of hooking on to a person, as if you were the only one in the room, and making you feel as if you mattered above all else. Anyone who might feel alone or...unloved would blossom from just being around him.

In the end, though, she was better for Sadie. But how to convince him of that?

Dear Reader,

Welcome to the second book in my miniseries, A Ranch to Call Home. You might remember Brock Holloway from *A Family for the Rancher*. There, he was a freshly retired cowboy shy of little humans and confrontation.

But in this story, an unexpected death demands that he take care of his four-year-old niece and contend with her aunt, Natalia. Brock and Natalia grew on me and I really wanted them to work things out...every bit as much as their matchmaking niece!

Glory to the internet for its information on horse therapy from veteran professionals. Thanks also to the team of editors, copy editors, proofreaders and the incomparable art department that make this story and all my others as good as they can, given what I hand them.

And thank you, reader, for letting another one of my stories into your life again, or for the first time. Your support means so much. I love to hear from you. Reach me at mkstelmack.com. I'm also on FB and Twitter. You can also leave a review on GoodReads or BookBub.

Happy reading!

M. K.

HEARTWARMING

A Family for Thanksgiving

—

M. K. Stelmack

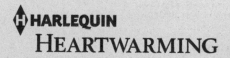

HARLEQUIN
HEARTWARMING

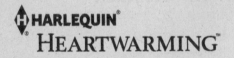

HARLEQUIN®
HEARTWARMING™

ISBN-13: 978-1-335-47553-4

Recycling programs
for this product may
not exist in your area.

A Family for Thanksgiving

For questions and comments about the quality of this book,
please contact us at CustomerService@Harlequin.com.

Harlequin Enterprises ULC
22 Adelaide St. West, 41st Floor
Toronto, Ontario M5H 4E3, Canada
www.Harlequin.com

Printed in U.S.A.

M. K. Stelmack writes historical and contemporary fiction. She is the author of A True North Hero series—the third book of which was made into a movie—The Montgomerys of Spirit Lake series and the A Ranch to Call Home series with Harlequin Heartwarming. She lives in Alberta, Canada, close to a town the fictional Spirit Lake of her stories is patterned after.

Books by M. K. Stelmack

Harlequin Heartwarming

A True North Hero

A Roof Over Their Heads
Building a Family
Coming Home to You

The Montgomerys of Spirit Lake

All They Want for Christmas
Her Rodeo Rancher
Their Together Promise

A Ranch to Call Home

A Family for the Rancher

Visit the Author Profile page
at Harlequin.com for more titles.

For Auntie Patti.
The Stelmacks will always
remember your Thanksgivings.

CHAPTER ONE

NATALIA GARIN GLARED at the watercolor, scarcely a foot square, that hung in the art gallery. The painting depicted a wide curve in the Peace River, the mighty artery that cut across Northern Alberta. Cliffs bound this section of the river, rising and then leveling off to the suggestion of meadows and pines beyond, unmarred by human presence.

"Pretty," Brock Holloway said, beside her, his voice echoing through the sloped gray-walled walkway where other paintings of the Peace Country were exhibited.

"That's because it's missing the flies, heat, cold, swampy smells and crazed bison."

"True. Painting would need to be bigger to get all that in."

Was he making a joke? Humor in conversation threw her like a stick in wheel spokes. But then, most everything about this man threw her. His very presence in the Grande Prairie courthouse had sent her, dry-mouthed and shaking, into the women's washroom to regain her composure. On top of the heartache of the past few days, he had walked in and proposed to take away the one good thing that remained from her brother's sudden, recent death.

He had applied for guardianship of her four-year-old niece, Sadie Garin. Technically, their niece. Sadie's mom and Brock were siblings, until Abby had died from childbirth complications. Natalia was sister to Sadie's dad, until Daniel's death eight days ago. Drowned in the frigid April waters of the same river that flowed wide and gentle in the painting before her. His body was found two days later caught up in shore debris. Local police had identified the body. She was spared that particular horror.

Natalia turned away from the canvas with its misty blues and greens and browns, and pretended interest in another painting of trees in autumnal shades. This one showed a sturdy log cabin amid dense, tall trees, not much different than the prison she'd grown up in. Daniel and Abby had taken it over after marrying, a wedding gift from the Garin parents who retreated farther north into the Yukon wilderness. A chamber of bad memories for her, as it had to be now for Sadie. She'd sat with her doll for hours, waiting for her father to return before calling for help on the ham radio.

These false images sickened Natalia, but the gallery provided a quiet space for her to hash it out with Brock. The judge had cleared both of their applications and turned it over to them to come up with a workable solution.

They'd left the courthouse and begun walking together because, Natalia supposed, together was what the judge had ordered. Half a block away she'd glanced over at the art gallery, and he'd asked if she'd wanted to go inside. It was starting to rain and she had no idea where else to go. So yes, she'd gone inside with Brock, and they'd drifted into the exhibit.

"Too bad we can't hear from Sadie what she'd like," Brock said. He'd stayed at the first painting, perhaps sensing her desire for space. "I'd like to know her thoughts, and take them into consideration."

It irked her, too, that the authorities hadn't allowed either of them to see their niece. Both her parents and Brock's parents south in Arizona had declined to travel, and had shown no interest in their grandchild. Her own parents had gone so far as to tell her that death was not to be mourned and Daniel's remains should be returned to the wild. He rested in an urn in her hotel room because she would not abandon him to bug-infested muskeg.

Brock and Natalia had asked separately and together to see Sadie, who currently resided with a foster family. But to avoid more turmoil in Sadie's life, the deal had been that they would first hammer out an arrangement. Dangling a carrot, the judge was.

Sadie would choose Brock. He was a typical handsome cowboy—tall, broad-shouldered and lean-jawed. Not that Sadie would register his good looks, but she would pick up on how Brock hooked onto a person, as if you were the only one in the room, as if you mattered above all else. Anyone who might feel alone or...unloved would blossom from just being around him.

In the end, though, she was better for Sadie. But how to convince him? She could sell candles and home décor like there was no tomorrow. If she had to sell herself, she'd gather dust before expiring on some discount table.

She touched the ammolite pendant on her necklace. "I'm not sure how much weight we could place on her thoughts right now. She's grieving."

Again, his warm gaze rested on her. "You are, too."

There, that…pull, reeling her into his orbit. She wrenched herself away to focus on a stylized map of the local area, part of the exhibition to show where each of the paintings came from. There was no marker even close to where Daniel and Sadie had lived, thirty miles east of Fort Vermilion, which itself was a hamlet of a few hundred. Most were clustered around Grande Prairie. The first time she'd come here when she was seventeen, Natalia had really believed it was a city. Until she'd rode the bus farther south to Edmonton. In the fourteen years since, she'd traveled on holiday to Singapore, London, Buenos Aires and dozens of other spots, including Amsterdam, when the Canadian embassy there contacted her about Daniel. Those were cities. This so-called city was a scraping out of streets and buildings from the surrounding wilderness.

"I'm fine," she lied. Her last visual contact with Daniel had been four months ago, at Christmas. She had sent Sadie a huge box of gifts she'd wrapped in rolls of thick glittery gold wrapping paper with intricate red bows, and Sadie had opened them over a video call from the Fort Vermilion library, where there was cell reception. They'd talked regularly since then over ham radio. The last time she heard Daniel's voice was when he extracted a promise from her to do a video call when she arrived back from Amsterdam. Among all the promises she had broken to him, this was the one she would've loved to have kept.

"Still," Brock said. Abby had been torn from him the day of Sadie's birth. He must have had the same aching hole inside she now had. Might still have it.

But mutual sympathy would not resolve their present dilemma. Best get on with it. She forced herself to look into his mesmerizing eyes and say her piece. "I don't doubt the sincerity of your intentions, but I think I'm a better fit to be Sadie's guardian. She wouldn't be alone. I work, but I have found a day care close by. There are other kids her age and programs, lots of stimulation."

"That in Calgary?"

"Yes. I manage a warehouse there. I also make sales calls."

"What do you sell?"

He didn't know? Then again, how would he know that his chance remark at their siblings' small wedding eight years ago had sent her career on a completely different trajectory? "I'm a partner in Home & Holidays. It's a home décor company. We sell into shops."

"Sounds as if it keeps you busy."

She detected censure. "No busier than your work. You still on the rodeo circuit?"

He shook his head. "I got out of that racket last fall while I still had all my body parts. I'm working full time at a ranch near Red Deer."

"Oh. Is that...stable?"

From the slight thinning of his lips, he had understood the bend of her question. "My position is secure. I know the owner well and we get along." He paused. "You?"

She had single-handedly pulled the business operating out of her landlady's triple-car garage into a going concern with twenty employees. A landlady and roommate who became her boss and was now her partner. "My company is secure, too."

The corner of his mouth flicked upward. "I guess we're even on that score. What hours do you work?"

"It's not a nine-to-five job," she said. "But the day care has flexible hours."

"After the kids go home, Sadie would be there, waiting for you?" Brock stood higher up the sloping walkway, making him rise above her even more than he normally would.

Natalia leaned against a railing to appear relaxed, though really it was for support. "They close at seven, so obviously it wouldn't be for too long."

"Seven. That's practically bedtime. Definitely past supper time."

He was right. "It wouldn't be every day. Once a week at the most. What about you? I imagine your hours aren't regular."

"I spoke to that in the report. I stay on the ranch. It comes with its own support system. Knut—the owner—already said he'd back me up. And his daughter, and her husband. They've got a boy. A one-year-old. And then in a pinch, there are families around. There'd always be someone around."

He had her there. She was pretty much on her own. She had Gina, but she had no experience with kids and probably wouldn't want to babysit during her precious free time. And she had no friends close enough to call upon for emergency childcare.

Natalia crossed her ankles to bolster her relaxed vibe. "I don't intend to raise Sadie apart from others." With its one and a half million residents, Calgary must have some kind of support for single caregivers. "Far from it. She'll be fully immersed."

"Immersed?" Brock walked down the tilted walkway toward her, slow and easy. She tensed.

"Given opportunities. Allowed to make friends. Go shopping. Use playgrounds. Go to the zoo, the science center. I will see to it she has everything she wants."

Brock leaned against the railing alongside her and stretched out his legs. Was he trying to project the same ease? No. Nothing rattled him. "What if she doesn't want that?"

Natalia blinked. "Not want what?"

"What if she doesn't want to live in the city? With all the people and noise? What if she wants a life closer to what she had here?"

"You have obviously not led the life she has or you would not even consider the idea."

"What are you saying?"

"Daniel's—Daniel was a great father, but there was nothing, nothing for her in that place."

"It might've been quiet, but then again she's only four—"

Natalia pushed off the railing and paced the flat portion of the walkway. "Four is old enough. You stay in the bush too long and you're stunted forever. Any ability to communicate with others, to laugh in the right spots, to make friends, to…anything." Her voice was quivering. She clutched the ammolite. Its deep rainbow colors complemented her every outfit, and her every mood. It never failed to calm her.

"The ranch isn't isolated," he said softly. "Sadie wouldn't be alone. If she didn't want to be."

And if he made a point of socializing Sadie, which she didn't trust him to do. Still, he had an available network and she needed time to build one of her own. "If she stayed with you," she said, "would she have her own room?"

"I already talked to Knut. We can live in his house, and there are three available bedrooms."

"And how far from the nearest town are you?"

"Quarter of an hour along graveled roads and pavement. Town's population is around ten thousand. Stores, schools, playgrounds."

"Would you take her there?"

"If she wants."

"Oh, she'll want. Trust me. And is there a chance for her to socialize? A kindergarten or a prekindergarten?"

"I imagine so. One of the moms up the

road takes her daughter into some classes. I could find out."

"I'll find out. And I'll pay for that."

Brock stiffened and blew out his breath. "Fair enough. Are you saying that I get her, then?"

Natalia had been grinding through her own mental calculations. "Three months. How about you have her for the first three months, until the end of July? I will take the next three months to the end of October, and then we can reach a decision about her permanent home. This way Sadie will see both kinds of life and we can feel assured that her wishes are rooted in knowledge."

Brock looked through the wide windows at the lazy spitting rain. Finally, he brought his gaze back to her. He had the darkest brown eyes she'd ever seen. She hated all shades of brown. It reminded her too much of the spring mud in the Peace River. But there was a quality to his brown. "That works."

Natalia found herself smiling, without even trying to. "Then let's go tell Sadie that she has a home now."

SADIE WAS A dead ringer for his sister. Brock had visited Daniel and her a couple of times, but seeing her now on the couch in the foster parents' living room, he was struck by how she seemed like a smaller replica of Abby. Same thin face, same watchful dark eyes, same boniness, same quick, birdlike hands. Only her hair was different, redder and curlier, like her father's. Like Natalia's. A reminder that as much as he might not like it, Sadie was not his alone.

The foster parents had a busy household. There were toys, backpacks, kicked-off shoes everywhere. A bike lay on the carpet with its front wheel missing. Some kind of long vine crept along the back of the couch above Sadie. Natalia, sitting next to her, had repeatedly eyed that plant, as if it might lunge and strangle their niece. Protective...or paranoid.

A social worker sat in a kitchen chair off to the side, pen over notepad, poised to record the slightest misstep. Brock kept forgetting her name, but he did recall how she'd said three times in five minutes that she was retiring in less than four months. In other words, she was counting the days and Sadie was just one more kid to deal with. Good thing he and Natalia had worked out an arrangement to get Sadie away. One that made him the caregiver of a small child he'd only met three

times before, and talked to for as many minutes on the phone. Three months under the
scrutiny of her suspicious aunt. Nothing in
his thirty-three years had prepared him for
this pressure.

"So, Sadie," Natalia said, her long, pale fingers coming to rest on the cushion above Sadie's head in such a way that the vine fell
down behind the couch, "what do you think
of our plan?"

If possible, Sadie hunched her shoulders
even more and darted a look upward to Natalia before staring down again, her knees
pressed together so hard they'd leave red
marks. She opened her mouth but clamped it
shut again. In awe of her aunt. Brock could
relate. The first and only other time he'd seen
her in person, at his sister's wedding, she'd
left him dry-mouthed, heart racing. Like he'd
slipped onto the back of a bronco.

He crouched down in front of Sadie, taking a page from his friend and neighbour Will
who did this when reasoning with his three-
year-old daughter.

Up close, Brock saw that maybe it wasn't
just his sister's looks that Sadie had inher-
ited, but the same fear that the entire world
was about to crush her. He had failed to res-

cue Abby from that fear. He wasn't about to fail her daughter, too. Even if it meant dealing with Sadie's intense, determined aunt.

He remembered a technique from when, as kids, he'd try to draw Abby, three years his junior, into conversation. "Do you want help saying something that's hard to get out?"

A sharp nod.

"Okay. Is it something you want to tell me or Auntie Lia or us both?"

"Both," she whispered.

"Both, then. Is it okay to tell us here or do you want to go someplace else?"

The social worker shifted, probably to state some policy, but Sadie whispered again. "Here's okay."

"Okay. Do you like it when you answer my questions? Or do you want to talk on your own now?"

Sadie pointed at him. "You ask me."

"I can do that. Is it about staying with me or Auntie Lia?"

A nod.

"That's good because it's important to both of us you say how you feel about our plan. We can always change it."

Sadie nodded again and then shook her

head. "I want to stay with you, but… I don't want to live with Auntie Lia."

He saw Natalia stiffen and take hold of the gemstone at her throat.

"That's honest. That's good. You want to tell us why?"

She pulled on her T-shirt until the hem stretched over her knees and said nothing. Natalia was biting her lip so hard that it had gone white around the dark pink skin. Her hand still over the gemstone, she said quietly, "Would it be easier to talk to Uncle Brock, if I left?"

Sadie swiveled to her aunt. "No! Don't leave me!" She gripped Natalia's sleeve. If she hadn't, Brock might have himself. Whatever their disagreements, he most definitely wanted Natalia to help Sadie and him hash this out.

Natalia relaxed in her seat. "Okay. I'll stay and listen."

Still holding on to her aunt, Sadie turned to Brock. "Auntie Lia lives in the city. And Dad said we can only go to the city together."

There it was. "You don't want to do anything your dad might not have liked."

Sadie's face cleared. "Yes."

"But he didn't say you couldn't go to the city?"

"No."

"Well, since your father has…is—Since your aunt and I are looking out for you now, you don't need to worry about disobeying your father. It's on your aunt and me to make sure we respect your dad's wishes. All right?"

Sadie nodded and then addressed her aunt's knee. "Is that all right with you?"

"It is."

Natalia's support emboldened him. "And Auntie Lia is welcome to visit us anytime. Okay?"

Sadie's grasp on Natalia turned into a full-on hug. "You can come stay with me and Uncle Brock, too."

Over Sadie's head, Natalia's eyes widened on Brock. "A visit," she said quickly, "is a short stay. One or two days."

Sadie sank back and her lower lip trembled. Brock and Natalia exchanged looks of mutual fright. She fussed with the stone on her necklace and then, in a single swift motion, removed it, the stone nestled in her hand. "This is the first time you've seen it for real, isn't it?"

"It's the most beautiful thing in the world,"

Sadie said with all the conviction of a four-year-old.

"I think so, too," Natalia said. "I don't know if I told you that ammolite is only found here in Alberta. Down south of Calgary. It's that rare. I think this piece has every possible color."

Sadie studied it. "Blue. Red. Orange. Wait, I see purple! It does have every color." She reached out a finger, then stopped.

"You can touch it," Natalia said. "It won't break or scratch."

Sadie stroked it softly, as if the stone were a kitten.

"Remember the story of how I got it?"

Sadie curled into Natalia and her arm banded around Sadie in a half hug. The tension in Natalia's posture eased, and Brock returned to his chair. *There, all good.*

Sadie drew a deep breath and, on the exhale, began. "You were shopping for a wedding gift for Mom and Dad, and you saw this necklace and you told Dad about it, and he called up the store and bought it over the phone for you and said that you had to come to the wedding in person to thank him for it. Only you came to the wedding but forgot to thank him. And every time you talked to him since then, you thanked him. I remember you thanking him. And Dad would always say, 'About time, Lia.'"

Natalia clipped the ammolite around Sadie's neck. "You keep it while you live with Uncle Brock. It's a little magical. When you feel stuck, it will help you find a way through. There are lots of pretty things like that where I live," Natalia said. "When you come to see me, I will show you them."

Lots of pretty things where Brock came from, too. Providing he kept Sadie safe and sound to show them to her. Hopefully some of that magic rubbed off on him, because he was pretty sure he'd need all the help he could get for the next three months.

CAROLYN'S COLLECTIBLES LOOKED like Black Friday after closing. Brass gargoyles peeked out from under throws, plaques were slotted together like books instead of their words of wisdom facing out, candles were jumbled into a bin, a stack of hats curved up from the floor like a wobbly palm tree. Natalia ached to right the retail chaos.

But she would focus on her job or, in this case, that of her salesperson who had begged off from dealing anymore with Carolyn presently slouched behind the store counter.

"If you would like help displaying our merchandise, I'm more than happy to help," Natalia said brightly.

Carolyn rolled her shoulders as if she had an itch square in the middle of her back. "I don't need help. I need time."

"The former often produces the latter," Natalia said as she gave into impulse and plucked Home & Holidays soaps out of a very not-H&H ashtray and re-homed them in a company glass bowl. The owner watched like a drugged sloth. This was not like Carolyn. She was normally an A-list client; her reorders came in like clockwork. The drop-off two months ago on the spreadsheets had alerted Natalia, but she'd never supposed Carolyn would let her shop fall into such disarray.

"We would like you to be able to show off the Home & Holidays line, and we could assist with that so you can concentrate on other…things." Like folding throws or hanging pictures or mopping the tacky floor or doing something about the smell of wet dog.

Limp, gray hair flopped over Carolyn's smudged glasses. "I can't focus. I'm worried to death, is the thing. It's my son and grand-sons."

Oh, no. She was going to tell Natalia a sad tale and expect kind words in return, a shoulder to cry on or something that would make her feel better and not as if life was hopeless. "I'm so sorry to hear that," Natalia said. "How about I just slip to the back, then, and bring out our merchandise?"

She didn't wait for an answer but scooted around the counter and dived into the dim cavern of the back room.

Her phone rang. Brock.

She held her breath. Since Sadie had taken up residence with Brock a month ago, she'd talked twice weekly to him, and he'd reassured her that everything was going well. Sadie, too, seemed happy enough and kept asking when Natalia could come up. She had put her off. Brock had never renewed the invitation, so she'd supposed that he'd only said it to pacify Sadie at the time. Besides, she was swamped with work.

For the first time, he was calling her. "Hello? What's the matter?"

There was a breathy pause on the other end and then came a voice strained and wavery. "Auntie Lia?"

"Sadie? Are you okay?"

"I'm okay."

Natalia sank onto an authentic cow stool. "Hey, sweet daisy-do. Good to hear from you." Natalia had read that kids liked pet names, and she and Sadie had spent ten whole minutes coming up with one. It was the most satisfying conversation Natalia had had in years.

"Good to hear from you, too," Sadie repeated back.

"What are you doing?" Natalia had learned the usual "How are you?" proved to be an astonishingly abstract question for Sadie. "Besides talking to me." She stuck to small talk, hoping the reason for the call would naturally tumble out.

"Nothing much. Sitting on my bed."

"Oh. How was school?" Natalia had enrolled Sadie in a morning prekindergarten program.

"I don't know. I didn't go."

"Why not?"

"Uncle Brock didn't take me. He said I didn't have to go if I didn't want to."

Natalia didn't think he had made much of an effort, either. Never mind that she had paid for those classes. "I see. What did you do instead of school?"

"I visited the kittens, and me and Pike went for a walk." Pike was the Australian shepherd and lab cross puppy Brock had bought her from a local rescue sanctuary. Apparently, Daniel had told Sadie that he'd get her a dog for her fifth birthday, and they'd settled on Pike for a name. Brock had seen fit to move up the timeline. Score one for him.

"Where did you walk?"

"I don't know," she said and added in a rush, "but it's okay. Uncle Brock found me."

Natalia breathed and then breathed again. "That's good. Could I speak to Uncle Brock?"

"No. He's not here."

"Could you call him?"

"No, he's gone off in the truck. The cows broke the fence again."

"You are there alone?"

"I have your necklace. And it's magical. It said to call you and tell you that I'm okay."

Natalia found she was shaking so much she could barely hold the phone. At least Sadie had someone to call. Not like her parents, who had regularly gone off into the bush with Daniel and left her alone all day. Once overnight when she was just eight. "Sadie. How would you like me to come up and visit you?"

Her voice brightened. "Okay. When?"

She could clear Calgary in two hours, be at the ranch in another two. "In time to tuck you into that bed you're sitting on."

CHAPTER TWO

NATALIA CREPT HER SUV to a stop at the end of the lane that her GPS identified as the co-ordinates for the Jansson ranch. Except it couldn't be. In a previous conversation, Brock had mentioned a long lane that split for the house and barn yard. Before her now was a much shorter lane that emptied out at a mod-ern bungalow and beyond that a huge steel shed big enough to play soccer in. A horse arena, she surmised, given the five horses grazing under the early May sun in a pasture by the lane.

She could call Brock, but she wanted the element of surprise, provided that Sadie kept her arrival a secret.

The house door opened and out came a mom, about Natalia's age, tipped sideways to hold the hand of a toddler in rubber boots. In her other hand she held an aluminum baking pan wrapped in foil. The mom spotted Na-talia's car and scooped her son into her free arm. As much to reassure the woman as to get directions, Natalia turned in and parked her SUV in front of the house.

The woman still held the boy, who also eyed Natalia warily.

Still in her skirt and blouse, Natalia fit the type of a sales solicitor. "Hello. I'm sorry to disturb you, but I am a little lost. I was wondering if you might know where Knut Jansson lives?"

The toddler reached over and patted the shiny foil, the crinkly noise adding a scratchy beat to the talk. "I do. You know him?"

"Yes, no, that is, it's not so much him I'm looking for but someone on his ranch. Brock Holloway."

"Okay, yeah, I know him, too." The mom said nothing more, clearly expecting Natalia to carry her end of the conversation.

"I was actually coming up to visit his niece, Sadie."

"Sadie! Sadie!" the boy said, squirming to get down.

The woman held on. "Yes, Sadie," she said to her boy. And to Natalia, "How do you know her?"

Natalia bristled at the nosy question, but refusing to answer wouldn't reassure the woman she was legit. "She's actually my niece, too. On her father's side. I am her father's sister." Her breath hitched. "Was."

The woman's face relaxed into a full smile. "Oh, you're Natalia. I'm Haley Pavlic. Knut's daughter."

Ah, part of the family support system Brock had invoked. Natalia's progress on establishing a network consisted of a phone call to a moms' group at the local community center. Her workload had been crushing.

"And this here armful of trouble is Jonah," Haley said.

He was too busy playing foil percussion to spare Natalia a glance. She tried, anyway. "Hello, Jonah."

Whap, whap. Haley jiggled her son's performing arm. "Jonah, say 'hi.' This is Sadie's auntie."

"Auntie," Jonah repeated. "Hi, Auntie."

Natalia's insides squelched. Haley laughed and Natalia took advantage of her good spirits.

"I know I'm close, but I can't seem to get my bearings." As if she ever had them in the first place.

"And Brock was no help?"

How to explain that she wanted to catch Brock red-handed mistreating their niece?

Natalia waved vaguely at her car. "He wasn't answering."

"That's funny. I just got off the phone with him. I'm bringing over Mateo's—my husband's—famous lasagna."

"How about I take it over? Save you the trip. If I know where to go…"

"Except I promised Jonah a truck ride to his grandpa's place, and if I break my promise, he'll break my eardrums. How about you follow me there?"

One more mile was all Natalia would have had to go to avoid that entire awkward conversation and the escort by a member of Brock's team to his place. Sadie's place.

The long lane opened up to a sprawling bungalow ranch house with a carport that extended across to smaller guest quarters. The exterior of the house was clad in blue siding, and a covered porch ran the length of the front. The attached quarters were also done in matching blue to create an aspect of spaciousness and connection. The place was much larger than the compact bungalow she shared with Gina. But her city home was a short walk to a recreation center and shopping.

Halcy led the way inside, calling out. Silence.

"They are—" Haley suddenly looked as if she had bit into moldy cheese. She set down Jonah and raced down the hallway. Retching rose from the bathroom. Jonah, free at last, sprinted through the kitchen to a back room. "Gapa!"

Natalia intercepted him at the back door and crouched to be at eye level. "How about we wait for Mommy?" She didn't know how long morning sickness—she recognized the signs from working with female staff—lasted, but she could watch over Jonah until his mom's stomach settled.

Jonah reached for the handle. "Gapa."

"All right, you want Gapa and I want Sadie, and the two might be in the same place." Natalia picked up Jonah and he lifted his knees to clamp around her sides and pressed against her. Like a cowboy swinging into a saddle. He'd clearly hopped a ride with others before.

"Haley?" Natalia said, heading down the hallway. She came to a closed door with a wood sign painted with daisies around the name "Sadie." She'd sent that up along with a table and two little chairs (an extra for a friend), a bed, a mattress, a dresser, all the bedroom fixings, even bright pictures. Curious, she opened the door.

A bed, neatly made with a lovely quilt. That was it. The table and chairs were still in the shipping box. No dresser. Nothing on the walls. What was going on?

"Yes?" Haley sounded as if she was hungover.

"I was thinking of taking Jonah for a walk to see Gapa. I mean, Knut, your father."

"Check the corrals. With the horses."

"Is there anything I can do for you?" *Please say "no."*

"Two months too late," Haley said. "If you could take Jonah to my dad, that's enough."

Outside again, Natalia made for the corrals, every stone and lump of dirt set to twist her ankles in her heeled pumps.

At the corral, two sorrels and two bays took note of her existence before returning to their horsey snuffling in troughs. There were no humans in sight, but the barn door stood open. Natalia directed her voice in that direction. "Hello?"

A tall man, gray hair showing beneath his ball cap, emerged from the barn. Jonah bounced in her arms. "Gapa!"

Jonah wriggled to get free and Natalia obliged. He made a beeline for Gapa, but not before a gangly puppy, knocked him flat. Jonah screamed in terrified excitement.

"Pike! Down." The puppy spun away from Jonah and made for Natalia. She braced herself, but it wasn't enough to stop the assault of licks and paws on her skirt. She'd never met a male so happy to see her. Except Daniel.

"Sit," Knut ordered. Pike dropped to his haunches but still looked up at Natalia, and she obliged by patting his head. From his new seat in Gapa's arms, Jonah pointed to Natalia. "Auntie."

"No—I'm Natalia Garin. Sadie's aunt."

"Pleased to meet you. I take it you figured out that I'm Knut." He stripped off a work glove and extended his hand.

Natalia took it, his grip warm and firm. "I was looking for Sadie. And Brock. But I ended up at your daughter's place first. She's in the house." She hoped Knut wouldn't ask for details.

Knut stuck to the first part of her explanation. "Brock and Sadie are out riding, I think. I haven't seen them in a while and his horse and gear are gone."

She'd known Brock would have Sadie on a horse and so she'd bought her a helmet and proper boots to wear around the heavy hooves.

But if the state of the bedroom was any indication, the riding gear might still be in a box somewhere.

"Brock has got a real knack with her," Knut said with almost fatherly pride. "He didn't mention you were coming."

"It was last minute," Natalia said.

Jonah pointed across the pasture. "Horse. Unca Brock. Sadie."

He was right. Brock had crested a small hill in the pasture and was coming toward them. Sadie sat in front. Without her helmet. For a cowboy who'd quit the circuit because of fear of injury, he didn't care about endangering his niece.

As the horse approached, Natalia spotted Sadie's sandals. Sandals while her uncle wore regular work boots. His eyes were guarded, watchful. He knew perfectly well that he was in the wrong.

"Auntie Lia! You did come." Sadie's genuine pleasure at seeing Natalia lit up her face, and for the second time in an hour, Natalia's insides experienced the same squelching as when Jonah called her "Auntie."

Sadie flipped up her leg to jump down, but Brock held her firm. "You know the rules," he said. Sadie lapsed back, and Knut came alongside with Jonah and with his other arm helped Sadie ease off the saddle. As soon as her feet touched ground, she ran to Natalia, but at the last moment she suddenly braked to a slow walk and touched the ammolite on her chest. "Can I still have it?"

"Of course."

Sadie ran the rest of the way into Natalia's arms. Between Jonah and Sadie, Natalia felt not quite loved, but, well, essential.

Brock flipped the reins over the railing, and the horse took the hint and stayed.

"This is a surprise," he said and gave Sadie a steady look. "Someone knows how to keep a secret."

"I didn't know for sure she was coming. Is it a secret if I don't know if it will happen?"

Brock answered her question with his own. "How did you know she might be coming?"

Sadie rubbed one sandaled foot over the other. "I called her."

Brock pulled his phone out from inside his jacket and thumbed through. He grimaced. "So you did."

"And I'm glad she did," Natalia said. "We talked about how things have been going for her, and I was anxious to see it all for myself."

Brock gave her the same tight smile he'd given the phone. "I bet you are."

And she bet he was scrambling to come up with answers.

KNUT SLID A cup of black coffee across the dining room table for Brock. "Does she know?"

Their evening coffee was a tradition dating back fifteen years when the Janssons had accepted Will's ask to give eighteen-year-old Brock a bed to crash on before they both headed off to a rodeo. Knut had offered him a coffee. Knut's wife, Miranda, had warned that not everyone had Knut's resilience to caffeine, but Brock had said that he didn't lose sleep over it. Knut had poured them each a cup and that became their routine whenever Brock had stayed over at the Jansson's. Now that he'd taken up residence in the adjoining quarters, it still remained a time for them to catch up and wind down, but not tonight with Natalia supervising Sadie's noisy bath.

Brock took a gulp of the scalding black coffee. "Not from me she doesn't. Sadie might've told her." Or not. Sadie's caginess and outright lies worried him. What else had Sadie kept from him?

He might never get the answer. She was one

big question in a little human form. Should he expect her to eat more than seven grapes and four crackers for lunch? Did wearing the same outfit five days in a row set a bad habit? Should he insist she brush her teeth every day if they were going to fall out, anyway? Knut wasn't much help. He couldn't remember what Miranda had done with Grace and Haley. Will and his wife, Krista, had provided some perspective, as well as Will's mother, Janet.

But none could advise him about how to deal with a little girl grieving for her father. Sadie would collapse wherever she was—porch step, grocery store aisle, on a horse—and cry loud and long. There was nothing he could do but pick her up and let her cry. He never knew what to say. Everything seemed a lie when the truth was that death left a hole that couldn't be filled.

At least, Knut and Sadie had bonded. The two played board games, trained Pike together, folded laundry, went for drives. Always coming up with one plan or another. As much as he appreciated Knut's interest, it made him feel even more inadequate.

Up the hallway drifted the suck of bathwater spiraling down the drain. The door clicked open. At his feet, Pike stood. "Stay." Last thing anyone needed was a pup underfoot.

"Into jammies," Natalia said. "Where are they?"

He stared into the dark abyss of his coffee.

"In Uncle Brock's bedroom. I sleep there."

There was the worst kind of pause. Knut was contemplating his coffee, too.

"But you have your own bed."

"Uncle Brock and I sleep in his bed. It's king-size."

"And your pajamas are there, too?"

"Because my bed is there, and bed and pajamas go together."

Brock could sense Natalia counting down slowly. "And where is his room?"

"Outside. Come. I'll show you."

They emerged into the dining area, Sadie pulling on her aunt's hand. Natalia's full lips had thinned to a pale pink line, and she shot him a scathing look as Sadie in her bathrobe led the way through the mudroom and out the side door to cross the carport to his quarters.

"You going with them?" Knut said.

Brock took another scalding swallow. "Sadie's got it under control."

"It's only temporary," Knut said. "You did what you had to do."

Natalia wouldn't see it that way. He rose and poured his coffee down the drain, the first time he'd wasted hot coffee. "Tell her I'm at the barn. I'll take Pike with me." There was a chance voices wouldn't carry to the house through thick walls and across a hundred yards.

He indicated the baby monitor on top of the fridge. "You'll keep an eye on things here?" Since Sadie slept in his quarters, separated from the house by the carport, he had set up monitors.

Knut nodded. "I'll switch it on after I tell Natalia where you're at."

BROCK SWITCHED ON an overhead light at the back of the barn and settled into one of two padded camping chairs, his feet on a saw-horse, Pike on a sack of straw. It was a quiet space to relax, but tonight he was strung tighter than barbed wire on a new fence. When Natalia entered through the barn side door, Pike scrambled to his feet, but at Brock's word, he stayed, though his tail wagged at full speed, ears and eyes fastened to Natalia.

Natalia wore a fluffy, pink coat that made her ginger-gold hair even brighter. She had switched out of her professional getup at some point and now wore leggings and white sneakers. They wouldn't stay white in this place. Not that she'd hang around long enough for that to happen.

Canuck Luck lowered her head invitingly as Natalia passed her stall. She paused and then pivoted to rub the mare's jowls. So…the city girl liked horses. Or at least knew how to make them feel special. When Natalia resumed her normal speed, pink filaments of her coat fluttering, he gestured to the empty camping chair. "Have a seat."

"No, thank you."

Pike couldn't contain himself and crossed over to her. She proceeded to rub and scratch the dog for so long he wondered if she'd forgotten his existence. Her next words proved otherwise. "She wasn't always scared of water."

"She's nervous of a puddle. Bath time is torture."

"I noticed. She didn't allow more than four inches of water and kept me right there."

"The whole time in a squat, right?"

Natalia nodded and the coil of tension eased inside Brock, only to snap tight again at her next question. "Why doesn't she have her own room?"

He launched into his carefully rehearsed

explanation. "We tried the house. I moved in from my quarters and took the room across from hers. Three nights in a row, she had nightmares about Daniel and drowning and being cold and alone. Each night worse than the last. No one was getting any sleep. The fourth night, I carried her from the house across the carport to my quarters so Knut could rest. Five minutes in my bed and she was out cold. She woke only once, and she fell right back asleep when she realized I was there. We all woke up feeling normal again. The next night, she headed straight to my bed, and that's the way it's been ever since. It's not ideal, but at least she's not crying all night for her dad."

Natalia's hand froze on Pike. "She misses him."

"It hasn't been much more than a month."

She dropped into the empty chair. "Thirty-seven days, actually." Pike pulled up close to her in search of more loving. Brock was about to order the pup back to his sack when Natalia reached out her hand, and Pike fitted his head underneath.

"If it's any help, thinking about him will get easier."

Natalia turned to him. Her light brown eyes

had taken on an amber hue. "When Abby... passed, Daniel always seemed lost...and stuck."

"Until she met him, Abby was lost." Because Brock had pushed her to become someone she couldn't be. "That's why Sadie sleeps beside me until she's ready not to."

"And are you waiting for her to be ready for school?"

"Pretty much. She doesn't want to go, and I'm not going to push her into something she doesn't want."

"It's quite possible to want something but not know how to go about getting it."

"She hasn't told me she even wants it."

"Maybe because she doesn't know what she's missing. Have you taken her to the psychologist I spoke to? Mara Flanagan?"

"I didn't need to. She lives down the road a few miles with her husband. He's got a canine rescue sanctuary. It's where I got Pike from. She met Sadie and didn't say a thing about her needing help."

Natalia slapped her thighs. "That's not how psychological help works. You take her to the office for an assessment. I told you I would pay for it."

Did he look that poor? "I've got the money." Or he'd find it. "Besides, there's a conflict of interest. She and Krista are sisters, and Krista's married to Will, my friend. I'm not having Sadie's feelings exposed like that."

"That's assuming she doesn't follow any professional conduct. I will call her and find out."

He could be as stubborn as her. "It won't change my mind. Sadie misses her dad, that's all. She's four. She doesn't need to put herself out there. It's my three months. It's my choice. You carry on with your life and let me do the same." A million doubts about raising Sadie, but of her right to be herself, Brock was dead certain.

Natalia crossed her legs, the toe of her shoe knocking the sawhorse, the vibrations coming through his feet. "You might be her guardian—for now, but I'm still her aunt. And it was me she called this afternoon. On your phone. Because you weren't there."

Of all the offenses she could pin on him, he hadn't foreseen this one. "What are you talking about? I've never left her alone. Even now Knut's in the house with the baby monitor in case she wakes up."

"Yes, she showed me. She also showed me the ham radio. Daniel's."

"She talks to Rudy before going to bed. A family friend, I guess."

"More like a lifeline. I used to talk to him for hours when I was a kid. Daniel mentioned that he still kept in touch, but I didn't know it was every day."

"That started since coming here, according to Rudy. Sadie said that Daniel taught her how to use it. I guess she's trying to keep connected to her old life." Natalia's slow nod suggested that, for once, he might be on the right track with Sadie.

She stroked Pike's ears. "You need to be properly licensed to operate the radio."

"I know, but I don't have the time to figure that out." He was too busy figuring out how to make ends meet. How to decipher Sadie's moods, eating habits, sleeping patterns. No way was he divulging his deficiencies to Natalia, though, with custody up for grabs. "And I don't care what the rules are if he gives her a bit of company."

Natalia bit her lip. Point scored? "You haven't answered my question."

"There's nothing to answer. She's never been on her own."

"She said she was alone in the house. That you had gone off because the cows had broken the fence."

Brock pulled out his phone and scrolled

to the time of the call. "The cattle did break through, but I called up Mateo and we handled it. I had Knut take Sadie up to the house. She had my phone in case she wanted to call, but mostly it's to play games. She must've called you then."

Natalia frowned. "I specifically asked her if she was alone, and she said that she had her magical necklace. Implying that she was."

"Well, she wasn't. Knut was there. Did you specifically ask her if Knut was there?"

She bit her lip again. Ah-hah. Two points for him.

Natalia fired another round. "She said that she had gone on a walk. Alone. And that you'd found her. Implying that she was lost."

None of this was making sense. "I have never lost her. She has never been lost. Closest we ever came to that was when she ran off over a bit of a rise in the pasture. She was out of sight, but I could hear her, and then she starts calling out for me all panicked. She was only lost in her mind, and that was for seconds."

"You're telling me that Sadie made all this up?"

"I'm telling you that it's not like how she made it out to you."

"But why would she lie?"

Brock could think of only one answer. It came from Sadie's excited wiggling in his arms when she'd seen Natalia at the corrals. From his own wash of pleasure when he crested the pasture hill. "Because," he said, "that's what it takes for you to come see her."

She flinched as if he'd snapped a whip over her head. Natalia had pointed out legit problems and he'd lashed out. An apology was on his lips when she said, "You never invited me."

"I did. That day up in Grande Prairie. A standing invitation."

Her hand on Pike's head stilled. "I didn't think you meant it."

What kind of person did she think he was? "I don't lie, especially to a little girl who's just lost her dad. Or, for that matter, to a woman who's just lost her brother."

She stood, the chair skidding back on the wooden floor. "I'm sorry. I was wrong. I'm sorry. I'll go." She nearly ran for the side door.

She left, exactly what he had not wanted.

Pike, who'd come to his feet the instant Natalia had, looked up at him, in silent plea for them to follow her. "No," Brock said. "We'll leave her be. I've stirred up enough trouble as it is."

NATALIA CHECKED INTO a hotel along Spirit Lake's waterfront, though it was wasted money as she lay awake, Brock's reproach growling in her brain. *Because that's what it takes for you to come see her.*

Daniel could have accused her of the same thing. When she left the bush at seventeen, she'd gone back only once to the family cabin to attend his wedding. She'd bolted off later that day, though Brock's wedding speech was really to blame. But she'd not gone back, not even after Abby's death, and despite Daniel's frequent, gentle invitations.

We could meet halfway, if you want.

Sadie's second birthday is next month. Her aunt would make a great gift.

How about we exchange Christmas presents in person this year?

She'd come up with any number of excuses. On a trip to Europe, slammed with work, icy roads. And once, on the very day they were supposed to meet halfway for a weekend in a mountain town, she called with the lamest one of all: she was sick.

She had been, in a way. The thought of heading into the sky-choking net of trees triggered instant claustrophobia, left her hyperventilating, dizzy, savage like a trapped animal.

She fingered the thin gold of her bracelet, her new talisman, now that she'd given her ammolite to Sadie. Daniel had sold firewood and saved to buy it for her fourteenth birthday. Her parents had said he'd wasted his money, but he seemed to understand that she craved pretty things. Jewelry and ceramics and flashy clothes proved that useless, beautiful objects still had value, even as he'd gone on to marry a woman whose only piece of jewelry was his wedding band. And when his wife had died, she had still been too selfish to give him what he wanted. Her company.

It had taken his death to bring her north again. Death and fear for Sadie was what it took for her to show up. She had failed Daniel. And now she stood to fail Sadie, too.

That had to change.

She dozed off, but by six thirty in the morning, she was walking along the waterfront, the rising sun useless against the chill breeze off the lake. She crossed to where shops and restaurants lined the streets, and her tension easing in the greater warmth.

She fell into her usual mental game of rearranging window displays. She rumpled the canvas drop cloth to create texture among the watercolors at the gallery, arched the mannequin arms at the casual wear store, tipped ever so slightly the display of cupcakes to catch the swirls of icing at the gourmet bakery. A check of approval to the sage-and-blue signage outside a spa: Because the Heart Wants What the Heart Wants. Simple yet stimulating.

Much like her own business motto: Love Makes a Home Out of Anywhere. Not her line but borrowed from Brock. Did he remember saying it at their siblings' wedding? She passed a restaurant, though tempted by the omelet special on the sandwich board.

A few shops down, she mentally enlarged the For Lease sign in the empty display window.

In her mind, she flung away the sign and dropped into the window space Home & Holidays décor—the rustic candelabra, the accent chair there, maybe a watercolor from the gallery to draw attention to the vintage wallpaper. Her imagination transformed the large display area into a cozy living room nook. There was nothing like this along the street, most definitely nothing that carried the Home & Holidays line.

Excitement bubbled inside Natalia. The last time she'd felt this rush was when Brock spoke of love and home to Daniel and Abby.

His words had sparked her resignation as a receptionist at a car dealership. She'd returned to the house in Calgary where she was renting a walk-out basement suite, headed straight to the garage where her landlady stood amid boxes of candles she'd dipped herself and a rocking chair she'd sanded down, and said she'd help make a living for them both if she'd let her stay a little longer rent-free.

And she had. Now, another opportunity, again spurred by Brock, had presented itself. Natalia logged into the real estate listing for the shop and read through the specifics on terms and permits. Tricky—cash flow might be tight—but doable.

Time to call her boss. Partner technically, though Natalia had always deferred to the woman who'd given her a home—and her trust—when she most needed it.

"Natalia, how are you?"

Most people used the greeting as a bridge to the real reason for the call. Gina asked because she meant it. "I am well," Natalia said, and given her rough night, she was surprised at the accuracy of her statement.

"And how's that little niece of yours?" Gina had shooed Natalia out the door when she'd asked for a day off, telling her that of course she could manage without her. Hadn't she just done that the previous month when Natalia had gone north and every time she traveled the world?

But then, she'd always assumed Natalia would return in a few weeks. This time would be different.

"That's what I was hoping to talk to you about. I was thinking that it's time we expand."

"Oh?"

"Into retail."

"Oh?"

Natalia always prepared her pitches; she discovered what a catastrophe it was when she didn't. But a little muddleheaded herself, Gina accepted that getting to the point might not always be a straight line. "Our big struggle with sales has always been placement. We're always competing for shelf space. So how about we eliminate the competition by opening our own store?"

"I'm listening."

Natalia peered through the dusty window of the empty store as she spun out her vision to Gina, who made encouraging noises on her end.

"Which part of Calgary were you thinking of opening in?"

Here was the part of the pitch Natalia could no longer avoid. "Actually, not Calgary. Here, where I am."

"Spirit Lake?"

"Yes, I was thinking of calling it Home & Holidays at the Lake. I think it would thrive here. The town's a year-round destination spot, with loads of tourist trade. It's got all the feels."

"Feels? Natalia, is that really you I'm talking to?"

"I know it's sudden, but I also think it's right. I haven't been inside yet, but I plan to recreate the interior of a pioneer cabin, like you might see at a historic site. Remember that huge woodstove I sourced and you nixed the distribution on? It would work perfectly here."

"I'm still not sure that—"

"I'll draw up a business plan and show you."

She spun off the details on the listing at the end of which Gina sighed. "Why don't you just say that you want to be close to your niece and leave it at that?"

Sometimes Gina wasn't so muddleheaded. "You're right. I want to be closer to her. I think she needs me."

"Her uncle not working out?"

"No, no, he's—" what could she say about Brock? "—he's well-intentioned. But he could do with help." Should she run her plan past him? No. If he really meant for her to be part of Sadie's life, this was the perfect setup. Nearby but not underfoot.

"You can manage her and a new shop?"

Each was a full-time job, especially after July when Sadie was officially hers. "Of course."

"Where will you stay in Spirit Lake?" Natalia still lived with Gina, though she'd renovated the en suite downstairs.

"I'm sure I can find a room somewhere. Or an apartment. I'm not worried."

"How long do you think it'll take to open up?"

Natalia thought on the fly. "The space advertises as move-in ready, and since we already have the stock, I could unofficially open in a couple of months. July, say. It'll be the height of the tourist season. And then I'll do the grand opening for Thanksgiving with our holiday stock." She might as well capitalize on that detestable holiday.

"But... Are you... Will you spend Thanksgiving with me as usual?"

Gina sounded wistful. Did she actually look forward to the holiday that they'd derided as a conspiracy among weight-loss companies? The holiday that expected her to be grateful even when it only called up old resentments? This year would be different. This year, she'd have Sadie to ease the sting of the past. "Of course, I'll be there. And then I'll be back to stay at the end of October, two weeks after Thanksgiving."

"You promise to come back?" Her voice held a note of pleading, like Sadie's when asking Natalia to come visit.

Stay in Spirit Lake? She looked across at the icy lake and the long, empty street. "I'll be back, Gina." An easy promise.

CHAPTER THREE

"AUNTIE LIA'S STAYING! She's making breakfast!" Sadie burst into Brock's quarters and jumped on the still unmade bed.

"Off," Brock said automatically from the adjoining bathroom, where he was shaving. Sadie bounced off and continued to jump up and down beside the bed. "Staying? How do you know this?"

"She's here and she said so herself. I'm going to eat."

Here, now? He'd got the water pumps on for the cattle and horses and done his usual round of chores to let Sadie sleep, and then come back to shave and shower. Natalia must've pulled in while he was in the shower.

She certainly looked as if she was moving in, from the way she bopped around the kitchen. Her bright hair was pulled back into a swinging ponytail, and she wore a red-and-yellow outfit that made everyone look as if they had on mud-colored clothes. From the corner of his eye, he caught Sadie staring at her aunt, as if she were a goddess. Even Pike at the entrance to the mudroom tracked Natalia.

"Sadie," he muttered across the table. "No staring."

Knut leaned close and said even more softly to Brock, "That goes for you, too."

He had not stared. Knut chuckled and took a bite from his half a grapefruit. In all the years and meals Brock had shared with Knut, a grapefruit had never passed his lips.

"Not bad," he said. There was a leaf off to the side.

Natalia set down a grapefruit in front of Brock, sectioned, with its own leaf. She smelled of citrus and herbs, and his stomach growled.

Her eyes went to Knut's plate. "It's mint. You can eat that. It's good for digestion. And your breath."

Knut dutifully ate it. Brock waited until Natalia had returned to the stove before he asked Sadie quietly, "You ate yours?"

"It's gone, isn't it?"

Brock gave her a long look. He didn't like how she'd played loose with the truth, even if her lies had brought Natalia here. He added a raised eyebrow to his death stare.

She tugged the leaf out from underneath her grapefruit. "Oh, here it is."

He gave her this small manipulation, especially since Natalia was bringing over omelettes, fluffy and lumpy. Sadie didn't like lumps of any kind and she definitely didn't like her vegetables cooked. He'd learned that the hard way when she'd gagged on green beans.

"Looks delicious," Knut said. They usually ate porridge and toast. On good days, neither was burnt.

Sadie pulled a face and Brock widened his eyes at her in warning. Too late, Natalia had intercepted it.

"What's wrong?"

"Nothing. Thank you very much," Brock said, and Sadie quickly picked up her fork. Brock sliced off a mouthful, which included yellow pepper.

Natalia still had a suspicious frown. "I didn't salt them. I didn't know what everyone's taste was. You might need to use salt. And pepper. To taste."

She was nervous, trying to be at home. For Sadie's sake. And for Sadie's sake, he'd make it easier for her. "It's delicious." No lie there. "Sadie tells me you're sticking around for a while longer."

Natalia turned her attention from Sadie's tiny forkful to him. "Yes, I am. I spoke with my partner this morning and we both agreed that I should open a store in Spirit Lake."

"A store?" Knut asked. "What kind of store?"

"Home décor," Natalia said. "We specialize in Alberta-made products. Candles, blankets, pottery, furniture, that sort of thing."

Sadie jumped off her seat. "Can I help? Can I?"

Brock could see that it was on Natalia's lips to decline the offer and then she smiled. "I'd love your help, Sadie. I could pick you up after school, and then you could come help in the afternoons."

Sadie's excitement at her aunt's first words had now completely faded away. Had Natalia not heard a word he said last night?

"I don't want to go," Sadie said quietly and looked at him in appeal.

"Then you don't have to," Brock said. "You can start when you're ready."

"Is it because you're scared?" Natalia said. Sadie nodded.

"I get that. I was much, much older than you when I went into a classroom. And I was shaking. I couldn't look anyone in the eye. I had so looked forward to going to school and then I didn't know what to do when I was there."

Natalia tucked Sadie's hair behind her ear. "I'm a little busy the next few days but how about I come with you next week?"

Sadie lit up as if handed a present. "Okay. Let's do this." She began wolfing down her omelette, lumps and all.

Natalia beamed at Brock in triumph. Well, she had found a solution that had never even occurred to him, probably because he hadn't tried to find one. Well, no argument from him. He could do with all the help he could get in the child-rearing department.

Natalia popped a spoonful of grapefruit into Sadie's open mouth, like a mama bird with her chick. No argument at all.

Sadie's eyes grew heavy after the third storybook, all Christmas books that Natalia had shipped up last year. "I like the colors," Sadie had said over the video call at the library.

"Me, too," Natalia had said.

Tonight, Natalia rubbed the picture with the suffused yellow and red lights on a Christmas tree, remembering. "I like the colors," she said, more to herself than Sadie.

"Me, too," Sadie said and ran her hands

over her twin French braids. "Oh, I forgot to tell Rudy about my hair."

He had listened to Sadie's prattling as if it were the latest headlines. Just as he had with her fifteen, twenty years ago. How old must he be now? Did he live alone or with family?

"But tomorrow you can tell him about how wavy it made your hair." Natalia leaned in and hugged her. "Good night, sweet daisy-do."

"Good night, Auntie Lia. See you tomorrow."

Except she wouldn't. Natalia planned to drive the two hours back to Calgary tonight to get a head start on loose ends. She wouldn't return until next week at the earliest. But to tell Sadie that now might upset her.

Sadie tapped her cheek.

Natalia sucked in her breath. Daniel had taught his daughter that move when she was a year old. He'd sent Natalia a video that she'd replayed countless times. He tapped his cheek and Sadie kissed him there, then clumsily patted her own cheek. And he gave her a loud squeaky kiss.

She kissed Sadie and then tapped her own cheek. Sadie gave her own noisy kiss in return and snuggled down.

Natalia stepped outside into the crushing quiet. No motors sounded, and instinctively she strained her ears for noise, any noise. Nothing. She scampered across the carport like a rabbit, and into the lit house. Brock sat alone at the dining table with a cup of coffee. Down the hall, she could hear rustling and thumps from the guest room.

"Knut's there, getting the room ready for you," Brock said.

"But I'm not staying. I'm going back to Calgary."

Brock looked out the kitchen window at the falling light. "Now?"

"I want to get an early start at the warehouse tomorrow. Put in orders, pack up a few things. I won't be back until next week."

Brock's mouth twisted. "We were all under a different impression."

"I'm sorry," she said. "I'll call Sadie tomorrow first thing, so she's not thrown for a loop."

"You didn't tell her?"

"I…I didn't want to upset her sleep."

Brock speared her with a hard stare. "That's awful close to lying."

"It's not lying. It's—" She was saved from further explanation by Knut coming up the hallway.

"I thought I heard you," he said. "The room's more or less ready. Sheets, blankets. Not fancy, but it'll do."

"She's not staying," Brock said.

"Not staying?" Knut echoed.

Why were they making her feel bad for not inconveniencing them? "I'm sorry for the misunderstanding."

"That's okay," Knut said. "I had to get the room ready anyway for when you move in."

Move in? She glanced at Brock, hoping he could clear up the matter, but he was staring into his coffee. "I'm not...living here," she said.

Knut edged toward the coffeepot. "I assumed...from what Brock was saying that..." He switched direction and headed to the mudroom. "You know, how about I check on...the horses. Yeah, that's right, the horses. Come on, Pike." Man and dog left out the back door.

"Coffee?" Brock indicated the pot. "It's fresh."

He spoke as if they were supposed to talk about this. "No, the caffeine will keep me up for hours."

"Isn't that what you're going to be, anyway?"

"Look, I appreciate the offer you and Knut are making, but I'm not staying here. It's not necessary, I can live on my own and I have since I was seventeen. I can pay my own way."

He looked down at the floor. "I didn't mean... I know... I know you can provide for her better than me. You've shown me that every package of the way."

"That wasn't ever my intention. I wanted to help out, that's all. For Sadie's sake."

"You say that, and then you ditch her."

"I'm not ditching her. I'm shifting my whole career, my entire home, to be closer to her. I'm risking everything for her sake."

"Then, what's the big deal about staying here?"

The big deal was the big space crushing her.

He pushed away from the table. "I'm sorry. Last thing I want to do is trap you into being somewhere or with someone you don't want to be with."

Strangely, his position saddened her. She might like him to trap her. That wouldn't happen, given her track record with relationships. She was here for Sadie and Sadie alone. "Why is it so important to you that I stay on the farm? What's the difference between me being here and fifteen minutes away?"

Brock locked his eyes on hers. "Because Sadie needs the both of us together. Right from the start, she didn't want to choose, and all I'm asking is that for a little while we don't ask her to. She doesn't need kindergarten or swim lessons. She took one look at the pool and suckered to my leg like a leech. Right now, she needs family and we're all she's got."

He was appealing to her emotions, and it was working. It also made sense. It would give her a bit of breathing space to find the perfect place for her and Sadie, while she was also trying to organize the opening of the store.

"All right," she said. "I'll stay here."

He grinned, and his eyes filled with his trademark bone-melting warmth. "I look forward to it."

"Me, too." What a stupid thing to say when she'd opposed it. She fumbled for her purse and gave him a little waggly finger wave. Stupid, again. "See you later." At the front door, she turned and walked back to the island where she'd left her car keys. "I'm going now."

"See you next week," he said softly.

She didn't look his way, in case she tripped and fell flat on her face.

"Bye," she said to the living room floor as she crossed it. This time, she made good on her escape, only to realize that she'd parked not in front, but around the side in the carport. She should've left through the mudroom door.

She stepped off the porch to take the long way around. No way was she going back inside within eyeshot of Brock.

BROCK STARED IN dismay at the walls of the guest bedroom. Sadie had opened Natalia's recent gift of a set of watercolors and applied flowers, rainbows, a house complete with figures that could be Knut, him, Natalia and something with four sticks. Either Pike or a knobby potato. Knut looked like a blue lollipop. Natalia had hair like a red tornado and a yellow circle around her arm. The gold bracelet. The figure he took to be himself had a huge grin and a too-small hat and feet like a clown.

"Oh, hi," Sadie said and turned back to brushing on pinkie-purple paint in wavy upward lines to join other waves of blues and yellows. Ribbons? Fireworks? "Auntie Lia said that we'd decorate when she came back, but I know she's busy with the store, so I'm helping out."

He had made the mistake of going horizontal on the couch and his body only knew that to be the posture of sleep. He didn't even remember closing his eyes.

Sadie could've wandered off. Instead, she'd made a royal mess. The walls could be washed off—and her brand-new shirt and matching capris from Natalia. And the floor. And the curtains, the window ledge, her hair.

"Auntie Lia meant painting a picture to hang on the wall, not to paint the wall itself."

Sadie shook her head. "No, Auntie Lia sent me a picture. Check your phone, I'll show you."

He dug it out of his back pocket. The thing had become a communication device for Sadie and Natalia that he just carried around. There were painted walls but no words since Sadie didn't know how to read. "We talked about doing a mural and she said she'd send pictures of ones she liked."

"For her room or yours?"

Sadie looked down at her feet, and Brock braced for an incoming lie. "Auntie Lia said she liked it, so if she wanted it for me, she'd want it for herself, right?"

"That's not the way it—"

Pike bowled his way past Brock, his tail brushing against Sadie's family portrait.

"Pike, no!" Sadie screamed and pushed him away. He backtracked onto the tray of paints and knocked over the jar of water. Brock grabbed for his collar. Pike probably knew this wouldn't end well and ducked away, Brock in pursuit. He caught up to the puppy at the back door and let him out.

Knut, coming along outside, frowned at the painted tracks Pike left on the carport pad. "Is that what I think it is?"

"It is. Sadie's taken it upon herself to redecorate the guest room with the watercolors Natalia gave her."

"Huh. That's…thoughtful."

The corner of Knut's mouth was slanted down in a clear effort not to laugh. Sadie could do no wrong in Knut's eyes. Brock swore the two conspired against him.

"I should leave it. Let Natalia see the consequence of giving unclear instructions."

"You could. She might also see that Sadie was left unattended to carry out those instructions."

And there'd be consequences for that. Brock turned to halt action on Sadie's project, but Knut added, "Sadie's got a point, in a way. It still looks a bit like a nursery from when Haley and Jonah lived here. Sadie probably saw those clouds and tree Haley stencilled on there and thought to add her bit. I suppose I could repaint it myself."

Knut had spruced up the white trim on the barn last fall. Paint everywhere, some even where it belonged. Fifteen years of living with Knut, Brock knew where this was going. "You want me to paint the room?"

"It might mean more coming from you. Might make her feel more welcome."

"I already told her I'd like her to stay for Sadie's sake."

Knut removed his cap, scratched his forehead. "That's not quite the truth, is it?"

Brock looked down at his feet. He wanted Natalia here, even if she called into question his every move with Sadie. No, because she did. She challenged him, but at least she assumed he had a plan and it was only its merits that were up for review. Equals, he realized. She treated him as if he brought as much to the table as her.

Which wasn't the case. It was Knut who had opened up his house, really. And it was Sadie who had brought her here and was now applying elbow grease to the project. If he really wanted Natalia to relax into her stay for however long it lasted, it was on him to make his own personal contribution.

During Brock's brief absence, Sadie had tried to repair Pike's contribution, but it had devolved into an abstract smear. Distress creased her face, like when she'd worried about choosing between Natalia and him that day on the foster parents' couch. "Uncle Brock, do you know how to fix this?"

"I might. Could I see the brush?"

Sadie handed it over, pink water dripping onto the area rug. He dropped the brush on the palette of colors and dried his fingers on his jeans. There'd likely be more paint on them before he was done.

He opened his phone and typed in *female bedrooms*. Walls—pale pink, pale yellow, pale purple and white—rolled along. He tilted the screen to Sadie. "See, that's more how women like Auntie Lia like their rooms."

"Auntie Lia likes gold. She told me."

Brock surveyed the green-brown tree with leaf stencils spreading out randomly amid uneven bluish clouds, the furniture that would have to be pulled away to give him access, the nail holes in the wall, the smudges to clean, the edges to tape, all that he'd have to do before he could apply a lick of paint. He thought of Natalia's face when she came home to her new room.

"C'mon, Sadie, let's go to town and make this happen."

CHAPTER FOUR

NATALIA CREPT TO a stop in the Jansson carport, the interrogative beam of the motion-detector light stinging her tired eyes. She had been prepared for the physical and administrative burden of the past five days as she juggled the lease paperwork for the Spirit Lake property, the reassignment of her workload and her personal packing. But the emotional reaction from the staff floored her. Her first hire broke into tears and another seized her in a neck-snapping hug. There had been moans and cries of disbelief, as if she'd abandoned them in a ditch. She'd not known that they cared so much.

And then there had been Gina. As she'd handed over Natalia's ice-cream maker, she'd confirmed their plans for Thanksgiving.

"Where else would I be?" Natalia had said.

"With your niece."

"And I will be. Here with you." It flitted through her mind that the custody arrangements excluded Brock from Thanksgiving. Well, if Sadie really wanted him at the table, she supposed he could travel to Calgary for the day.

No sooner had she killed the engine than Sadie burst from the house. "Auntie Lia! Auntie Lia!"

Natalia opened her door to her jumping niece and a barking Pike. Sadie launched herself into Natalia's arms and didn't let go, wrapping her legs around Natalia's waist as she stood. "Oof, you weigh a ton. Are you eating rocks?"

It was a line Natalia had overheard a co-worker say to her child, and it produced the same reaction with Sadie. Giggles. Behind her, the house door yawned open again.

"You're here," Brock said. He seemed to realize his obvious statement and gave her a small, diffident smile. He lifted his chin to the crammed load in her SUV. "Open it up and I'll bring in your things."

"I can—" But he was already moving to the back of the vehicle. Natalia pressed the release button. "I've marked which room the boxes go to."

"Why does that not surprise me?" he said as he lifted the hatch door. He sounded amused.

Sadie wiggled from Natalia's arms and tugged on her hand. "Come in. Let me show you what we did!"

She led Natalia down the hallway, Pike spinning around their feet. The smell of fresh paint hit her and then Sadie pushed open the door of the guest bedroom. "What do you think?"

Pale golden walls under the glow of low-lit bedside lamps. New bright white wooden blinds and sheer curtains in red-gold. It was the same bed, but now covered by a homestead-style quilt in brilliant sunset colors and an antique wooden trunk at the foot.

"Do you like it?" Sadie asked, jumping on the bed. "Uncle Brock picked the curtains because it matches our hair."

"Off the bed," Brock said at the door. He was holding her box of bedding.

Natalia drew in her breath, but it caught in her throat and she had to swallow before speaking. "You...did this?"

He exchanged a quiet look with Sadie. "With help."

"And I painted this." Sadie pointed to a picture in a wood frame on the wall. "Do you like it?"

Natalia could make out herself with red

squiggly hair in a green triangle of a dress and Sadie as a smaller version. Brock in a hat floating over his egg-shaped head stood on the other side. Sadie's arms were stretched to hold their hands. The standard picture of a family. There was a sun and a blue curvy line. A river. The Peace?

"Very pretty," Natalia said. It was the best she could say about an image that projected a togetherness that didn't exist and a body of water she detested.

"Is the paint smell too much?" Brock said. "We threw open the window all day, but you can stay in Sadie's room for a night or two."

He sounded so anxious to please. "No, I'm one of those weird people who finds the smell of paint kind of refreshing. But... I'm only here for less than two months and you went to all this work."

"Sadie wanted you to feel welcome. And I thought she had a point. That's it."

"But I didn't expect..." She gestured to the bed, the walls, the ceiling, the bedside lamp with the price tag still affixed. She recognized the tag from a national secondhand store.

Brock moved to the bedside lamp and peeled off the sticker. "Sorry."

"You shouldn't be," she said. "I always brag to Gina when I find an amazing bargain."

He slanted her a look. "Others might think I'm cheap."

She sat beside Sadie on the quilt and glided her hand over its warm textures. "You didn't cheap out here. This is gorgeous. A work of art."

"That's what I keep telling my daughter," Knut said from the doorway.

Natalia mentally adjusted her store display. "Does Haley sell them?"

Knut snorted. "She probably would sell them out from underneath her sister. It's my other daughter. Grace. She makes them for fun. She's a lawyer in Calgary."

"I'd love to have her work displayed in my store."

Knut rubbed a finger across the bridge of his nose. "Well now, I suppose you could try."

"Haley says her sister doesn't listen to anyone," Sadie explained, bouncing on the mattress, jiggling Natalia, too.

"Neither do you," Brock said. "Didn't I tell you to get off the bed?"

Natalia didn't care if Sadie tested the mattress springs, but neither did she want to undermine Brock's authority.

But how would that work long-term? Never mind, that was a can her exhausted brain was only too happy to kick down the road. "Come, Sadie, let's get you into pajamas."

That got her off the bed. Natalia took Sadie through her bedtime routine while Brock unloaded. By the time she tucked in Sadie and stepped onto the covered deck that ran the length of his bunk quarters, her vehicle was dark and still. A light bobbed in a corral and a horse whinnied. Brock with a horse. She'd overheard him tell Knut about a mare he would try in the corral. Whatever that meant.

She could hear him, not the words but the pitch, exactly as at the wedding—affirming, intimate. She envied the mare. Then again, it was her, not the mare, that had received a newly refurbished room. Complete with totally new bedding. Or so she thought until she checked the pillowcases. They were the exact same yellow as Brock's. Were they—the hem had the same fraying—they were. Brock had donated his own bedding.

Love makes a home out of anywhere. Of course, Brock hadn't given them out of love, unless it was for Sadie. Still, it was a thoughtful gesture from the man who had given her the Home & Holidays tagline.

It had happened at the wedding of Daniel and Abby. She'd arrived at the last possible moment, partly because of a tire blowout and partly because she planned to reduce the time spent in the company of her unforgiving parents and her childhood home to the absolute minimum. Her decision also meant less time with Daniel, but she would not exactly be his top priority that day.

But Daniel pressed her into a hug the second she arrived. "Happy you're here, Lia," he'd said into her hair.

Her cheek mushed against his boutonniere, she regretted not having come sooner. That hug proved to be the closest they would get the rest of the day. Her late appearance had held up the outdoor ceremony, and so it began immediately. Right after, it segued into a supper buffet hosted by her parents. She had dutifully offered her help but got a frosty brush-off.

That left her to make small talk with the twenty or so guests milling in and around the cabin. She cobbled together a little talk but gave that up all together when she'd made the blooper of asking Abby's parents how they knew the bride and groom. She'd hugged Abby because, well, they were sisters of a sort, but she'd gone rigid in her arms. "A case of stranger danger," Daniel had joked, but Natalia stayed away from her after that. Even worse than being socially awkward yourself was to be with someone exactly like you.

She'd not really noticed Brock until he stood to give the speech to the bride. She had focused on Daniel and Abby during the ceremony, and then apparently he'd slipped off to write the speech he now gave. Natalia couldn't remember the exact words, but the tenderness, the quiet wonder in his voice, the intimate warmth, had riveted her to him. Somewhere in his final words, he said, "Love makes a home out of anywhere."

She had given the cabin another look. Abby and Daniel had been renovating it in the past months. They'd knocked out a segregating wall, installed a large window and replaced the ancient appliances with shiny new ones. They had taken her childhood prison and made it a home because they loved each other.

Sitting there at the far end of the reception tables, Natalia hatched a plan that eight years later had transformed her own dingy residence in Calgary into a little house of wonders from the profits off an enterprise that created homes.

All because of Brock. She doubted she'd ever tell him how much he'd influenced her life, but she could repay him by helping to create the best possible home—best possible *temporary* home—for their niece, their common love.

From inside a small box tight with bubble wrapping, she withdrew Daniel's urn. She couldn't bear to leave it behind, and what place was more fitting than where his daughter lived? She set it up on her closet shelf. She might find a better spot later, but at least it was safe there.

"I'll take good care of her," she whispered. "I promise."

Starting tomorrow with the small, soulless room across the hall.

Tomorrow, after Sadie's first day of school.

THE DEAL WAS Sadie had to stay in the classroom until after snack time, which happened after a little more than an hour into the two-and-a-half-hour class. It was a plan concocted by Natalia and Sadie's teacher for all of June, at which point the school year ended. Sadie had insisted that Natalia wait outside the classroom. Precious time lost at the shop, but it would be worth the inconvenience for Sadie to acquire social skills.

The teacher emerged with a scowling Sadie a bare half hour into the class.

"Hello, Natalia," Ms. Whitby said in an extra bright voice. She had purple glasses and hair to match. "I thought we'd both come out to talk. I have a couple of minutes while my helpers are with our friends."

Sadie took the chair next to Natalia. "After, we can go. She said we could." Leave it to Sadie to strike a deal.

"We were just going over some of the rules," Ms. Whitby said. "How to sit next to our friends, how to take turns, how to listen to others, that sort of thing. Sadie struggled."

Natalia felt herself flush, as if it were her that had misbehaved, even though parenting books warned about not taking criticism of your child—your niece—personally. "Is that right, Sadie? Was it hard?"

Sadie nodded. "Yes. No one gave me my space and no one listened to me and no one knew the answers and I was bored."

A chip off the old Brock. "I see." She turned to Ms. Whitby. "I'll talk with Sadie, okay?"

"Sure. Give me a call, please. We might need to come up with a different plan."

"A different plan?"

"It's already late in the year. And with Sadie facing…facing adjustments…"

She was kicking Sadie out of school. "I'm sure that Sadie will do better next time. No one can argue that she isn't capable, right?"

"Very capable," Ms. Whitby rushed to say. "A great thinker, a great planner. When she wants something, she sees it through to the end."

The forced chirpiness implied it was not a compliment. What exactly had happened? Natalia took Sadie's hand and stood. "I'm sorry it didn't work out today, Ms. Whitby. We'll try again on Friday."

She didn't give Ms. Whitby a chance to decline. It wasn't as if Sadie had set fire to the place or punched a kid.

"Are we going to the store now?" Sadie said as they walked out into the wind and sunshine.

"First we need to pick up the key to the place," Natalia said.

Sadie's eyes widened. "Can I turn the key? Can I?"

Was that all it took to make her happy? Bright, shiny objects. That was all it had taken for Natalia. She glanced down at her bracelet. And someone who cared enough to give them to her. "Sure."

Natalia wanted to know what had happened in the classroom, but all she felt right now was the same frustration, fear and shame from her one public high school year where she was a social loser.

She would not make Sadie analyze herself, but would take on the burden and then help her.

With Brock.

He needed to know Sadie was struggling, how critical it was that she learn how to socialize for her happiness. And if that meant Natalia opened a vein to her own sorry past, so be it.

NATALIA FOUND BROCK that evening as he loped a horse around the corral. Beside her, Pike barked and the sorrel threw up her head and broke sideways.

"Easy," Brock said, "easy there. You got yourself a pup, that's all. You're good." He brought the horse to a stop on the far side of the corral. "She's not fond of dogs."

"Oh," Natalia said. "We'll go, then. I'll catch you later. I should get Sadie into bed." Knut and Sadie were inside playing checkers.

See, Ms. Whitby? Sadie's perfectly capable of taking turns.

"Hold on," Brock said. "You wanted to talk?" He nudged the mare a few steps forward, her ears pricked toward Pike sniffing the grass.

"I do, but not if it'll cause you to get bucked off."

"Whole point is to get Molly used to farm animals," Brock said. "And I'm not easy to buck off."

"Right, you've ridden horses for money."

"You know your way around horses, too." He spoke it like a fact.

"From traveling a bit. Just recreationally."

"Where?" He spoke as if he might recognize the places.

"Here, of course. Trail rides in the mountains. Australia. The States. England. Argentina, once."

"You like traveling." Another statement.

She opened her mouth to give the standard response about how new places had taught her so much about the world. "Traveling means you don't have to worry about never feeling at home."

He tipped back his baseball cap and studied her from across the corral. No, no, he must not ask what she meant by that. "Your horse. She scared of all farm animals?"

He took her cue. "More like she's not used to them. She was stable-raised, and when she moved to a farm, she couldn't handle anything smaller than a steer. The owner doesn't have the time to fix her, so that's what I'm doing."

Natalia sensed an opening. "You're…socializing her?"

He shifted in his saddle. "You could say that."

She rubbed Pike's head. "I thought we might work on our niece's socialization."

"I see."

"Did Sadie talk about her day at school?"

"It didn't come up."

Because school didn't interest either of them. "Her teacher said that Sadie was… pushy and rude and unkind. I told her I'd talk to Sadie."

Brock straightened. "Sounds as if that teacher is the one who needs talking to."

"She didn't say that, but that's what she meant."

"What exactly did she say?"

"She said Sadie didn't like sharing space

and wouldn't listen to others. Sadie admitted as much."

"Sounds to me like she wanted to be left alone."

That was what Brock wanted, but it wasn't good for Sadie. "She can't be alone. She can't. Let her be what she can be, or else she'll grow up alone and unloved and unhappy, wondering what she did wrong."

Her voice had risen an octave. She stopped, her heart pounding out her fears. She squatted to pet Pike and he put his forelegs on her thighs with enough force to plunk her on her bottom. He immediately crawled into her lap, his legs sticking out.

The clip of Molly's hooves drew up her gaze. Brock had halved the distance between them. Molly still had her large brown eyes on Pike, but with Natalia's hold on him, she looked more at peace.

"I don't think," Brock's voice came soft and steady, "we're talking about Sadie anymore. Am I right?"

She ached to escape, but the sooner he understood what happened to those isolated from others, herself as a case study, the sooner he'd be persuaded to work with her to help Sadie succeed at school.

"I grew up not talking to anyone but my family for months at a time. Nobody but Mom, Dad and my brother. Daniel was the only one who tolerated me for more than five minutes. Winter was the worst. The three of them were happy to sit around the fire and read or play Scrabble. Chop wood, cook up pots of stew. My lifeline was the computer for outreach school and the occasional internet when literally the stars aligned.

"There was this boy in high school. He and I became friends online. I unloaded how horrible it was, and he said that I could stay at his home four hours away in Grande Prairie. He had okayed it with his parents. All I had to do was get down there.

"I did the obvious thing. I asked for my parents' permission, but they said no, outright. I pestered them enough so that in November they agreed to take me for an outing to Fort Vermilion. I had a plan. A stupid plan only a desperate seventeen-year-old could dream up.

"Dad kept money locked up in the glove compartment. While we were in the grocery store, I told him that I'd forgotten my purse and could I have the keys? I...I took it all. Nearly five hundred bucks. I'd timed it with the bus down to Grande Prairie, bought a ticket and left. It was all done in a quarter of an hour."

Natalia looked up. Brock had rested his hands over the pommel. His eyes had gone all warm and soft, like at the wedding. No…that was only how she wanted him to look at her.

She ducked her head down again. "I got to Grande Prairie and called my friend from a payphone. His mom answered, and she knew nothing about me. She hung up on me." Natalia drew breath. A dial tone rang horribly in her ears to this day.

"I ended up at the police station. They contacted my parents over the ham radio, but they didn't want to have anything to do with me because I stole their money. Daniel persuaded them to find me a place to stay. A room in a boardinghouse. I was lucky Daniel was even there at the time because he was working stints at a Fort MacMurray oil camp.

"First day there, I'm more alone than when I left. I was no wiser than Sadie is now about how to make friends. And it didn't get better. I was rude or awkward or just plain weird. I inserted myself into circles of friends where I was shouldered out, I was 'bossy' in science projects, and on Friday when parties were arranged, no one ever invited me.

"Instead, I'd spend the weekend holed up in my room, critiquing my every move and every word and planning for a fresh start on Monday. By Friday, I was heading once more for my basement room, alone."

Natalia stopped, breathing as if she'd just sprinted a mile uphill. Years of therapy and still the past left her gasping. It was why she had contacted Mara Flanagan today, after the debacle at school. Mara had freely disclosed that not only was she a sister to Krista who was married to Brock's friend, Will, but also a sister to Bridget who co-owned the restaurant below Mara's office located just a few doors down from Natalia's shop. Natalia was sure that the family ties would all be too cozy for Brock, but then Mara presented the perfect option. Instead of Sadie, Natalia could come for her own grief counselling, and for guidance on how to be there for Sadie. Natalia booked sessions on the spot.

Brock dismounted and led Molly over to the fence. Pike and the horse perked their ears at each other, but Pike stayed soft under Natalia's hand. She waited for Brock to say something, but why should he? He gave therapy to horses, not dysfunctional women.

She came to her point. "I want a different outcome for Sadie. If we help her now when she's young, she doesn't have to turn out like me."

Brock rubbed Molly's neck. "Abby was like you were in school. A loner, not because she didn't know how to get along like you, but because she didn't like people much or only certain kinds. Sounds to me as if your parents were like my sister.

"But they should have seen you were different and given you a chance to be with others. We're all different. I get along well enough with people and I always wanted Abby to, as well. After she met Daniel, I didn't push it and came to see her solitary ways as almost a strength. I should've told her what I'm telling you now. There's nothing wrong with you. You are fine just the way you are. Don't convince yourself otherwise, Lia."

Lia. Sadie and Daniel called her that. A family pet name. Coming from Brock, it didn't feel intrusive. It felt…intimate. Not as intimate as laying open her past to him. She'd done it for the sake of their niece, but she couldn't deny it felt good to hear Brock Holloway say she was fine the way she was.

"I look fine, but I'm not, believe me."

He drew Molly a yard or so closer to Pike, who seemed content to lounge in Natalia's lap. She waited for him to say something but realized that it wasn't in his nature to persuade her to his way of thinking, even though she sort of wished he would.

"I think Sadie was scamming you."

She blinked, her mind trying to catch up to his words. "Scamming me?"

Brock braced a foot on the railing, Molly's reins loose in his hands. "I think she knows exactly how to be with people, but she just prefers being with you. And that's my fault."

Natalia waited him out.

"I might've told her that if she didn't behave, they'd kick her out. And she took me at my word."

He was accusing Sadie again of deception. "She intentionally did this?"

"I don't think she set out to do it, but if the teacher warned her that she might have to leave, then maybe she saw an opportunity. She didn't actually push or hit another kid, did she?"

"I don't think so."

"Well, then. You're right. She's bright…and stubborn. She doesn't mind doing whatever's necessary to get her way."

"So what should we do?"

"Tell her that if she pulls the same trick again, she can't go to the shop with you."

"I don't know if that's much of an incentive."

"It will work. She'll be chumming around with the kids fine on Friday."

"That fast?"

"She's a charmer. Before school's out, for sure."

"And if she's not?"

He swung back into Molly's saddle and gazed down at her. His eyes were warm and soft, and a small smile played at his mouth. Like how a man might look before asking a woman out on a date. Or maybe to go riding together. "Then we'll talk again. All right?"

In a wild flash, Natalia hoped Sadie would be an unholy terror. "All right. Let's hope for the best."

MIDNIGHT, AND PIKE licked Brock's face. Beside him, Sadie slept on, arms splayed. Since Natalia had moved in, she'd not woken once during the night. Brock dragged on his jeans and opened the door. Pike shot out and did his business, but instead of coming back, he trotted in the direction of the main house door.

Brock leaned over the side railing of his bunkhouse to call him back but saw Pike's reasoning. A light was on in the room meant for Sadie, and through the window he spotted Natalia on a ladder. He recalled chatter between her and Sadie at supper about decorating. But at this hour?

He switched his bed T-shirt for a regular one and wiggled into his running shoes. He switched on the baby monitor on Sadie's bedside table, and then with Pike tight on his heels, Brock opened the back door of the house using the key under his mat. That summed up the high-level security system at the Jansson ranch. His key under the main house mat, and the main house key under his. He needed to upgrade, if Sadie stayed on past October.

Inside, he activated the monitor on top of the fridge and followed Knut's snoring rolling up the hallway from the master bedroom like a jet on takeoff. Brock drew even with the closed door of Sadie's room, and knocked before opening the door.

Natalia yelped, teetered on her ladder and

fell, landing softly on Sadie's bed, a plastic cover crinkling underneath her. Brock jumped to her side, Pike already there with licks, but Natalia easily sat up.

"What are you doing here?" she whispered.

He cast his eyes about the wallpaper, the shelves, the drop cloths. "I was curious."

She brought a finger to her lips. "You're going to wake Knut."

"The only thing that wakes Knut is daylight," Brock said in an ordinary voice. "Partial deafness has its benefits. Does he know what you're up to?"

"I asked him if I could do some renovations and he agreed. I don't think he quite knows the extent of them. I'm trying to keep it a secret from Sadie."

"Why?"

"I thought she might like the surprise. And…and I thought that maybe if she liked what she saw, she'd want to sleep here."

"Are you saying my place is too ugly to sleep in?" It had taken him three years to string a curtain across his two windows and he still didn't have enough hangers for his shirts.

"Not ugly, the quilt is gorgeous, for instance. But maybe…empty."

"This is a lot of work to fix up her room. Especially if she's only here for another couple of months. Unless you plan—"

"I'm planning nothing like that. I'll keep to our arrangement. She stays with you until the end of July, and then me to the end of October. But whichever way this goes, Sadie is your niece, too, and will spend time here. Why not give her a beautiful room she can choose to move into when she's ready?"

She was still whispering, and her lowered voice added more spit to her words, as if they were sharing a secret. And in a way, they were. He hadn't just walked into Sadie's room but into Natalia's acceptance of his right to care for their niece, when he doubted it himself.

"And…" She hesitated. "I'm doing it for you, too. To thank you for—" she waved across the hallway "—for making me feel at home when there was no reason."

"There was reason," he said quickly. "Sadie wanted you to feel at home, and I… I wasn't opposed to that." That barely scratched the surface of his feelings. He hadn't found the words earlier that evening, either, when she said she was damaged. No words, but he had two hands. "What can I do to help?"

She held up the electrical drill. "Let's test your theory about Knut's snoring."

He and Natalia spent two long nights in the room, leaving him to stagger sleep-deprived through his days. Then she said that the rest was just tidying and sorting, and she could take it from there. He backed off, not without regret. It was nice to work alongside someone who didn't smell like a barn and, from what he dared risk from the corner of his eye, who looked like a million bucks even in paint-streaked clothes.

Three days later at Sadie's bedtime, he realized what Natalia meant by tidying and sorting.

He and Knut were having their evening coffee on the front deck when Sadie yelled his name from inside. "Uncle Brock!" She cycled his name over and over.

"You'd think the place was on fire," Knut grumbled.

Sadie burst—the girl always burst—onto the deck. "We finally get to see my new room."

Knut set his cup on the railing. "About time."

Natalia stood at Sadie's door as the three came down the hallway. Her hair was swept up into a messy ponytail and she wore an old saggy shirt with pajama bottoms made up of tumbling cats. This was Lia at home, the one the world didn't get to see, and Brock felt honored.

"Welcome," she said with a flourish, "to the grand opening of Sadie's room." She clicked open the door and waved them in.

Sadie led the way. "Oh, oh, oh!"

Brock and Knut popped their heads inside. Even after all his help, Brock barely recognized the room.

The bed frame was a new bright white and seemed three mattresses higher, and with a pile of pillows but with the same rainbow-y quilt from Grace. There were wooden shelves with odds and ends that Sadie was already exploring, an enormous beanbag chair and a basket of books nearby, and in the opposite corner was a small table with matching chairs. The closet contained a white organizer with spare hangers. The curtains, made somehow from the same material as the quilt, were trimmed with a string of small lights.

"This is mine?" Sadie said. "This is all mine?"

"Yes," said Brock and Natalia together. Their eyes met, and she blushed, and he suddenly wanted to take her hand and go on a long walk with her, alone.

"How about I read you books on the new chair?" Natalia said, lowering into the bean-bag chair that rustled like dry cornstalks.

Sadie hopped from the bed to Natalia's side.

They looked so good together he itched to take a picture, but that seemed kind of presumptuous, as if he had a right to record Natalia's relationship with Sadie. He straightened up from where he was leaning on the door frame. "Books, then out to sleep."

Sadie frowned. "But I have my own bed now."

Brock looked to Natalia again, both of them biting back smiles of triumph. "I suppose you're right. But what if you wake in the middle of the night?"

"Auntie Lia's right across the hallway. I'll go there." She twisted to look up at her aunt. "Can I?"

Natalia gave an indifferent shrug, though Brock knew she must feel near to busting, too. He heaved a reluctant sigh. "All right, then. If that's what you want."

Sadie cuddled tighter against her auntie in reply. With their twin heads of bright hair, they looked like mother and daughter, as if they belonged together.

Together, but here with him. Which wouldn't happen. Natalia was doing time on the ranch until she got her store up and running and could escape back to the city. His place in her future was only as Sadie's uncle.

CHAPTER FIVE

BOTH LEANING ON the corral railing, Brock and Knut watched the horse trailer ease down the long lane before swinging onto the graveled road. A long denim-covered arm stretched through the open window and waved. The two men both raised theirs.

Molly's owner was a grateful client. A very grateful client. Knut pulled a wad of fifties and hundreds from his pocket and held it out to Brock. "Here's your cut."

"I was there when he paid. That's not a cut. That's the whole thing."

"You did the work, you get the money."

Natalia had done her bit, too. The break-through with Molly two weeks ago had come with her and Pike playing together outside the pen. Molly had finally understood that a dog wasn't to be feared. Though maybe Molly was more taken with the way Natalia's hair shone or how light she was on her feet or the wideness of her smile.

Brock couldn't stop staring at the stack. "What about Mateo? He brought the client to us."

"He agrees with me. You've brought him work, too."

That was true. Years on the rodeo circuit had put Brock in contact with a network of horse owners that trickled in clients for Mateo's business in training cutting horses.

Knut shook the money at Brock. "Here, take it. I'm not putting it back in my pocket."

Brock took it, and Knut said, "You got a talent for problem horses. You could get a good sideline going with that. Maybe even full-time work."

Brock had already thought of that, especially now that Sadie was in the picture. The courts had accepted his income, but it had come with a lot of questions. The judge hadn't liked that the accommodations for Sadie were at the good graces of his boss. Natalia would've scored much higher in that category. He'd overheard her talking to Sadie about buying a house in town. She'd come a long way from that high school girl, alone with five hundred bucks to her name in a strange town. Though she didn't seem to believe it.

"I rely on you for the stables."

"I don't see how that's a problem. Plenty of space, now that Haley and Mateo have horses over at their place."

Another example of Knut's generosity. Haley kidded that her dad saw Brock as the son he never had. Knut had never said anything one way or another. What could be said when Brock already had a real father? A father he hadn't seen in years, and both not minding at all. His dad had spent more time away than at home as a military engineer, and his mom had worked at whatever base they ended up at. It had mostly just been Abby and him raising each other. He had gathered friends and their families as a way to replace his own disinterested parents. After meeting Knut and his wife, Brock no longer sought those connections. The Janssons and this ranch gave him all the sense of belonging he needed.

"Thanks, Knut. You let me know if you change your mind on that."

"You need the money more than I do."

That stung. "Is it that obvious I can barely keep myself in oats, much less take care of a kid?"

"You're not the only one taking care of her."

He meant Natalia, who right now was inside giving Sadie a bath. That had become their routine since Natalia had moved in. Bath—one that Sadie actually sat in now—bed, books and Sadie was out like a light.

"She isn't going to be around forever."

"But isn't that your plan? To make it forever?"

Brock stared at Knut, who gave him a blue-sky stare right back. "What? You mean, me and Lia?" Just like that, her shortened name, the name only her family used, slipped out.

"You're the one who wanted her to move in."

"For Sadie's sake. And into your house. You're making it sound like something it isn't."

"You're not interested in her, then?"

Brock glanced up at the house, halfway expecting her to be listening in. "I recognize she's single and pretty and she loves Sadie. I mean… I guess you could say that I'm interested that way."

"That way," Knut repeated, his tone both thoughtful and questioning.

Lia fixing her most precious possession around Sadie's neck. Lia playing with Pike. Lia looking up into his eyes and then away, flushing.

Her in a pretty gold-and-green dress, her arms bare, her gaze intent on the wedding ceremony of her brother and his sister. Off to the side, he had stolen one look after another at her, his own sister in a long, white dress coming in a pale second. Lia had been so wrapped up in the moment, as if she were caught up in a high drama. At the point where Daniel and Abby were declared joined, she'd brought her ammolite to her lips. Now that he understood she saw the stone as a kind of charm, it was as if she'd given her own kind of silent blessing to their siblings.

He had hoped to visit with her after the ceremony, but he had a speech to come up with, and then after the meal, he saw her hug Daniel and Abby, and then vanish. Back to Calgary. He never saw her again until the courthouse in Grande Prairie. Now they were a daily occurrence to each other, and he still stole looks her way, still in awe of how much she changed things simply by believing in them.

"Yeah," he answered Knut. "That way."

A FEW DAYS LATER, Brock came around the side of the house to find Sadie on her knees planting marigolds. Pike was digging the holes with Knut's help. Lia had said that they were the perfect flowers for the garden, and, of course, if Auntie Lia said it, Sadie took it as the gospel truth.

Brock had agreed to take Sadie into Natalia's shop, but it seemed that they hadn't finished yet.

"When will the wedding be?" Sadie said to Knut, nearly shouting. Sadie near-shouted everything anyway, and with Knut's hearing sometimes on the fritz, her voice drifted easily across to Brock.

"I guess there are a whole lot of steps before we'll see your aunt and uncle come down the aisle together."

Brock braked so hard he could have left skid marks in the grass. He stepped into the shade of the house, visible to the conspirators only if they looked his way.

"What steps?" Sadie poured water and some actually got on the plant.

"Well, I don't think they've even gone on a date."

"What's a date?"

Knut pushed the short shovel blade into the ground. "A date is when two people go out to places together and have fun and get to know each other. Like out to eat or dance or out to a movie."

"We have movies!" Sadie said.

"Yeah, well, the idea is that they do it alone without us around."

"We don't have to be around."

"The problem is more getting them to want to do it."

"We could ask them," Sadie said.

"I don't think that'll work," Knut said. "They have to come up with the idea on their own."

"Rudy said the same thing."

Knut started another hole. "If you got agreement between two old men, it must be a good thing."

"But think if they did get together," Sadie said as she patted a marigold in place. "I'd have both a mom and dad like other kids."

Brock shook his head, but thankfully Knut was there to say it for him. "Well now, Sadie," he said gently, "they'd still be your aunt and uncle."

"I know," Sadie said, "but they'd be married, taking care of me, like a mom and a dad. I've never had that."

Her voice was so wistful, so hopeful. Like Abby's, when he'd cautioned her about how remote she and Daniel would be from everyone, and she'd said, "I don't care. We'll be together."

He and Natalia were as close as they could be without actually being…close. But if he let it happen, Sadie and Knut would push them both into the arena. "Hey, Sadie." He advanced quickly as if he'd been on the move for a while now. "You ready to go see Auntie Lia?"

She looked at herself. "I don't think Auntie Lia would approve."

But she did of the quick clean-up from the smile she gave Sadie when they entered the shop. Brock had discovered that Natalia noticed everything, and would reach across and adjust a hair tie or smooth a ruffle in a shirt, or adjust the necklace, her fingers lingering for a moment or two. Sadie submitted like a cat being petted. Brock thought he might do the same thing, if she were to straighten his collar.

To avoid looking at Natalia, he took in the space. Shelving units stood askew, boxes piled high created tunnels to walk through, paint drop cloths crowded the floor.

Sadie echoed Brock's own thoughts when

she asked, "How can I help?" All polite, as if she'd never been rooting in the dirt an hour ago.

"Are you ready to count these?" Natalia pointed to a box of candles. "I think I've been shortshipped, so we need to take stock."

"But there are hundreds and I can only count to twenty-nine."

"That's fine. I need you to make rows of twenty. Like this." Natalia knelt on the floor beside Sadie, and together they made a row of the different colored candles. "And now you make a new line, right below them. Okay?"

"Okay, Auntie."

Natalia smoothed Sadie's ponytail and then dropped a kiss on top of her head. Brock hadn't seen her kiss Sadie before, and her tender affection for their niece stirred something deep inside him.

Natalia stood and started as she turned to him. "You're still here."

"Yeah…there's something that I wanted to go over with you." He hadn't intended to mention the matchmaking plans to Natalia at all, since there was no way Sadie could pull it off, but that kiss had him thinking.

They sat on the ledge of the store display, their backs to the window. The sun warmed his back, shone on Natalia's hair and her cheekbones. "I overheard Knut and Sadie," he said in a low voice. He caught the scent of vanilla and honey. Those candles, no doubt. "They've got plans for us."

He hit on the highlights of the conversation, while Natalia's expression wavered between amusement and incredulity. She flushed, and he liked that she wasn't unaffected.

"What did they say when you told them that you and I weren't happening?"

Why hadn't he said anything? Why had he pretended not to overhear? "It never occurred to me."

"Never... So Sadie thinks... You left her and Knut thinking there was hope?"

Hope. That was it. He hadn't wanted to crush Sadie's hope. And maybe...maybe he hadn't wanted to crush something inside himself that had grown since the day Natalia had decided to stay, grown with their every conversation over renovations, school, horses, daily schedules. Two equal partners sorting out problems and life.

Like a couple in a relationship.

"Sadie sounded so...charged up. I couldn't disappoint her. I think Knut felt the same way." He chose not to add the bit about Knut asking him point-blank about his intentions toward Natalia.

She looked across the room at Sadie and heaved a sigh. "You're leaving it to me to break her heart."

"Break her—No, I mean, do we need to?"

She frowned at him. "What are you saying?"

He hardly knew himself, but the one thing he was suddenly certain of was that he liked the idea of Natalia and him acting as if they were a couple. "I dunno, maybe for a while we could pretend. I think for her it has more to do with having a family, and for her right now that's having something like a mom and a dad. Or an aunt and an uncle but together."

"But this'll make it worse. We'll raise her hopes and then eventually we'll have to crush them."

He glanced over at Sadie, whispering the numbers as her line caterpillared along. He hated to disappoint her, and, well...he didn't want to disappoint himself. Not yet, anyway. "There are other outcomes, you know. Maybe she just sees us together often enough so that she gets used to us being who we are. If she just goes on seeing us being friendly together, sitting together like we are now, she'll figure out that what we have now is solid enough without stacking it higher."

"What we have now?"

"You know…friendship."

Natalia's hand fluttered to her bracelet. "Friends," she said flatly. "I suppose we are that."

"And friends," Brock pursued, "hang out." Hang out? What kind of high school kid was he? "Go out and eat. Dance. Well, okay, maybe not that," he added hastily as Natalia sucked in her breath. "But…watch movies."

Natalia's finger stilled on the bracelet. "Go riding together."

She flushed and this time he could feel warmth rising in him, and it wasn't entirely from the sun beating on his back. "I'd like that very much."

He'd negotiated friendship, but that had not addressed the dryer-like tumble and thudding inside him.

Tea lights fell and rolled everywhere. Sadie sat among them and the upended box, something that wouldn't have happened if she was paying attention and hadn't her eyes on something—or someone—else. And from the wide grin on Sadie's face, Brock knew she'd been looking at them staring into each other's eyes like a regular romantic couple.

Brock had given her hope. Maybe he'd given himself some, too.

FOR THE NEXT WEEK, Natalia captained her own special operation, running forays between her shop and the Calgary warehouse, making sales calls, keeping her psychologist appointments and showing up for Sadie, even though technically she didn't take charge of Sadie for another six weeks.

She still hadn't secured lodgings for them. All of the vacancies were located on the outskirts of town, backing onto construction sites and open fields. Better to find a home more central, more settled for Sadie.

As she finished up at the shop late in the afternoon, Brock's number rang. Probably Sadie wondering when she'd be back, even though they'd talked a bare half hour ago. Time for kids not yet five ran five times slower. "On my way, sweet daisy-do."

"Uh, hello." Brock.

Lovely. A little endearment for the fake man in her life. How did this ruse work? Did they arrange a time and place to meet as they did for Sadie? Or did the traditional codes of dating apply and she waited for Brock to ask her out? Or was she supposed to take the lead? "Sorry, I thought you were Sadie."

"That's okay," he said. "I've been called worse."

"I doubt that." An unintended admission of her attraction to him. Heat rushed to her cheeks. At least she was spared him cracking a little smile whenever she blushed.

But she detected a trace of laughter in his reply. "We're all over at Mateo and Haley's having supper. You're welcome to come over if you want."

She didn't want, but then she heard Sadie's excited pleading in the background and she was hungry, and she and Brock had agreed to do things together.

"Sure, thanks."

He must've given a thumbs-up to Sadie because Natalia could hear her "Yay!"

"You know where they're at?"

Above the sound of clinking plates and cutlery, she could hear Haley laugh and say, "Yeah, she knows."

They'd eaten by the time Natalia arrived. "They've gone to see the horses," Haley said, leading her into the kitchen, a stainless steel and granite showpiece. It seemed out of character for casual, earthy Haley. "Sadie's with them. Jonah's there because his dad is. And because of Sadie. Four years old, and she already has an admirer."

"She's quite sociable," Natalia said, relieved that someone else had seen it, too. The second attempt at school had gone just as Brock predicted, though all parties involved thought it best if Sadie left an hour earlier than the others to keep the experience upbeat. Summer break was only three weeks away, anyway.

"Have a seat." Haley pointed to a bar stool at the counter. She opened the fridge. "I set aside a plate for you. Pepper steak and grilled vegetables okay with you?"

"Sounds delicious."

Haley put the plate in the microwave and set it humming. "That's because I didn't make it. Mateo's the reason I put on pounds." She patted her lower stomach. "He's also the reason I'll continue packing them on until Christmas."

Natalia couldn't tell if Haley was annoyed by her condition or not. "How are you feeling?"

"Tired. Due to puke in twenty minutes. That's why I'm hanging around, while the rest are having fun outside."

Meaning she wasn't there to socialize with Natalia. The microwave beeped to a stop and Haley set the plate and cutlery in front of Natalia with disinterest, as if pouring chow for a cat. More thirsty than hungry, she didn't know how Haley would react if she requested water or, worse, got a glass for herself.

"Fork on the wrong side?" Haley asked.

It was. "No. Everything looks great. I was wondering if I could get something to drink."

"I knew I'd mess up somehow." She threw open the fridge and stepped aside for Natalia to view the drinks lined on the door. "What would you like?"

"Just a water. Thanks."

"Can or do you want it poured into a glass?"

Natalia preferred a glass with her meal. "Can is fine."

Haley plunked the can down in front of Natalia's plate. She suddenly closed her eyes. "I am sorry. This is so mean girl of me. I'm tired, I'm grumpy and I was cooped up in the house all day and I had to play nice with the guests. And then you show up, looking all put together. Krista's the same way. Why are all the women in my life so perfect all the time?"

Perfect? *You're fine just the way you are.*

Did Haley honestly think that, too? "That's the last word to describe me."

Haley bugged her eyes. "Are you kidding me? Sadie reset the table because the forks weren't on the left side. Because that's the way Auntie Lia does it."

"I just watch videos."

"About table settings?"

Natalia cracked open her water to hide her embarrassment. "Good manners make for repeat invitations." Not that it had worked tremendously well for her.

"Don't get me wrong. It's better than picking cutlery from a beer mug. I'm no good at doing the feminine things. All the hosting, cooking, keeping house. If this kitchen wasn't here when I married Mateo, if he couldn't cook like a pro, we'd probably be eating canned corn off a camp stove."

"I'm sure he had other reasons for marrying you."

Haley smiled, her gaze shifting out the window to the training arena. "Yeah, he tells me every day. Sometimes with words."

When her eyes drifted back to Natalia, they'd softened. "Anyway, the Jansson ranch needs more of your civilizing touch. You did the bedrooms up nice. Hardly recognized my old bedroom."

"Is that—"

"Sadie's. Your bedroom was Grace's, then Jonah's nursery."

"Brock painted it. His color choice, too." Natalia heard a note of pride creep into her voice.

"I got the impression he was keen on you moving in."

Moving in, as if they were romantically involved. Why had Brock allowed the truth to be misrepresented? "I'm leaving in a month. Brock and I have a deal with the courts. He gets the first three months with Sadie and I get the next three months. The switch is the end of July when we move together into town."

"So, why are you living with Brock and Sadie now?"

"Sadie wanted both of us there."

"And at the end of July she won't?"

Natalia had thought of that. Sadie was feeling more and more at home, but... "I'm not staying there."

Haley slotted a plate into a dishwasher rack and reached for another. "Look, I moved out a year in October, and there's nowhere I'd

rather be than with Mateo and Jonah and—"
she pointed at her belly "—this one. But
Dad's place still felt like home. A place to
go and remember Mom and growing up. But
then Sadie moved in, and Dad got all excited
about her and I don't blame him. Everyone
loves her. And then you come along, and he
changes out the bedrooms and that makes
sense. I say nothing, because I have no right.
Grace keeps telling me to move on, which is
rich coming from her."

Natalia had spoken to Grace on the phone
about bringing her quilts into the store. Grace
refused to sell something she did for fun but
took Natalia's suggestion that the proceeds
go to a charity of Grace's choosing, in this
case, the local pregnancy center. Grace had
not made one reference to Natalia's living arrangement, other than to ask if she should
send the quilts to the ranch or the store.

Haley slid the rack back into the dishwasher. "I guess what I'm saying is that I can
deal with you taking over the ranch house,
because it makes everyone there happy. But
you better think hard about your next step,
or you're going to disappoint people I care
about."

Had Natalia misunderstood Knut's hospitality? "I don't mean to upset your dad. I had no idea he hoped I'd stay on. As perfect as you think I am, I'm lousy with understanding people."

"Then you don't know how Brock feels about you?"

Natalia froze, steak juice dripping from her fork. "I'm sure I don't."

"Brock asked Sadie if he should invite you for supper, not Sadie. And when Sadie told Brock that you two should watch a movie together, he said that was a good idea and then grinned at the rest of us. That kind of fat-cat grin that means he's making a play. You know anything about that?"

Brock wasn't playing, so much as playing along. But to tell Haley that was to tell everyone. "I'm sure I don't."

Haley closed the dishwasher door and pushed buttons. She leaned on the counter, her face close, as if about to pass along a secret. "Please find out. Brock matters to all of us, and we're especially interested in whoever he dates." She suddenly straightened, and her face paled. "On the dot. You think on that. Meanwhile, I've got a date with a toilet."

CHAPTER SIX

SADIE ROPED BROCK and Natalia into movie night that Friday. Brock hadn't put up a fuss, had even wound up his work with the cattle in time to catch a quick shower and a change of clothes.

"Uncle Brock," Sadie said, "you smell nice."

"It's the aftershave," he muttered while Knut grinned openly.

Natalia didn't seem to notice as she flipped through a basket of DVDs by the television. She looked pretty in a filmy top and her hair coiled up. Probably playing up the dating aspect. She looked at them. "How about *Rapunzel*?"

"Uh...no," Brock said at the same time as Sadie voiced her downvote. She added, "I get nightmares about people stepping on my hair."

They went through a half dozen like that, Brock remembering again why movie night wasn't such a great idea. Knut might need to join this decade and consider streaming services.

"*Up?*"

Sadie shook her head. "It gives Knut nightmares."

Knut hitched in his easy chair. "Not nightmares. Brings back memories, is all."

Of his wife, just like for the curmudgeonly widower in the movie. Knut had watched that movie with his hand over his brow as the widower had gone through the photo albums of the times with his wife. He had risen stiffly from his chair afterward and not come out from his bedroom for their traditional coffee. Brock had tiptoed down the hallway and thought he heard the quiet, distinct crackle of the heavy pages of a photo album being turned. He'd tiptoed back.

He caught Natalia's eye and gave his head a slight shake. She slipped the DVD back in. "Well, that's about all—Oh, wait, what's this?"

She reached her hand under the couch and Brock's heart sank. She pulled out the DVD he'd deliberately hidden there. "*The Lion King.*"

"Lions?" Sadie peered over Natalia's shoulder.

"I don't think—" Brock tried to insert, but Sadie didn't seem to hear.

"It has baby lions," she said.

"A baby lion. Natalia, don't you remember it?" She looked at him and he frowned to convey his disapproval, but Sadie plucked the DVD from her hands. "This one! Let's watch this one."

He'd shoved it under the couch when Knut had brought the bunch home from some garage sale. As Sadie inserted it into Knut's ancient player, Brock edged close to Natalia beside him on the couch. "The dad lion dies," he whispered, "and the uncle is evil."

"Oh." She shrugged. "I guess we'll see how it goes."

He knew how it would go. "You'll have to deal with the nightmares."

She paused. "If there are any."

"I remember this one," Knut said. "Miranda and I took the girls to see it at the movie theater. Gah, that must've been thirty years ago or so."

Brock still sat close to Natalia, a position that he didn't mind, and since the whole point was for them to look friendly, he didn't see any reason to shift away. It might even be interpreted as rude.

But Sadie opened a space as she squeezed between them. Brock and Natalia exchanged looks of quiet amusement. At least, if Sadie was going to be traumatized, they'd both be here for her.

Brock touched Sadie's bright head. "Any of this get too much for you, we can always turn it off."

"It's animals. I can handle it."

But then Simba's dad died, betrayed by his brother, Scar. And Simba blamed himself. Tears leaked from Sadie. Brock grabbed the remote and clicked it off.

He shouldn't have allowed Natalia to talk him into this.

The sudden blank screen sent Sadie over the edge. "No, I need to know what happens to Simba. Does he live? Does he survive? I need to know."

Was there life after death? Would Simba find happiness? Would Sadie find happiness? He glanced over at Natalia, who gave him a faint sympathetic shrug. He switched it back on and Natalia handed Sadie a tissue. Sadie blew her nose and sat glued to Simba's journey.

As the show credits rolled up with Elton John belting out "Circle of Life," Sadie fell back against the couch. "Are there more like this?"

"I think there's a sequel," Knut said.

Quiet, Knut.

"Can we watch that one?"

"I don't know if we—"

But Sadie was already reaching under the couch. "Here it is. It has a girl lion."

"Couldn't exactly hide just the one," he whispered into Natalia's ear. She smelled of vanilla and sugar, like a cookie, and if they really were dating, he might have taken a nibble.

"It's got a girl and a boy lion," Sadie said, picking up on the cover photos. "The same lions from this story. Do they get married?"

"I guess we'll have to watch it and find out," Knut said.

"With Uncle and Auntie. Or maybe they can watch it on their own."

Sadie lacked any subtlety. And it didn't help that he and Natalia were brushing shoulders. Had through the entire movie. Close enough for him to count the seven freckles along her cheekbones, the streaks of blond in her hair and how her eyes widened and her hands twitched according to the unfolding drama. She still observed life with the same intensity as at the wedding.

He'd been wrong to keep Sadie away from

sad stories. He'd only seen that a dad had died because of a mean uncle. But it was also about how someone little can overcome pain and guilt with the right allies. He shouldn't have doubted Sadie's resiliency.

Or Natalia's faith in it.

NATALIA WOKE TO Sadie crashing open the door. "Simba drowned!" The mattress jostled underneath Natalia and the bony force of Sadie fell against her. She wrapped her arms around her niece.

"It's just a dream—" Natalia began and then stopped. Of course, Sadie had figured out it was no more than a nightmare. But no less, either. What did Brock do to ease her fears?

Holding on to a trembling Sadie, Natalia understood why Brock had hid *The Lion King*. And she'd not listened. Her turn to deal with the nightmares.

Her mattress jostled again and there was joyful padding and sniffing. "Pike," Natalia said, "aren't you supposed to be out with Brock?"

"He was probably on his mat in the mudroom. Uncle said he might let him in after his midnight pee." Brock had suspected Sadie might have a nightmare, and prepared a remedy. Pike wiggled between Natalia and Sadie and relentlessly licked hands and faces, even as they squirmed and dodged. Sadie broke into giggles, and relieved, Natalia joined in.

He finally collapsed between them and succumbed to slow petting from Natalia and Sadie, his soft, sturdy body warm and trusting between them.

"Do you want me to turn the light on?"

"No," Sadie said. "I know you're here."

Natalia smiled at Sadie's vote of confidence.

"Simba didn't drown. That was a dream. But Daddy did." Sadie's voice was sad but matter-of-fact.

"Yes," Natalia said. What had Brock told Sadie about Daniel's death?

"I don't understand," Sadie said. "He knew how to swim. How could he drown?"

Her sessions with Mara might finally pay off as Natalia eased into an explanation. "There's a place that studies how people had their accidents. It's called the coroner's office. They said that your dad bumped his head and fell into the water, or fell into the water and then bumped his head. The bump was hard enough to make him dizzy and he might have fainted."

She and Sadie had fallen into a rhythm of

petting Pike. When Natalia reached Pike's butt, she lifted her hand away as Sadie started at the top, their hands slowly cycling together. Pike melted under the constant stroking and his pup pants settled into snoring. Someone was getting their sleep.

"Daddy didn't know he was drowning, then?"

"The truth is that no one knows. And no one will ever know because no one saw what happened."

There was a quiet heaving of breath from Sadie. Natalia thought she was struggling to hold back tears, but it was something different. "Can I tell you a secret?"

"Sure."

"You have to promise not to tell Uncle Brock."

Good grief, what was she going to say that couldn't be told to Brock? "I can't promise that, Sadie. But I'll only tell him if it's something that I think he needs to know so you can be happier. Okay?"

"It'll make him unhappy. He won't like me anymore."

"I don't think there's a danger of that, sweet daisy-do. He likes everyone."

"But what if I was the only one he didn't like?"

"Not possible," Natalia said. "You're his family. And we both know you're a good kid."

"Okay." Sadie stopped petting Pike and whispered, "Dad wanted me to come with him and I said I wanted to play house, and he said 'Fine, let's do a little test with you by yourself' and he made me go over again what to do with the radio and he said that he would be away for fifteen minutes, but I started playing and forgot time. But if I hadn't forgotten, I would've gotten help sooner. Auntie, I failed the test."

Mara had cautioned against magical thinking with children. They would invent stories from loose facts to ease the horror of the death. This was magical thinking, of the worst kind because she was using the facts to increase the horror. Natalia clasped Sadie's hand in hers. "It's not your fault. Hear me? It's not. It was an accident. Like with Simba. It wasn't his fault his dad died, and it's not your fault what happened to your father. Even if you had gone, you are too small to have pulled him out of the water. You did the right thing. You called for help. Your dad was checking to see if you would be safe even if he wasn't there. You passed that test with flying colors. He would be so proud of you. I am proud of you. But there are still things out there too big for you to defend yourself against. That's my job. Your uncle's job."

"What's my job, then?"

"To be the best possible you, and you're doing a fabulous job of that."

"Okay." Sadie cuddled down, her head tucked beside Pike's. "Can I sleep here tonight?"

Letting her stay was a step backward for her sense of security. But all they had to do was close their eyes.

"Sure."

Sadie didn't respond. She'd already fallen asleep.

THE NEXT MORNING, Brock met Natalia as she opened the the carport entrance to the house, Pike on the dead run for his pee. Despite living in close quarters, Brock had not seen Natalia in her pj's before. He liked the rumpled look.

"Long night," she said. "You were right. Sadie had a nightmare."

As he'd feared.

"Thanks for giving us access to Pike. He helped. We talked…about Daniel. She was curious about what happened. You never told her, I take it?"

"She never asked, and I thought it best to leave well enough alone."

"That's pretty much your motto, isn't it? Leave well enough alone." Natalia might not look ready to take on the day, but she already had him in her sights.

"Given last night, it turns out to be a pretty good one."

"What did you tell her whenever she had nightmares?"

"We talked about what we were going to do the next day, and then she'd fall back to sleep. After we got Pike, it got easier."

"You avoided the subject altogether?"

"I let it be, yeah."

She worried the bracelet at her wrist. Sadie had informed Brock that her dad had chopped wood to buy the bracelet because he knew that Auntie Lia liked pretty things. Natalia let go of the bracelet but not the subject. "Look, a dog's great for helping through the bad times, but he can't help with explaining to her why she's having the bad times."

"If she'd asked, I would've told her. I didn't want to say the wrong thing and confuse her."

"I understand that, but—" Natalia stepped onto the mat. Her toes must be freezing, yet she wasn't giving up.

"But what?"

"She told me a secret last night…and I helped her work through it. It was mostly magical thinking."

"Magical thinking?"

"Mara Flanagan explained it to me. She said—"

"You're taking Sadie to her? I thought we'd agreed—"

"I'm taking myself there."

That didn't sound much better. "There's nothing wrong with you, either."

"Do you want to hear about magical thinking or not?"

He gave a clipped nod.

"It's where you think up scenarios because of misunderstanding or not knowing facts. But that's not where I'm going with this. She…she specifically told me not to tell you."

"Then don't."

"And I won't, but she didn't want you to know because she thought you wouldn't like her anymore. And believe me, if you did know, you wouldn't stop caring for her. You'd probably love her even more. But why would she say that? Especially when you like everyone. Honestly, it's me you'd think she'd want to keep secrets from."

"But you have a theory."

Natalia wiggled her toes and he scrunched his own toes in empathy. "I do. I think…and I'm not sure she's even aware of it, but she doesn't want you to think badly about her in case you don't want her here."

He liked her theory because it meant that Sadie wanted to stay here. Which meant… "You figure she still doesn't want to be with you."

Natalia bit her lip. "I can't help thinking that."

"I think she wants what she's already made clear. She wants to live here with the both of us."

Natalia gave him a look as if she were about to serve up bad news. "Brock, I can't do that. I can't live out here. This is your home… not mine."

He tried to see it from her point of view. How she might feel trapped. "But you've got your store. You've got life on asphalt. You can come and go as you please. It's not like life in the bush. We got electricity and internet and people all around."

"It was only ever going to be temporary. This isn't my home."

"You could try to make it one," he said.

"For Sadie's sake." *For my sake.* "I don't mind if you do. Place looks better for it. I think Knut's happier, too."

Too. She lifted her eyes to his. He was happier to have her here, but telling her right now sounded like a con. His turn to look away.

"Living here…it's not me," she said. "I tried, but I'm still planning to get my own place. For me and Sadie."

He'd indulged in his own magical thinking. Pike returned, bumping against Natalia, his direct ask for affection. "This matchmaking game we got started, then…it's over?"

Natalia scratched Pike's head. Her fingernails could've come out of a salon, pale pink with a flower on her pinkie, but they were shortish. Pretty and practical, like her. "I'm not moving out today. Last night didn't seem to go so badly, did it? I mean, outside of daddy lion dying and uncle lion being a murderous megalomaniac."

Her first joke. A good sign. He had a chance. It wasn't over, at least not yet. Like his career. One horse at a time, one evening with Natalia at a time. "I want us to—"

Sadie pushed open the door. She was carrying a brass rectangular box that could be mistaken for a little treasure chest.

But it was an urn. "I got this down from the shelf in your closet, Auntie Lia. What is it?"

"DADDY'S IN THERE?" Sadie pointed to the urn now relocated to the middle of the dining table like a macabre centerpiece. Knut had taken stock of Brock and Natalia seated with Sadie and the easily identifiable urn, and exited to the front porch with his morning cup of coffee.

Natalia had fumbled through an explanation of cremation as a special process where a body underwent intense heat to change form in order to fit inside a small space. She was on her own with this one. She had not discussed this aspect of grief with Mara, and Brock sat on the other side like a rock. A very unhelpful rock. He would probably be out there right now with Knut, if Sadie herself hadn't taken his hand and pulled him inside, after Natalia had rescued the urn from her.

"His body rests there," she emphasized.

Sadie frowned. "Knut said that when his wife died, her body stayed here but her soul went to heaven. Is that where Daddy's is?"

Natalia had never contemplated the existence of heaven. It had been enough to comprehend that Daniel was gone without contemplating where he had gone.

What had Daniel told Sadie about her mother? She didn't want to contradict him. *Be absolutely honest*, Mara had advised. *With her and yourself.* "I don't know where your daddy's soul is."

"Knut says that when he dies, he's going to be with his wife. Is that where Daddy went? To Mommy? His soul, not his body," Sadie added.

"I'm… I'm not sure," Natalia said. Why didn't Brock speak up? What were his beliefs? It was his sister, after all. "I'm not sure if there is a heaven or not. Nobody has gone there and come back." But what if Daniel had talked about angels and second comings? "At least… I don't know. Some people believe in heaven, others don't and I don't know what to believe myself."

Sadie turned to Brock. "What do you think? Are Mommy and Daddy together?"

"Yes," Brock said. His answer was so quick and final that even Sadie seemed taken aback.

"How do you know?"

"You don't need proof for these kinds of thing," Brock said. He stood abruptly from the table. "I'm going to make breakfast."

Natalia didn't know that he could, having let her dominate the kitchen in the morning. He was probably willing to walk on hot coals right now to avoid any more of Sadie's questions, leaving her to hold the ball.

Sadie settled back in her chair and regarded the urn. She didn't seem as concerned so much about the answer, but that there simply was one. One that sounded honest and that Brock believed in. Natalia attempted to take Brock's lead. "Right, then. Let's get dressed for the day." She reached for Daniel's urn.

"Are you going to put Daddy's body back in the closet?"

Natalia's hands stilled around the urn. "It will be safe there."

"But the closet is dark and stuffy. It doesn't belong there."

"What's your suggestion?"

"I have a shelf in my room. There's lots of room there."

It was fair, it did make sense…but it meant giving up Daniel.

An egg cracked into a bowl. "You two could take turns," Brock offered. "One takes him for, say, a week, and then the other for the next week. Back and forth, like that."

Sadie's face brightened. "Yes, let's do that,

Auntie Lia. Like you and Uncle Brock are doing with me. Taking turns."

Did Sadie see herself as a thing, a special thing but still a thing, swapped between two adults who couldn't make up their minds?

Natalia didn't know how to explain the difference to Sadie, and as Brock had already demonstrated, she might be overthinking all of this. "That sounds like a plan. How about you take Dan—the urn first?"

"Okay!"

"And the rule is that only I take it down from the shelf. Deal?" The urn sealed the ashes tightly, but Natalia felt certain her brain would explode if so much as a speck escaped.

"Okay!" Sadie hopped off her seat and down the hall to her room, Natalia to follow with the urn.

Another egg cracked. "You know that if you move out at the end of July, doing a weekly exchange isn't going to be so easy."

"Not if she's living with me."

"And after that? When things become permanent? What if she's living out here?"

"How about," Natalia said, "we leave things alone for now? I hear it's a philosophy to live by."

Brock's lips thinned and he cracked another egg. He didn't answer, appearing to concede the last word. But she had a sinking feeling that the subject was far from over for him.

CHAPTER SEVEN

BROCK WAS LEANING against the corral fence, his eyes on a quality dappled gray quarter horse, when he heard footsteps behind him. And very faintly, the scent of ginger and honey. A new one.

Natalia settled against the fence beside him. "Who's this?"

He had heard her vehicle roll in a half hour ago, and Pike's excited, welcoming yips for her and Sadie. They'd eaten in town, while he and Knut had a quiet meal of Natalia's casserole leftovers. Too quiet.

"My latest project. Persephone." Courtesy again of Mateo. He and Mateo had gone south to pick up a cutting horse. A promising bay by the name of Fifty-fifty. But the gray had whinnied and acted up the second the gelding was loaded. The owner said she was going to be nothing but trouble without her buddy, and Mateo had said that there wasn't a horse Brock here couldn't fix. Mateo and the owner struck a deal, while Brock saw to the loading of the mare. He hoped he wouldn't make a liar out of Mateo.

Natalia scrutinized Persephone between the railings as if in the business of equine therapy. "Other than an unfortunate name, what's her deal?"

"Scared of everything. I accidently kicked that chop pail—" Brock pointed to a spot ten feet away "—and that's why she's on the other side of the corral right now."

"So desensitization?"

"Some of that, but I got a bigger problem. She's only halter broken."

"You can't put a saddle on her?"

"Yep. Lots of work here. Owner's hoping to turn her into a cutting horse."

"Why is she scared of everything?"

The tension of the day seeped away as he settled into his one-on-one with her. "Owner doesn't rightly know himself. He got her as a yearling, and she was already skittish. Her mama died at birth, and she was stabled alone quite a bit."

Natalia snorted. "Nobody around. That would do it."

Bitterness sharpened her words, and the Brock of old would've let her be, but if he wanted her to stay, then he had to give her reason to feel that she belonged. "Seems to me you could give insight into this one here."

"You are asking me for horse advice?"

He could probably figure this out for himself. But it was nice to have her within arm's reach, smelling like dessert, and the setting sun catching fire to her hair. He itched to touch the red and gold strands. "I guess I am. I appreciated your help with Molly. I could do with more. I can pay."

She jutted out her hip as she leaned on the railing. "I'll help, but I'm not accepting money. I don't need it."

While he did. His hand-to-mouth existence had never bothered him before, but he had to become worthy of Sadie. And Natalia. To provide for one and to gain the respect of the other.

She turned to Persephone. "How about we consider our time with her as 'dates'?" She made air quotes. "It'll keep the matchmakers off our backs."

Did he pick up on a thread of nervousness in her suggestion, as if his answer mattered? She still had her face averted.

"Good idea," he said. "But Perse could do

with training every day. You up for that much dating?"

She glanced up at him, then away, blushing. "Yes."

His hand drifted up to her hair but stopped short at her next words. "I guess I need to step up my end of the game. You've got Haley convinced already. At the supper, I guess you said a few things to lead her to believe that you have...intentions toward me."

Her face was all kinds of pink. He couldn't blow this opening. "I admit that it has crossed my mind. I like you. I always have."

"Always have? We met once at the wedding eight years ago, and we didn't even speak."

Brock didn't think it wise yet to tell her how much simply setting his eyes on her had knocked him flat. He had to go slow, for both their sakes. "I guess I like what I've seen so far."

She fiddled with her bracelet. "That'll change soon enough. Once you get to know me better."

"I've seen you in your pj's. That was pretty raw."

She squinted up at him. "What do you mean?"

"Just a joke."

She gave the bracelet such a hard twist he thought it might snap. "And that is why we don't stand a chance. I have an abysmal track record when it comes to men. We will not work out. Let's commit to fakery only."

No. "I'm not like the other men you dated."

She laughed, a harsh bark. "Exactly. And that's why we don't have a future. We're just too different. I'm too different."

"I already told you there's nothing wrong with you. It's like with Persephone. You just need desensitizing."

This time her smile was genuine, even if it was small. "Increased exposure to you, is that it?"

"Exactly. How about I make good on that ride you asked for?"

She blew out her breath. "All right, let's prove me right. Tuesday evening?"

No, he would prove her wrong. Or at least she'd discover that if they were not meant for each other, it wouldn't be her fault. "Tuesday, it is."

TWO DAYS LATER, Natalia rode Crocus and Brock sat on a chestnut named Canuck Luck. They hadn't spoken much on their date. Brock looked happy enough to conduct the whole outing in silence, like an old married couple.

She reverted to her usual tactic of encouraging her "date" to talk about himself. "How's Persephone?"

"Best brushed horse ever. Likes my touch and that's about it."

Don't blame her, she very nearly said. His gaze drifted to her position in the saddle. "How many countries did you say you've gone riding in?"

"I don't think I did say. Not sure I even could, I've been to so many countries."

"How many?"

"Not sure. At least forty."

"Forty! Holy." He absorbed that for a moment. "How could you not know how many countries you've been in?"

"Have you seen the size of some countries, especially in Europe? You can literally ride a train through them and not even notice. I'm not sure I can count the ones I never stopped in. Or only stayed for a few hours."

"Which country is your favorite?"

"I'm not answering that. It's like asking which of your children you love the most."

He grinned. "We both know the answer to that."

Sadie, their niece. They could both make that claim. Brock pointed to a break in the trees that ran along the half-mile length of pasture. "See there? It leads down to a creek. Pretty little spot."

Tall, gloomy trees and thick, clawing bushes. Her heart rate bumped up. "I don't think—" She'd agreed to this date to show how wrong he was about her. Time to prove who knew her better. "Why not?"

Like a giant roller coaster, it started off easy enough. The ground sloped gently downward, and Crocus knew the way. Natalia pushed away a branch that Brock had set swishing back and forth. A bush nearby rustled. A rabbit might dart from the undergrowth and startle Crocus, throwing Natalia, snapping her spine, and she'd die in the bush just as she'd always feared.

Stop it, Natalia. She had gone on trail rides through bush before. But she had always chosen ones wider, more groomed, opening to vistas.

She peered through the trees. A crow cawed above, and she jerked. Crocus, bless her, kept going. She looked over her shoulder. Nothing but trees. She couldn't even see where they'd entered. Down they went. She

thought she heard the burble of the creek…
or was it the wind in the leaves?

She focused on the plaid-shirted back of
Brock, and then he and Canuck Luck's rump
rounded a corner. The fractal pattern of them
appeared through the blowing leaves and yet
her chest squeezed tight. Her breath shortened
to pants, she felt light-headed. She pressed on
the thick ridges of the stirrups, gripped the
pommel and clamped her legs against the sol-
idness of Crocus's flanks. She heard the rush
of the creek now, the clunk of rocks moving
in the current.

Like a head hitting a rock in the water.

Her world blurred and she closed her eyes.
Bright spots flashed in the dark.

"Make this stop," she murmured, not sure
if she was calling out to Brock or to the powers that be.

Crocus slowed and stilled. Natalia heard
Brock call her name, and she fought to open
her eyes, but if she did, she might fall off. She
clung to the pommel and opened her mouth
to explain.

"Brock," she said, his name low and strung
out. That took all her energy, and, she fell.

Fell into strong arms and then the sensation
of grass and the warm solidity of Brock's

chest. He smelled of soap and fresh air; she could have happily slipped into unconsciousness.

"Lia, you with me? Lia?"

His voice was soft and urgent…caring. For her. Her dark world still swirled, and she kept her eyes closed. "Could we stay like this for now?"

"We can do that." His voice rumbled at her ear. Like when he'd whispered to her during movie night. They'd sat so their heads almost touched through the whole movie, but not nearly this close.

He settled himself around her, one arm along her back, his other hand cupped over her knees as she sat between his legs, her head on his shoulder. Slowly, slowly the bright spots faded and her senses filtered in the crunch of horses grazing on grass, the rattle of harnesses and, beyond that, the rush— not in her head—but of the creek.

It wasn't loud, so the creek couldn't be that wide. She could face this, but then Brock brought his arms a little tighter around her, and she kept her eyes closed. She could soak him in, pretend that they really did have something together. One minute of him. He wouldn't notice.

The minute passed. She'd definitely open her eyes if he said her name. She couldn't fake it beyond that.

But he didn't. He held her in the circle of his arms as her world righted. In the end, it wasn't her name that he said. "Crocus, whoa. Don't you go in the water." Splashing told her that the horse had paid no heed.

She opened her eyes automatically. The horse stood up to her hocks in the water, the current streaming under the stirrups. Brock called to Crocus again, to no effect. Brock grunted. "She listens every single time, but when it comes to water, she becomes ornery."

Crocus dipped her mouth to the creek as if to demonstrate. Canuck Luck mowed the thick, high grass at the edge. It had to be juicy for her to eat wearing a bit.

"Crocus loves water," Brock said. "I've seen her stand in a puddle with the rain pouring down. She'll come out if we walk away. She hates being left behind."

He shifted his hands off her and onto his legs. He raised his knee and she rested her back against its support. Definitely overstaying her welcome, but what did he mean by setting his leg there? His gentle words only confused her more. "What happened there?"

How much to say? "I'm not that good in close spaces outside, trees and bushes. I get all kinds of phobic reactions."

"You could have told me," he said. "I didn't need to bring you here that badly."

"I thought I'd be okay."

"You started off fine."

"That's because I was with you." That came out wrong. "I mean, not you in particular. Just the idea of someone else being around."

Crocus kicked her back leg and a spray of water scattered, drops pebbling onto the saddle. "Quit that," Brock ordered her. He turned back. "She's eight and still acts like she's one."

Natalia was grateful for Crocus's antics, since it distracted Brock from his interrogation. "I am glad you brought me here." The flashing creek, the light and dark greens of the leaves in counterpoint to the white trunks, the resting horses, all made for a pretty spot. "It could make for a painting."

"Wouldn't it make you as cranky as the ones in the art gallery?"

For once, she wished he would let things be. Except hadn't they agreed to discover more about each other? "I hated—loathed—

that cabin. I hated growing up there. It stunted me, and don't say that I'm fine. There's a difference between being normal and acting as if you are. I'm always acting, but with first the trees and then the water, I couldn't hold on anymore." She recalled the firm hold of his hands, then his arms around her. "Thank you for...catching me."

"No problem. You had me worried there."

She'd let him worry, while she had faked her dizziness. "I'm sorry. It won't happen again."

"Because you don't plan on getting on a horse ever again?"

"No. I liked the horse riding."

"Then we'll do this again, but with no trees involved."

And no cuddles, either. "All right."

A RAP ON the glass door of Home & Holidays the next day jerked Sadie and Natalia away from the job of scrubbing down a woodstove. To play up the authentic pioneer vibe, she planned to use the stove surface as a counter, and the oven and firebox below for storage. The huge black range would anchor the kitchen part of the store.

Sadie tossed aside her steel wool pad and dashed to the locked door.

"It's a mommy and her daughter. Or maybe, an auntie and her niece." She waved to a girl with dark hair on the other side. A woman also with dark hair stood beside her and smiled through the glass.

"Can they come in?"

Natalia surveyed the unsecured bed frame with its heaps of quilts and clothing in the bedroom section, and the pottery and ceramics stacked along the long dining table, and the glass cabinet in the living room section, and wondered about the saying of a bull in a china shop. It turned out the mother had the same thought when she stepped in.

She took her daughter's hand. "You're not going anywhere unless Sadie's aunt says so."

She knew them?

"We're not stopping here for long. I'm Bridget Holdstrom. My husband and I own the restaurant just down the street. He said you and Sadie dropped in for supper the other night. This is my daughter, Penelope. Or Penny."

Sadie took Penny's hand as if they went way back. "Do you want to come play with me? I have paper and crayons. See?"

Penny wasn't given a choice as Sadie hauled her over to the craft corner Natalia had set up. Her hosting lacked grace, but not enthusiasm, and from Bridget's smile, that was all that mattered.

"Jack said that your Sadie and Penny got along well."

Your Sadie. It sounded…great, though Brock might prefer a more inclusive pronoun. "Small world," Natalia said, not really sure where this conversation was going. But that was the nature of small talk, countless online help articles had explained. The age-old bridge to the real topic.

"Isn't it?" Bridget said. "And then he says you're living at the Jansson place, and that's right close to where my sister lives with her husband. Krista and Will Claverley. Their oldest—Ella—is the same age as Penny. Three. Four in November."

"Sadie's four. Five in August." A full year seemed like a huge gap, but Sadie didn't seem to care as she offered her pinwheel of crayons to Penny.

"I was chatting with Krista, and we thought that over the summer, we should arrange for Sadie to be part of the girls' get-togethers sometimes. The cousins are besties, but it would be good if they had someone else to play with."

Besties. Natalia remembered how that worked. Best friends didn't like an outsider with their extra bright smile and secondhand clothes and awkward interruptions. No insult to Penelope and Ella, but Sadie didn't need that kind of stress.

Penny suddenly cried out. She had cut off a petal on the paper flower. Bridget darted forward, but Sadie picked up a roll of tape. "Don't worry. We can fix that."

This was a story to tell Brock tonight. The last thing she needed was for Sadie to lose a friend because her aunt couldn't get over her high school trauma. She turned to Bridget. "That sounds like a great idea."

Bridget tipped her head sideways. "Are you sure? I don't want you to feel that I'm ambushing you. Our other sister always warns Krista and me that we're a little overwhelming when we're together and apparently our daughters are the same."

Bridget seemed completely unaware that Natalia was Mara's client. She was right to trust Mara. *There you go, Brock.*

"No, that sounds wonderful," Natalia said. "I was actually wondering what activities I could get Sadie involved in over the summer." A thought she hadn't shared with Brock because she knew he'd be happy for Sadie to spend all her waking hours at the ranch.

"Perfect. Penelope, time to go." As she secured her daughter's hand, Bridget turned to Natalia. "I'll see you on Sunday, then?"

Wha—

"Every Father's Day, Krista and Will hold a barbecue at their place for the community."

Sadie's hand squeezed Natalia's. Painfully. Bridget's face fell. "Oh, I'm… I'm so sorry. I didn't mean… I wasn't thinking—"

"It's okay," Natalia said quickly. It was supposed to be, too. This was the one time with Daniel's death only a bare two months ago that Natalia had agreed with Brock to avoid the celebration. They didn't know if Daniel had introduced Sadie to the celebration, but it defeated the purpose to ask her. Natalia had arranged with Ms. Whitby for Sadie not to attend the day when crafts for father figures were made. Natalia had dodged shops with Sadie in case of displays promoting the event. Knut had received training not to bring up the barbecue. As for the day itself, they had settled on just another Sunday at the farm.

One look into Sadie's tear-filled eyes, and it was clear that all their good intentions were blown to bits.

CHAPTER EIGHT

BROCK KNEW SOMETHING was up before Natalia joined him that evening as he led Persephone around the corral. He'd wondered why Sadie had seemed down at supper and Natalia extra chipper. Foot on the corral railing, she recounted the Father's Day incident at the shop.

"I told her we didn't have to go, but that seemed to upset her more. She'd miss out on hot dogs and cake, and playing with Penelope and Ella. She's just…sad. And I don't know how to make it better."

Brock didn't know, either. "I suppose we can wait for Sunday and see how she feels then."

"I'm not sure if she understands her feelings."

Like his own for Natalia. "We didn't get an invite. Knut's going, but no one got in touch with me. Since it's out in the open now, I guess we could take her someplace else for the day." He suddenly liked that idea, the three of them going off like a family. "Drive down to Calgary, to the zoo or something. Or out to the mountains for the day."

Natalia shook her head. "I suggested it to her, but she wants to be fair to her daddy. *Respectful*, that was her word."

Persephone snickered and tugged on the reins. If he was reading her right... "I think she wants to meet you."

"She's just curious."

"No, she likes you." Brock flipped the reins over Persephone's withers and stepped away to give her space. "Climb in here with us and call her over. I bet she'll come right up to you. Let you touch her."

As Natalia had let him. A day later, he could still remember the feel of his arms around her. He'd been scared when she'd nearly fainted away, her body a full weight against him. She'd tensed as if coming to, but then she'd relaxed again with almost the same heaviness. It was that almost that had gotten him thinking he was holding a woman with her eyes closed but who was fully aware of her surroundings. Had she done it because she liked being held as much as he'd liked holding her? Who knows how long it might've lasted if Crocus hadn't ruined it all.

Natalia scaled the fence and held up her

hand. "Who wants some loving?" Persephone pricked her ears and came forward, stopping only once before Natalia's encouragement prompted her to close the gap.

"There," Natalia said, rubbing Persephone's neck. "That wasn't so hard, was it?"

Brock felt it was his own victory. "You've got a way with horses, Lia. I couldn't pull that off, and I spend hours a day with her."

Natalia sighed. "I wish I could solve Sadie's problem as easily."

"Maybe she has to come to us. The way Persephone did."

Natalia's mouth flatlined. "She did come crying. Her heart's broken. She's alone in her room right now with Pike and we've no clue how to make her feel better."

"It's natural that she'll feel bad."

"You and your 'natural' talk. There will be bad times, but we're supposed to have a way to help her get over them."

"She never will get over this," he snapped.

Persephone swung her head. Natalia ducked away in time to avoid contact and grabbed the reins. "Whoa, steady. Nothing going on except two people talking. You can handle that, right?"

It should've been him dealing with the horse,

but all he could think of was Abby. Sadie's birthday was always crowded out by the death of his sister. He would be fine and then it was like rounding the back of a horse that kicked for no reason. And from the sympathetic look Natalia gave him, she understood.

"We'll walk her around the corral," Brock said. "It'll settle her."

Natalia handed him the reins, but he shook his head. "You're good." He needed a moment to steady himself.

His phone rang. Will. He often called to offer extra work at the training arena he operated with Mateo. But not tonight.

"So Bridget got a hold of Krista and there was a bit of a mix-up about the Father's Day barbecue."

Brock glanced over at Natalia. "I'm just talking it over with Lia right now. All's good."

"We're feeling kind of bad about it. We didn't invite you because we weren't sure where things were at with Sadie, not because of who you are, but that wasn't our call to make. Just so you know, you are all welcome. It's Father's Day, but it's really about guys who take care of kids."

"Thanks for the thought, Will."

"No problem. Mateo was our token not-

father-but-father last year. You can be it this
year. If you want."

"How about I get back to you?"

"You don't have to. Come or not."

The call over, Brock caught up with Natalia.
"So much for using the lack of an invite as an
excuse not to go."

Persephone was snuffling Natalia, nibbling
on her sweatshirt. Brock pushed on her head.
"Perse, cut it out."

"Why's she doing that?"

"Because she smells apples and cinnamon
on you."

"How do you—It's that bad?"

"It's that good," he blurted.

She reddened, and he thought again of her
in his arms. He looked away, and there was
Sadie heading their way, hopping along, Pike
beside her. She waded into a puddle halfway
up to her boots and plowed through it, as if
she'd never experienced a second of fear over
water. He swiveled to Natalia, whose expression held the pleasant shock he was feeling.

"Progress," he said.

Natalia grinned. "Swimming lessons, here
we come."

Miles to go before that day, but no longer
an impossible dream. Knut stood at the house
and Brock waved to show he'd take over. Knut

returned the wave and went back inside to his photo albums.

Sadie began to climb the railings. "Hold it right there," Brock said. "This is the tricky horse, remember?"

Sadie looked over at Persephone nuzzling her aunt's neck, and Lia giggling. Huh. "You want me to saddle up Canuck, and we go for a ride together?"

Sadie shook her head.

"I came out to tell you how I can make myself less sad."

"That right?" Natalia picked up the lead reins and brought a willing Persephone closer.

"Can we bring Daddy to the party?"

She must mean the urn. Brock looked over at Natalia, but she had her eyes on Persephone, who in turn was regarding the vibrating noisy duo of dog and small human.

"Uncle Brock?"

"I guess." Was this healthy for an almost five-year-old to want? All he had to remember Abby by was a few out-of-focus wedding photos. Daniel had scattered her ashes in the river. "He'll have to stay in the truck. We don't want anything happening to him."

"Okay, he can wait in my booster seat. This way he'll still be there…like all the other dads."

"You understand that your dad…in there… it's not what you remember of him?"

"But, it is important that I remember him on Father's Day, right?"

"Right."

"And as long as I'm remembering, I can also have fun."

"That's…that's a good way of looking at things, Sadie."

She jumped off the corral railing. "I'm going to play tag with Pike, okay?" And she was off. Straight for the puddle.

Brock turned to Natalia. "There you go. We gave her space and she found a solution."

"Or she wanted to be with other people so bad that she was forced to find a solution."

Brock knew he was pushing it, but she'd practically said it herself. "True. One where she can be with people and live on the ranch."

Natalia shook her head. "Brock, I know you're talking about me. My life is not here. I haven't changed my mind."

Just when he thought that the creek incident had brought them closer.

FROM HIS CHAIR in the gazebo, Brock looked down the long sloping hill on the Claverley property to where a gaggle of kids, Sadie included, crawled about square bales, took turns riding an old saddle, fought invisible monsters and each other using broom handles, and healed the fallen with lilac blooms. Moms sat under an erected shelter nearby, chatting. Natalia stood closer to the kids, something Abby would have done. Ready to leave as soon as she arrived. Natalia even carried her purse, a great floppy bag, over her shoulder.

"Can't believe you found the one shady spot no one's at," Will said, coming from the house with Mateo. Both held beers and camp chairs, and Will handed Brock the extra beer in his hand.

Mateo surveyed the bunch below as he sat, and Brock, from two months with Sadie, knew his mind.

"You all right with Jonah on his own in the horse barn?" Brock asked, poker-faced.

Mateo straightened and then caught the joke. "Yeah, yeah," he said, sinking back into his chair. "I'd like to see you if I'd said the same about Sadie."

"True," Brock said. "She's kind of grown on me."

Krista walked over to Natalia and began chatting with her. He liked Krista, not the way Will did, but enough to have pushed Will to pursue her years ago.

"She the only one who's grown on you?" Will, it turned out, was watching him.

Brock kept his voice extra casual. "Me and Natalia? Yeah, we get along."

"She staying on at the house, then?" Mateo said.

Brock had to be careful here. Natalia hadn't budged yet on her commitment to leave at the end of July. "For the time being."

Mateo must have sensed Brock's awkwardness because he shrugged. "Then again, none of my business. I meant to ask if you'd practice on Fifty-fifty for me. He could do with the feel of someone else making the calls."

Normally, Brock would've latched on to that crude attempt at redirection, but these two were his buddies, especially Will. He and Will had traveled parts of the circuit together, shared campers and hotel rooms, and visited each other in hospital. He'd known Mateo for less than a year, but they worked well together. He had even played around with the idea of asking Mateo for a steady job. At any rate, he could do with serious feedback.

"Yeah, all right, okay," Brock said, as if the two had been pestering him. "There might be something between the two of us, but it's all pretty new and up in the air."

"I know how that works," Mateo said and took a pull on his beer. "I've been married to Haley seven months, we have a kid on the way, and it still feels up in the air. Sometimes she takes off in the truck and I haven't a clue where she's going."

"Krista goes off and I wonder the same thing," Will said. "Except I know she's told me and I've forgotten, and I'm going to get an earful if I call and ask."

"I'm at the stage of where it's none of my business where she goes off to," Brock said, "except that she tells me, anyway. And I tell her."

"Sounds pretty serious," Mateo said on another draw of beer.

Will pushed Brock's shoulder. "Yep, advanced setting."

Despite their teasing, Brock caught a dead serious glint in Will's eyes, and when Mateo left in search of his absent wife and son, his old friend said, "You are head over heels, yeah?"

"I know it's probably not the smartest thing. She's all city, and I mean hard-core city."

"I thought she grew up in the country."

"Yeah, but not like here, where we're all a two minutes' drive from each other and a quarter hour to a grocery store. She was raised in the bush in Northern Alberta. From what her brother told me, her family ran power off a generator. Ate only what they grew or hunted. Not even bread. Real survivalists. She's only here for Sadie's sake, and she eventually wants to take Sadie to Calgary."

"Joint custody, then?"

"That's a possibility, but practically, it'll be one or the other. We got until the end of October to figure it out between the two of us, or it's over to the judge to decide. And neither of us want that."

"What does Sadie want?"

"She hasn't changed her mind. She wants us together." Brock wavered about divulging her matchmaking scheme, but it was Will, after all. "Actually, she concocted this plan with Knut to get Natalia and me together."

"Together? As in…married?"

"That's how her four-year-old mind works. I thought Knut was doing it to humor her, but now I'm not so sure. He likes Natalia."

"And you know about their scheme how?"

"I overheard them. Natalia and I decided to

play along a little but not to the degree we're overcommitting."

"Overcommitting…as in getting married?"

Brock shifted in his seat. "Yeah, something like that."

"But you admitted that a relationship is brewing, which means that you two might end up walking down the aisle together."

"But she'd have to want to live in the country."

Will pointed down the hill to where Krista and Natalia were still talking. Krista was wildly gesturing, and Natalia was smiling. "I know a thing or two," Will said, "about a city girl and a country boy. And a guy a few years back who pushed me to go for it."

"And?"

"And today I'm that guy pushing." Will slapped Brock on the shoulder. "I'm off to find out from Krista what time she already told me to fire up the barbecue. Wish me luck."

Brock watched Will walk down the slope, his eyes drifting past to Natalia. *Go for it.*

Will reached Krista, spoke to her, and she raised her arms in clear exasperation. Natalia looked up the hill. To him. She sent him the tiniest of waves.

Good enough. The country boy rose and wound his way down the hill to the city girl.

Krista had led Will off by the time he came alongside Natalia. "You doing okay?" he said and casually raised his hand, intending to touch her braid of bright hair. Instead, he brushed her bag. Something hard and square.

She shot him an embarrassed look, her back stiff. "I couldn't leave him in the truck," she said. "I know we made a deal with Sadie, and then I go back on it but—"

He wrapped his arm around her shoulders and pulled her tight against his side, the urn jabbing into his hip. "Happy Father's Day, Daniel," he whispered against Natalia's hair, the color of her brother's.

She tugged her bag out from between them and hugged it to her front, leaning against him. "Happy Father's Day," she said. Together, they watched Sadie play with her new friends.

THE FOLLOWING WEDNESDAY, Natalia nearly executed a U-turn after seeing the location of the rental Krista had learned about through one of her spa clients. Krista had said it was close to the lake. No, it was on the lake. A strip of lawn separated the house from the water. Decent-sized, she'd said. No, it was a modern A-frame that must have at least four bedrooms. Not suitable for just her and Sadie.

But there was a yard, big enough for a trampoline, and a walking path. The property manager waved to her from the front step. She might as well go through the paces.

The property manager with bouncy blond hair led her up and down and around the house. It was beautiful and ridiculously big for Sadie and her, and possibly dangerous with the mezzanine railing that overlooked the living room complete with a full-sized fireplace. Big and overdone, and yet she could picture Sadie here.

She looked through the window at the clear blue lake beyond. Sadie's nightmare made real.

"Isn't that an absolutely gorgeous view?" The property manager was already heading to the stairwell. "Come, let me show you."

A cobbled walkway led onto the dock. The boards were spaced perfectly to grab Natalia's heels, so she stepped barefoot onto the dock. The property manager's shoes thudded on the wood, reverberating into Natalia's bare soles. The vibrations felt therapeutic.

"Do you have a boat?"

"No."

"It's a great place to just be, too." The property manager was nothing if not adaptable. "Lots of people bring out their deck chairs and enjoy the view."

Natalia squatted down, her skirt riding up, to check the depth of the water. She could barely make out the bottom. On impulse, she swung her legs over the side, immersing her feet and calves in the cold water. She sucked in her breath.

"That's the spirit!"

The one thing a lake gave was space. Outside of a couple of apple trees along the fence, there were no other trees on the property and the lake stretched to the horizon. Open and clear. She, if not Sadie, would have felt at peace here.

"Does your niece swim?" the property manager said.

"No. She's not yet five. But she knows the dangers." More than most kids.

"They learn so fast. My grandkids figured it out in a couple of afternoons in the water. Enough to float and dog-paddle and keep their heads above water. Now the trouble is keeping them out of water. Absolutely no fear."

Absolutely no fear. Wasn't that what she wanted for Sadie? No fear of people, no fear of water, no fears, period.

Sadie had already started the journey on her own. She navigated deep puddles, took baths past her belly button. At the barbecue on Sunday, the dads had set up a wading pool, and Sadie waded right in, saddened only because she didn't have a bathing suit so she could kneel and crab walk about like the others.

Here near the shore, a small school of minnows, a cloud of black lines, flicked past her legs and under the dock.

Sadie would've gasped with excitement.

Brock had invited her to stay at the ranch for Sadie's sake. But moving here was also for their niece's sake. To help her to accept not just the danger of water, but its charms, too.

Natalia turned to the property manager. "I'll take it."

KNUT WAS IN his rocking chair when Natalia and Sadie arrived back at the Jansson ranch a few days later in the middle of the afternoon She planned to make an early supper so she could help Brock with Persephone. In their little more than a week together, Persephone could now walk past a full trough of water without shying away. The horse and Sadie had something in common. She must warn Brock to watch Sadie around troughs now. The water was deep enough to drown a small child.

Knut opened his arms to Sadie. "Hello, girl." His voice sounded strained.

Something had happened. Brock.

Knut looked over Sadie's head to Natalia. "Brock's down at the barn. You might want to give him space."

Brock never needed space. He gave it. Knut's eyes held silent appeal. Did he want her to go to him? She pointed at the back door and then herself. He gave a quick nod.

"Sure, I'll go…for a walk," she said, edging away.

Sadie hadn't missed a beat. "Tell Uncle Brock we're having pizza tonight."

"Pizza? With lots of rubber tires?" Knut said, neatly diverting Sadie's attention away from Natalia.

"Olives, Knut. They're olives."

"Then how come they feel like rubber tires?"

Natalia closed the door on Sadie's answer. Knut derived untold pleasure from posing circular questions for which Sadie tried to give straight answers.

Inside the horse barn, Brock stood with his back to her, head bowed. He seemed to be thinking, but then his shoulders rose and fell like a man crying or trying not to.

Something horrible had happened, and that was why Knut had wanted her to come. Didn't he know that she had no idea what to do? She was hopeless at comforting a man. On her last date with one man, he'd told her how he'd set his pet budgie on the balcony railing and a magpie had swooped in and carried it off. Beset with guilt and grief, he had sat slouched at the restaurant table, and Natalia had listened because that was what articles advised. When he'd fallen quiet, she'd thought it was her cue to say something. She'd told him that her sister-in-law had died suddenly, too. He snapped that this wasn't about her. She'd only meant for him not to feel alone in his sadness, but maybe it had been selfish of her.

She didn't want to make the same mistake with this man. Since the Father's Day barbecue, they'd become more like partners. They trained Persephone together, coordinated times to be together for meals and for walks with Sadie. She squealed in delight at bringing them together, and they'd shared quiet smiles over her head at her little game.

Natalia had stayed silent about her lakeside rental. It would undo all the good rapport they were building. Brock wouldn't buy her argument that she was doing it for Sadie's sake. She didn't fully believe it herself. Even as they drew closer, it seemed more important that she strike a distance between them. All her romantic relationships had crashed because she crossed lines too early and came off as needy or awkward. Other than that little bit of fakery she pulled at the creek, she'd performed much better with Brock. But seeing him so broken and alone now, that could all change, if she wasn't careful.

She scuffed her feet. "Hey there."

Brock swiped at his face before turning. He didn't move, didn't speak.

She stepped closer, keeping it casual, like with Persephone. Giving Brock an out, and maybe herself, too. "Knut said you were here. He's in the house with Sadie. They're talking pizza."

Brock nodded. His eyes were red, his cheeks wet. Should she ignore his tears for the sake of his privacy?

"Fifty-fifty's dead."

Natalia gasped. She'd never seen the horse, but Brock had often mentioned him. "I'm so sorry. What happened?"

"It was his stomach. He must've eaten something out in the pasture. It was cutting him up inside. No way of fixing that."

Brock sawed his teeth on his lip. "Mateo came over and told me. Fifty-fifty had started going downhill the past few days, right after I'd gone over to work him. Mateo had the vet out but held off telling me until he knew something, and by then, it was already over."

Her budgie man had described the bird's death in graphic detail, and Natalia had secretly wished he'd stop. Brock's brief account shuttered his pain.

"These things happen, I know. Seen enough horses go down, and never shed a tear, but ever since—"

His hands hung at his sides, and with only a few steps, she could reach out and take them. He had comforted her at the creek. Her turn.

"Ever since Abby passed, I've been like this." He squeezed his eyes shut, the tears still seeping through.

How to reach him? She swam against the same helplessness that had weighed her down when Daniel had called nearly five years ago to say that she had a niece and then in the next shaky breath to say that Abby hadn't made it.

Still elated about Sadie's birth, she'd asked what he meant. "She died, Lia. She died." And then he'd burst into sobs.

"I bawled when Dan told me," Brock said now. "It…it came like a wave, the news. I could tell Dan was holding it in. He said he had to call you."

Daniel had let Natalia contact their parents. The conversation was short. She had called again to inform them of their son's death. Another short conversation. She didn't think she would ever have reason to call them again. "I remember," she said softly. "He cried with me."

"Did he tell you what she said? Before she died?"

Natalia shook her head. With her, Daniel had kept repeating "What am I going to do? What am I going to do?" And she'd had no answer, and to her everlasting guilt, she'd not gone to see him, to wrap her arms around him and tell him that everything would be okay, even though she wasn't sure it would be.

"'I don't want to die.'"

Natalia had never known the full reason for Abby's death. "What...happened exactly?"

Brock, his face red and blotchy, looked at her in surprise. "You don't know?"

Natalia shook her head. "Daniel didn't say. He never spoke about her...and I didn't ask." She'd let Daniel take the lead. She should've given him a chance to open up.

"She...she had a tear in her uterus, and they couldn't stop the bleeding. In any other hospital she would've been fine, but out there, there was no doctor and no blood to give her."

Brock's hands balled into fists. Natalia ached to wrap them around hers.

"You better get used to this," Brock said. "I haven't found a cure. Every time a horse I know dies, I cry like it's Abby all over again. Five years on, and I'm still no better." He smiled weakly. "Good news is that I do eventually stop."

Somehow his smile made him look all the sadder, and just as she had with Sadie when she'd come to her room after the nightmare, she held out her arms, and like Sadie, Brock fell into them.

This time, his arms around her were not loose and easy like at the creek, but tight as if she might float away, and he'd drown if he let go.

Finally, she'd gotten it right and not, she saw now, because she'd done anything so different, but because his belief in her powers to comfort had given her the strength to give him what he needed.

He rested his head on hers, and she let herself be his pillow and his rock.

CHAPTER NINE

WHAT A JERK thing to do. He'd blubbered about Abby, when Lia's brother had passed not three months ago. What did it say about a guy wanting to offer his support and then folding like a teddy bear in her arms? He had apologized when he'd found the backbone to pull away, more for wetting her with his tears than for not recognizing her own grief.

She'd handed him a tissue and the conversation had eased into the usual, if shaky, back-and-forth of their day and it wasn't until he lay in bed that night before the extent of his selfishness hit home.

He would've apologized the next morning but she had already left and for the next two days he barely saw her. She'd tucked Sadie into bed the first night, gone back to her shop and not returned until nearly 1:00 a.m. And then today, he'd had Sadie all day because she was in meetings down in Calgary. She'd texted to say she was coming back late.

He was on his deck counting stars when he heard her SUV roll into the carport.

Her door slammed and he began to rise in his seat to join her when she rounded the corner of his deck.

"Saw your light on. Sadie's in bed?"

He gestured to the empty chair beside him. "Yeah. She talked me into watching *The Lion King* again."

"Am I on nightmare watch then?" Instead of sitting, she stretched, arms high and back arched. He liked that look.

If he was going to make a big apology, he might as well start with a small one. "I confess that she has already watched it, since her nightmare. It was pouring rain one afternoon, and she talked me into putting it on. I forgot to tell you that night, and the next morning, there was nothing to report."

"That's a relief."

She swept her arms down to touch her toes. He liked that look, too. "How's Calgary?"

"Good. I went out for dinner with Gina, and it looks as if we're on track to open late July."

"July? I thought the plan was Thanksgiving."

She straightened and then tilted into a *k*-shape. "All the fixtures are in place, and it's a question now of last-minute stocking. We decided to have a soft opening for the summer inventory, work out the kinks, see the kind of stuff that grabs attention, source out more local crafters."

She moved into a reverse *k*. "But before all that can happen, I will have to start hiring next week."

"Hiring?"

"For the shop. I'm hoping to find someone local. It'll be easier for…later."

Later. "You mean when you go back to Calgary?"

"Yes."

"You could stay here," he said quickly. "Just putting that out there. Again."

She stood straight and faced him. "Thanks, but I don't think it's for me."

"You're good with horses and—" he brought himself forward so his elbows were on his knees and he was closer to her "—and with crying cowboys."

She smiled and folded herself into the chair. "No worries."

"I owe you an apology. I'm not so macho as to criticize a man for crying, but it was selfish of me to lean on you when you are grieving for a sibling, too. One gone for only a few months."

Her smile dropped away. "I... I'm doing okay. He's staying with me this week. I don't chat with him the way Sadie does, but it helps me to think about the past. My—our parents find it easy to let go of things, even their son. I'm not so good at that."

"I'm living proof that it's nearly impossible." Two days later and he still felt a little winded.

"That's not a good prognosis for Sadie."

"Death changed her the day she was born."

Natalia wrapped her arms around her waist. He shook out the jacket shirt he'd taken off earlier. "Here."

She hesitated, and her gaze flew to his face, searching. What? She gave a short sigh and then slipped across to the seat beside him. She must've supposed he was holding it out for her to come to him. This worked, too.

He spread the shirt across her lap as casually as he could manage. At some point, with her body tight against his in the barn, he'd become acutely aware that he was holding her less for support and more for his pleasure. Besides the apology, he'd occupied his spare thoughts with how he might precipitate a repeat hug solely for the purpose of their mutual pleasure.

"It's your choice if you want to stay or not, Lia. I talked with Knut and he's okay with you staying on. I just want you to know that this is an option. It would be good for Sadie."

Natalia pulled the jacket up around her shoulders, the collar snugging her neck. "And you, Brock? How would you feel about me staying?"

It would rank as the top event to have come his way in a long time. He leaned back on the bench beside her, her red-gold hair grazing his shoulder. He picked up on the same scent he'd breathed in the barn. Vanilla and cinnamon. "You know I like you. More each day. We get along. It feels as if you're part of the place."

She tipped her cheek to him. "Sometimes it feels right to be here. Like when I drove up and your light was on, I thought that this is where I want…where I might want to be."

His heart thumped, like when the rodeo announcer broadcasted his name just before his ride. *Keep it casual.* "You're welcome on my bench any day of the year."

She searched his face for confirmation of his soft invitation. Silently, he gave it to her.

Her eyes sparked in answer, and her chin lifted. Their lips touched, the kiss slow and tender. He pulled her tighter into his arms, deepening the kiss. And she let him. A small part of his rational brain kept ticking, though, and he pulled away. "That was incredible, but I hadn't intended to take it this far."

She stiffened and dropped her hand from his cheek. "I'm sorry. I misinterpreted."

"You didn't. It was my fault. I don't want you to feel pressured into thinking that you staying here requires us to be together, too."

"Right. Of course." She stood and began to fold his jacket shirt. "I'm not good when it comes to…relationships. I tend to overreact… make assumptions. You're not the first." His jacket shirt was folded like the day he'd bought it off the shelf. She set it down on the bench beside him. "I'm sorry. You were being… welcoming, that's all." She backed down the steps. "I'll see you tomorrow. Good night."

She was gone before he could stop her, and maybe it was for the best. He'd set out to give her space, and then with the kiss had sucked it all away.

Neither could he just let her walk away. Because even that one short kiss was more powerful than anything he'd experienced before.

And he was sure the attraction was reciprocal. He had to find a way to make her want to stay without making her feel trapped. For Sadie's sake, and their own.

USUALLY, SHE GOT through the first kiss without screwing up. She could extend it for a few more dates, even a month or two before the guy stopped calling, stopped answering, just stopped. Brock had called it quits in the middle of their first kiss.

Mortification kept her awake half the night. And yeah, her heart was sore, too. She turned to the silhouette of the urn. Sadie had placed it on her bedside table because, as she explained, Natalia could whisper to him without anyone hearing. "I screwed up again, Daniel. But I promise I won't let it hurt Sadie."

A restless night led her to sleeping in two extra hours. Fortunately, Sadie was with Brock this morning. She pulled on shorts and a top, bundling her hair into a scrunchie. Caffeine first.

Knut was washing dishes as she beelined for the coffeemaker. "You'll have to put on a fresh pot," he said.

"That's okay, I'll just press a cup for myself." She reached in the cupboard for her single-size French press, which she hadn't used in nearly two months.

"I was planning on treating myself to another cup, anyway," Knut said. "Brock pretty near drained the entire pot himself this morning."

Had he not slept well, either? She slid the press back inside the cupboard and took down the coffee can. "Is he out with Sadie?"

"Yeah, they went riding off together. We're all going into town later for July first celebrations. You coming?"

She'd not forgotten about Canada Day. Even though the store wasn't open yet, she had jazzed up the window display with pioneer collectibles, red-and-white maple leaf flags everywhere. Never too early to catch the interest of passersby on what Bridget rated as the busiest weekend of the year. She expected to stay busy inside, setting out the last of the stock for next week's soft opening, and to read through submitted résumés. And she didn't think Brock really wanted her too close.

Knut's cell on the island rang. His hands still in the soapy water, he asked, "Who is that?"

Natalia glanced at the caller ID. "Grace."

That father-daughter conversation was never quiet. "You want me to take over there?"

"No time. Answer it before it goes to voice mail. Hard enough to get a hold of her as it is."

Natalia quickly gave her name to Grace. "Your dad's here, but he's washing dishes."

"Ask her if she's coming up for Thanksgiving."

"He wants to—"

"I heard him. Can you put us on speakerphone, please?"

Natalia did and brought the phone closer to the sink.

"Dad? Can you hear me?"

"How could I not? You're like a fire alarm. You coming?"

"You don't need me there. There'll be Haley and Mateo and Jonah. Brock and Natalia and Sadie." Natalia swallowed at Grace's grouping of her with Brock and Sadie, as if they were their own family.

"Of course, I got people. You don't. I'm asking for your sake, so be selfish and enjoy your family for one weekend of the year. Where else you got to go?"

"Thanks, Dad, for pointing out my relationship status."

"We have the same status, dear," Knut said quietly.

There was a pause, and while Grace's next words weren't exactly apologetic, the sharpness had gone. "I'll come, if you want it so much."

"I wouldn't be calling three and a half months ahead if I didn't. Just so you know, you'll be staying over at Haley's. I've got a full house here."

He wouldn't by then.

"Great, you're kicking me out before I'm even in the door."

Natalia couldn't keep pretending. "You can have your old room, Grace. Don't worry. I'm leaving in a couple of weeks. I've already found a place."

Knut looked at her as if she'd announced plans to skip the country. "I'll call you back," he told Grace and, without waiting for her reply, ended the call, soapy water and all. Instinctively, Natalia wiped the phone dry with the hem of her shirt.

Knut pulled the sink plug and dried his hands on a towel.

"Now, why would you leave us?"

He looked disappointed. Did she really mean

that much to him, or was she over-reading the situation as she had with Brock?

Sadie's high voice sounded from the other side of the back door and she came through, chirpy and bouncy, Brock behind her.

Natalia and Brock exchanged quick glances and then looked away. Brock turned to Knut and frowned, no doubt taking in Knut's glum expression.

Sadie hadn't clued in. "Did Grace call back?"

Knut wiped around the sink, his back half-turned to Sadie. "She did. She said she'd come."

"Yay!" Sadie hugged Natalia around the waist, jumping up and down, a lift and a drag. "Are you surprised, Auntie Lia? We're going to have a big, big, big Thanksgiving. Knut invited the guests, and you and me can decorate, and you and Uncle Brock and me and probably Mateo can cook. And can we use that big, big, big table from the store? If it hasn't sold. We can put it back afterward. We have enough plates. I counted. Knut and I have planned it all out."

Another disastrous scheme in the making. Natalia couldn't let Sadie continue to believe that she would get her dream Thanksgiving, but neither could she crush her heart. "You've put a lot of thought into this, Sadie."

"I have. Nobody will be alone."

Natalia took hold of Sadie's shoulders, pressing down just enough to halt the jumping. "I'm more than happy to help with Thanksgiving, Sadie. But you have to remember that Thanksgiving is a full three months away. It'll be in October when summer is gone." And she'd promised to spend Thanksgiving with Gina.

"That's fine," Sadie said. "I can wait."

Brock, for his part, had taken a seat at his usual place at the table, the one nearest the back door. Sitting sideways, he looked ready to exit.

Natalia cupped Sadie's cheeks in her hand and dealt the blow. "Just so long as you know that we won't be living here."

Sadie pulled free of Natalia. "What do you mean we won't be here?"

She looked from Knut to her uncle; both kept their heads down.

"Remember the agreement. Three months with Uncle Brock, three months with me. You start living with me at the end of this month. In Spirit Lake."

"But I don't want to. I want to stay here with you."

"And you will stay with me. Just not here.

I found a terrific place. It's a house right by the water."

Brock's head shot up. "When did you arrange all this?"

She couldn't look him in the eye. "A couple of weeks ago." While they'd taken walks together and trained Persephone. She had not wanted to ruin those times. Well, she was paying for it now. Yesterday's delay translated into today's betrayal.

Sadie rushed to him. "Tell her she has to stay. You want her to stay, too. I know you do."

"She has a right to go if she wants," Brock said quietly. "And by the law, you need to go with her."

Brock was right but she couldn't drag a rebellious Sadie along with her, legalities aside.

She sat at the table to be closer to Sadie. "All right, you can stay. If that's okay with Uncle Brock. I won't force you to come with me. I'll set up my place and maybe you can stay the night now and again. Longer, if you like it. Does that sound fair?"

"I stay and you go?"

"Yes."

Sadie clutched the ammolite. "Can I still keep the necklace?"

"Of course. For as long as you want its magic."

Sadie turned to Brock. "Will that be okay with you?" Her shoulders were hunched, her voice timid. Exactly like the defeated girl they'd met in Grande Prairie more than two months ago.

Brock pulled her onto his lap. "That's plenty okay."

"Can Auntie Lia come visit?"

"Whenever she wants," Brock said. Natalia doubted that, but she appreciated how sincere he sounded.

"And can she sleep over here, like me at her place?"

"Whenever she wants."

"And if she wants to move back, can she?"

Brock hesitated. Leave it to Sadie to put them in a sticky situation. He smoothed her bright hair and quietly said, "Best let things be, Sadie."

He couldn't have said it more gently, but Sadie looked between the two of them and burst into tears as if her heart was breaking.

THE TEARS ONLY drew to a hiccup-y end when Lia promised that she and Sadie would plan a beautiful Thanksgiving, and that, yes, she would definitely spend the entire day on the ranch from beginning to end.

Brock couldn't bring himself to say anything through it all. Kept himself quiet and still, especially when the curve of Lia's cheek and her soft lips had come close as she talked to Sadie on his lap about how everything was going to be okay and they would have lots of good times together. And that, of course, Uncle Brock was welcome to visit anytime he wanted at her place.

He couldn't wrap his head around visiting her at a home that wasn't also his. A place she'd plotted to escape to, even as he hoped to ignite a romance between them.

The next day, Lia took Sadie to see the new place and she came back raving about the upstairs-downstairs house, the view, the fish and how she was going to have a trampoline.

"You can have a trampoline here," he said. How much did those things cost, anyway?

"Don't waste your money," Sadie said. "I can just use Auntie Lia's."

That house would cost a pretty penny each month, especially since it was the tourist season, and Lia could swing that while sinking money into the store. The knickknack business proved more profitable than horse therapy.

Lia moved out two weeks later during which time by tacit agreement they'd not worked together on Persephone. The mare had regressed, not focusing, preferring her own company. Her horse sense had picked up on something amiss. In the evenings when Lia usually visited, Persephone hung around at the gate and eyed the house. He didn't blame the horse. He'd caught himself doing the same once or twice.

About a week after Lia moved out, Brock retreated one evening to his barn den, feet up on the sawhorse, when Persephone gave a snicker of recognition. Like a stupid fool, he hurried to the entrance.

It was Knut, feeding Persephone a wedge of rindless watermelon. Knut had bought a watermelon for Sadie, but she'd stayed in town for a playdate and eaten supper with Natalia at *Penny's* restaurant.

"Might as well feed it to her," Knut said. This was the gloomiest Knut had been since Miranda's death more than ten years ago. Brock had worked five winters at the ranch by then, and after her death, Knut had insisted Brock come and stay whenever and for however long he wanted. Brock drifted off for the summers and came back in the fall to winter over. Brock provided company to Knut but Sadie had restored his boss's joy of life that he once had around his wife.

"The stuff keeps," Brock said. Pike sat politely beside Knut and he threw a chunk into the grass. Pike dived after it as if hunting a gopher.

"Not for long enough," Knut said. Watermelon filled a plastic tub.

"I thought of taking Perse out with the other horses. Put the saddle on, no rider, and lead her," Brock said. "Want to come with me?"

Knut shrugged. "Lia's dropping off Sadie soon."

"She texted. Not until seven thirty or so. Sadie has a playdate with Penny. Jack and Bridget's daughter."

Knut sighed, and riding across the pasture only elicited more sighs. He finally twisted in his saddle to face Brock. "What happened? You and Lia seemed to be getting along just fine."

"Nothing happened, Knut." There was a kind of truth to that. "We had an agreement with the courts and we're sticking to it."

"Sadie still lives here. That's not according to the courts."

"For now."

"You think that'll change?"

The reins to Persephone jerked in his hand as she followed with her head too high, on the alert for anything. Or hoping to see her special human. "It might. I think the only reason she's not living there full-time right now is because she's scared of water."

"If she's so scared, why did Natalia pick a place right on the lake?"

She hadn't explained herself to him, but knowing her philosophy about fears, it probably had something to do with desensitizing Sadie to deep water. "There's lots she likes there."

Including proximity to shops. It seemed every day Sadie came back with a new top or toy or restaurant leftovers. He could not provide for Sadie the way Lia could. Down the road, sure. If his reputation grew, but right now, he'd come to depend on Lia to help him with that. As much as it hurt to say, Knut deserved the truth.

"She's got money. I saw the supporting documents she submitted to the court. It was this thick." Brock spread his hands a foot apart. "I'm exaggerating only a little."

"How much money do you need?"

"I'm not asking. I got to look good based on my own assets. Which aren't anything. I don't own the horse I'm riding or the land she's on. I got a truck that's only a speck of rust short of passing inspection."

"There's more to a man than what he owns."

"Tell that to the courts."

"What kind of assets do the courts want?"

"I dunno…land, a business, a professional income."

Knut pulled Crocus to a stop, and Brock followed suit. All three mares shook their heads, lifted hooves, and Crocus pricked her ears toward the slough at the edge of the pasture. The horses wouldn't stick to this holding pattern for long. Knut had better get to his point quick.

He did. "Would a couple of quarters do?"

Brock couldn't mistake the intent in Knut's blue eyes, but he asked, anyway. "What are you saying? Your land? To me?"

"That's what I'm saying."

Three hundred twenty acres. That would do it. "But that's upward of a million dollars, Knut. There's no way I could pay you that back."

Knut twisted in his saddle, rested his hands over the pommel. "Brock, I've already willed it to you. Now, the government, being the greedy lot they are, will grab their share, but it's yours for the asking."

Brock looked at Crocus's head, the cattle like black boulders resting in the shade, Pike checking out a gopher hole. He was like a lottery winner, stunned, checking the numbers again. "Are you sure, Knut? There's still no guarantee Sadie will come stay with me, and it's not as if living with Natalia is such a bad thing for her. I appreciate it and all, but it doesn't seem right. Give it to Haley. Keep it in the family."

"You are family," Knut said fiercely. "There's a reason Haley kids you about being my son. Because…it's the truth."

Knut had always chosen to give a secretive smile whenever his daughters groused about his third child. The unspoken closeness between the men had layers Brock had never dug too far into, never supposed he had the right to.

"I'm not out to replace your dad. But right from the time you showed up with your duffel bag and that same truck fifteen years ago, I kinda took you on the same way I took on the girls."

"You were legally obliged to take them on,"

Brock reminded Knut. "They're biologically yours. Not me."

"It didn't feel different. It felt like I had no choice, like I didn't want a choice, either."

Brock understood. That perfectly described his feelings for Sadie. So much the harder for Sadie torn between two people she loved.

"So… Haley has six quarters and Grace's got her quarter down in the Foothills. Which suits them fine. That leaves you to take care of."

"You don't have to take care of me."

"I just got through explaining how I do. And if you don't want to think of yourself, think of Sadie. You could pass the land to her, or to one of your own kids."

"If I ever have any." His thoughts ricocheted to Lia and then he smacked them away. But Knut had a point. Sadie would always have a home with him. Lia had guaranteed as much when she decorated Sadie's bedroom months ago.

"You drive a hard bargain," Brock said. "I accept."

"Good," Knut said. "Now there's no reason on God's green earth that you can't go after Natalia."

It was Brock's turn to give a weary sigh.

"Knut, I know about the little matchmaking scheme between you and Sadie. I overheard you two talking in the garden way back at the start of June when you were planting flowers. It's not going to work."

"It's not going to work because you don't want it to or because you tried and it didn't work out?"

"The latter case, I suppose."

"Well, we're going at it again, then."

"But Lia doesn't want it."

"She's a woman. It's her prerogative to change her mind. Our job is to give her reason to."

Brock didn't argue in the face of the old man's unswerving conviction. He nudged Canuck Luck forward, Persephone in tow. Knut could give him every square inch of his land, and it wouldn't change the sad fact that if it weren't for Sadie, Lia would not step foot on the property.

CHAPTER TEN

NATALIA SPREAD THE three résumés along the polished stove top that now served as her counter. The candidates all sucked for one reason or another. Inexperienced, inflexible, disinterested.

"Auntie, can we go now?"

Sadie had been patient through the interview process. She'd amused herself with paints, and for the last one, Natalia had given Sadie her phone to play games on, the interview punctuated by Sadie's triumphant cries when another level was achieved.

"Yes," Natalia said, piling the sheets together. She could sleep on it, but she had to decide soon. Here it was, the first of August and no staff. She'd delayed her soft opening to help Sadie adjust to her new watery home, but now her own business drive—and Gina—was pressuring her to get a move on. As it was, she'd probably missed the window to open this coming long weekend. She could try running it herself, she supposed, but that would only work on a very short-term basis. Sadie was her top job.

The front door gave a glassy rattle from a series of knocks. A woman waved. She looked familiar, but only when Natalia opened the door did it click.

"Carolyn! Come in."

"I'm sorry to come unannounced," she said, "but I heard from Gina that you were looking...and I came up. I was wondering if you'd be interested in talking with me about the position."

Natalia took in the short hair dyed autumnal shades, the stylish blouse and pants, the alert aspect. Hard to believe that this was the same dispirited, slouched woman from the Calgary store.

Wanting to manage Natalia's pet project.

"Sadie, I have one more person to talk to, and then I promise we'll leave for the day."

"I'm sorry," Carolyn said to Sadie. "I'm interrupting time with your auntie." And to Natalia, "I can come later."

It was the way Carolyn apologized to Sadie first that melted Natalia. Sadie had her eye on Carolyn's hands. "They're so beautiful."

Carolyn stretched out her fingers to better

show off her nails. "Aren't they? Lake and beach themes. Look, there's a shell on my pinkie. See?"

Sadie inspected the pinkie and the nine other fingers, Carolyn giving her all the time in the world to do so. Was this really the same woman? And if it was, what if she slid back to her earlier dysfunction?

"Is it okay if I talk with your auntie for a few minutes?" Carolyn knew how to ask for the sale.

Sadie nodded. "I can wait." She returned with Natalia's phone to her seat at one end of the long dining table.

Natalia showed Carolyn to the other end of the table and opened with the obvious question. "What happened to your store?"

"You don't know? We're doing what you're doing here, converting it into a Home & Holidays store."

Gina had told Natalia none of this. Wouldn't a partner consult before implementing a change, as she had done before starting this shop?

"My shop's undergoing a makeover, like I did." Carolyn laughed, a warm and light crescendo that had Sadie lifting her eyes away from her screen. "With Gina's help. The store, not me." She trilled again, a bit more of a nervous jingle. Nervousness denoted interest.

"Gina sent me to you. She told me not to waste a moment. That you were expecting me." Carolyn scanned Natalia's face. "But you weren't."

Maybe a message had come through while Sadie had the phone. Natalia would give Gina the benefit of the doubt.

"I am taken by surprise a bit," Natalia admitted. "I hadn't expected you."

Carolyn spread her hands flat on the wood table. "This is the thing. Back when you last saw me…you caught me at a weak moment. I was having health issues, I was depressed, I was worried. It's my son. He lives close to town here. He's a single dad with two young ones, nine and six. He farms with his uncle, my sister's husband, but he needs someone close by to help with the kids, even if it's only his mom. But how could I help him?

"Then Gina comes along a few weeks ago and proposes a change to the store. I take it because I like the idea of a partnership and I've always liked the Home & Holidays line. Then today we get to talking, and she tells me where you're opening up, and I say that my son lives here. She came up with the idea of a swap."

"Yes!" Sadie fist-pumped the air. "Fastest time ever, Auntie!"

"Good work," Natalia said automatically. She had good reason to say that a half-dozen times a day. "Swap?"

"I manage this store and you manage mine. After Gina has set it up right."

Natalia fought the urge to call Gina right then.

"This is the first I've heard of the arrangement."

Carolyn stilled at the sharpness in Natalia's voice. "I'm sorry. I thought Gina had told you…"

Natalia pulled herself up sharp. Carolyn was only acting according to Gina's machinations. And Gina…well, a memory tinkled at the back of Natalia's mind. Over dinner, before the doomed kiss between her and Brock, she and Gina had talked about expanding the retail concept to Calgary locations, and the name of Carolyn's Collectibles had floated over their wineglasses. Gina had acted on what Natalia had assumed was only an idea.

Besides, she hadn't indicated to Gina that she wasn't returning to Calgary. Now that it had all gone sideways with Brock, she was back to her original plan. Except that she'd started to dream a little of something more permanent involving Sadie and her at the lake house with a thriving store walking distance away.

"It doesn't matter, Carolyn. I do need someone I can trust and who knows a bit about the business."

"Then I'm your girl," Carolyn said on another high-pitched laugh.

"What do you think of the store here?"

Carolyn looked dutifully around. "It's beautiful. Well laid out." Her gaze dwelled on the neatly stacked jars of herbs atop sacking on the table beside them.

"Thank you. Any suggestions?"

Carolyn's glimmer of a smile registered Natalia's challenge. "I think, and this is just what I see off the top…but, well, it seems to me that it's almost too well laid out."

"Oh?"

"I mean…look, I know my store was a mess and I'm not suggesting that you turn this store into that, but I got my best sales when people felt they were on a bit of a discovery. That they could touch things. And then you know once they pick things up, it's harder to set them down again."

Sadie did that all the time. She had carried

around a cow stuffie and Natalia removed it from inventory and bought it for her. All because Sadie had been able to sample the wares.

"You might have a point," Natalia admitted.

Carolyn brightened. "For instance." She took the jars of herbs and batted them onto the sacking. The thuds and knocks of the thick jars startled Sadie and she looked wide-eyed at her aunt.

Carolyn smiled. "Doesn't it just make you want to pick them up?"

It most certainly did. And while Carolyn could contribute to the store's success, she wasn't going to turn her store—and it was entirely hers in spirit, despite her business partnership—into a bargain bin heap. She'd return to Calgary when she was good and ready, and not according to Gina's program.

Natalia set one jar beside another, labels facing out. "Can you start this weekend?"

BROCK SLAMMED HIS truck door shut. He had to, otherwise it wouldn't catch. It was always a small miracle that it didn't fall off. The crush of steel on rust brought Sadie to the front door of Natalia's place.

"Uncle Brock! Won't you come inside?"

Sadie was inviting him into a house he could barely afford to drive by, a so-called cottage with its soaring A-frame and solid stone framework. He sat on the bench outside and pulled off his boots. The scuffed pair looked totally out of place on the deck with its stone vases.

"We have a closet," Sadie said. "You don't need to leave them out here."

"I think Auntie Lia would prefer it," he said, but Sadie had already disappeared inside, hollering his arrival.

Stepping inside, he had to look up to see Natalia, who stood at a railing that overlooked the living room. She held a laundry basket, her hip jutting out. She wore a huge smile. Happy to see him? "Thanks for coming, Brock."

"Thanks for having me." He sounded trite, but he meant it.

"Just trying to get ahead of a few chores. I hired someone yesterday, so looks as if it's a go to open this weekend."

He'd wondered if she'd opened yet. A little more than three weeks since her flight from the ranch, and they were losing touch. "Sounds good." Another stilted answer.

Her cheeriness faded and she stepped back.

"Anyway, I think Sadie wants to show you around."

If Lia had been happy to see him, she clearly wished for better company now.

Sadie conducted the tour as only someone not quite five would. They bypassed Natalia's bedroom and spent a good amount of time in hers. It was decorated much like on the farm with a different quilt of Grace's, and the addition of a lava lamp. "In case I want to stay over," she said. She lay on the bed and waved her arms and legs, as if making snow angels.

"You can if you want," Brock said.

She gave the answer he selfishly wanted to hear. "No." And hopped off. The tour of the kitchen focused on the fizzy water and yogurt tubes in the stainless steel fridge, and the popcorn maker for movie nights. The living room, with its big-screen TV the size of his truck box and the couch with the hidden cubbyholes built into the armrests. Front and center on the coffee table sat a ham radio, like Sadie's. Lia's, then. Did she talk to Rudy, too?

Lia glided in the background, light-footed in a short skirt and loose top.

"Beautiful place," he said.

This time her answering smile was stiffer,

hesitant. "Thank you. I was hoping that you would like it."

He might have liked it better if she hadn't left the ranch to live in it. "What's not to like?"

"It doesn't have Knut," Sadie said. "Or Pike."

"True," Natalia said. "I miss them." She turned to Brock. "And Persephone. How's she doing?"

"She's restless. Misses you, too."

"I'll have to come out and visit her."

"You're welcome anytime," he said. He thought he hadn't given away how much he missed her, but Lia reddened.

Sadie looked between them, wide-eyed like the day he'd brought Pike home. "Auntie Lia's not working at the store tomorrow because Carolyn's there. She can come tomorrow, anytime."

Still up to her matchmaking tricks. Lia made shooing motions at Sadie. "Go on, show your uncle the lake."

It was hard to miss. The wide windows displayed the blue spread of water, glinting in the early evening. Sadie tore across the grass in her bare feet and jumped up and down on the dock. Brock considered his sock feet. He could go back and get his boots or… He stripped off his socks and followed Sadie across the grass.

"The ground's pokier than Sadie makes it appear." Natalia followed a step behind him in sandals. "Somehow she misses all the little rocks and pine cones."

"Between here and the ranch, she probably has got soles like leather," Brock said.

"Remember the rules," Natalia called to Sadie, but it appeared she already knew. She hopped on one foot and then the other at the dock's edge, but only when Natalia had stepped on it first, did she follow along. "Good. And what's the other rule?"

"Walk or sit or lie down."

When Sadie adopted the last option to look for fish, Natalia turned to him and spoke quickly, so quickly his brain scrambled through the first bit to keep up. "I'm really sorry about not telling you about getting this place right away. I took the place to help with Sadie overcoming her fear of water. And you can see it's working. It wasn't…personal. But I can see that you might take it that way."

The horse-heavy weight on his chest lifted and he took her hand in his. "I get it. Thanks… for telling me. We're good, okay?"

Her hand softened inside his. "Okay. I'd

like you to have a house key, just in case you ever need to get in. Is that all right?"

Letting him into her house…and her life? "Sure is."

She did that adorable thing where she blushed, bit her lip and avoided his eyes. She didn't wiggle her hand out from his. "School's starting in a month."

"Shouldn't be a problem. June ended well, right?"

"Better than it started, but it's a new year, a new teacher."

"And a new Sadie. I'm not worried."

He could feel her relax. He missed their daily talks, and maybe she did, too.

"Swim lessons start back up in September, too," she said. "I enrolled her."

And paid for it, but with Knut's offer, he could soon pull his own weight. "Good idea."

Natalia tilted her face to him, squinting an eye against the sun. It was like a long, slow wink. "Somebody's birthday is coming up in less than two weeks."

Sadie turning five. Five years since Abby had passed. He usually kept busy that night. And to himself. He made for miserable company every August the twelfth. He released Lia's hand. "Yep."

"I thought, maybe so it's less of a reminder of Daniel not being here for it, that we—or I—might give her an entirely new memory. And, well, maybe you, too."

She hadn't forgotten how painful the day was for him. He reached for her hand again, but she'd tucked it inside her skirt. "That's... kind of you."

"I arranged a party. At the pool." She said it quickly as if ripping off a bandage.

And to Brock, it felt like one. "But Sadie and water. She'll be scared."

"She likes water. Look at her." Sadie's head had disappeared over the edge, and the lake water sloshed as she swept her hands through it. "She even told me last night how the lake here is like the Peace River. 'Daddy and I fished in a river like this lake.' I honestly think she's ready, Brock. And she won't be scared at all, if you're there."

"You're asking me to come?"

"Of course, you're her uncle. I've invited everyone she knows. And that means everyone you know. Will, Mateo...the community."

She was turning it into a party for him, too. As much as you could when it involved a bunch of screaming kids. "You don't have to worry about me," he said. "I'll come if you want me there. What does Sadie think?"

"I haven't told her. I wanted to talk to you first."

"Shouldn't that discussion have taken place before you booked?"

She closed her eyes, and when she opened them, they reflected regret. "You're right. Gina went over my head recently, and I didn't like it. I'm sorry. I can cancel."

He didn't like seeing Natalia so beaten down. "Look, her birthday falls in your months with her. It's your call in the end. I appreciate that you asked for my input. Could we do what we usually do and get her opinion? I don't want her to feel pushed into it."

"Fair enough. Mara didn't like that I'd booked without getting Sadie's input, either."

Brock riled at the thought of Lia discussing Sadie's welfare with the psychologist, but he took a calming breath before speaking. "Since Mara and I agree on this point, maybe you could trust me on other Sadie issues?"

"It's not you I don't trust, it's me. I tripped up already and have to make it right. Sadie?"

She spun on her stomach to face them.

"Uncle Brock and I were talking about your birthday."

"We'll need five candles and a cake. Can I have balloons?"

"Yes, of course. We were thinking of having a party. With Penny and Ella and their families, and Mateo and Haley and Jonah. And anybody else you might like."

All bobbing around like peas on the boil. He couldn't think of another place he'd rather not be. Sadie pointed to him. "Will you be there?"

"Wouldn't miss it for the world."

"I—The thing is, we were thinking of having the party at the pool." Natalia was, not "we," but united front and all. "Would you like that?"

She didn't wait for Sadie's answer. "The pool isn't super deep like the lake. It has a whole area where it won't come up above your head. There are slides and bubbly water and a tropical rainfall and toys like you're at a beach."

Sadie frowned. "I don't know how to swim."

"I'll be right there with you, and if you want, you can wear a life jacket or water wings, even in the shallow end. Or you can sit on the edge and watch."

Sadie twisted her mouth. "That won't be fun."

"It's only for an hour and then they have

a special party room for cake and opening presents. And balloons."

"Penny likes water," Sadie said softly. "And Ella. They told me they've been on a boat and been in real deep water in the middle of the lake."

They weren't lying. Krista and her sisters co-owned a boat. Will often talked about his list of excuses to avoid those outings. He liked water as much as Sadie. "I won't be a good friend," Sadie said, "if I say 'no.'"

"It's your birthday," Brock said. "You can refuse if you want. We can have cake and balloons at the ranch."

"But…" Sadie stared down into the water. "I want to." She raised her head. "If you go, I'll go." She wasn't letting him off the hook.

"Deal."

He could hear Natalia expel her breath. Sadie spun away to look down in the water. "Then I'll go."

He didn't like throwing Sadie into a situation she didn't feel ready for, but he'd have to trust that Natalia was doing what was best… for Sadie and him.

NATALIA HADN'T REALIZED how complicated a party for a five-year-old could be. Moms called to confirm time and place, despite text invites. Moms called to ask if it was okay if siblings came. Some of the same moms called to ask if they needed to stay. The bakery called to say that they didn't have a *The Lion King* stencil. The party place filled balloons that read Happy 2nd Birthday!

But like most parties, it came together, even as Natalia herself unraveled. She now sat in the pool, Sadie lightly bobbing beside her. She'd taken to the water well enough. But her eyes were on her little friends who were in the deep end, splashing and flapping about their parents like ducklings. Penny's older sisters swung off a rope and cannonballed into the water. The lifeguard wandered around. Clearly this was an easy hour for her.

Sadie had jumped in herself, her water wings buoying her up. It had been a big step, but her smiles had faded away as she saw her little friends have much more splashier fun.

"Would you like to try that?" Natalia said. She glanced over to where Brock was in the deep end. He and Krista, along with Jack, were playing some sort of game that involved picking up rings from the bottom of the pool while one of them tried to prevent them.

Krista let the whole pool know when she recovered one.

"Can you take me there?"

They skirted to the deep end by edging along the wall, so Sadie could feel safe. The instant they crossed into the drop-off that marked where the adults were, Sadie called to Brock in an excited voice. "Come get me. Please!"

In a couple of strokes, he glided over. Natalia hardly recognized him or any of the ranchers, bare except for swimming trunks.

"Auntie Lia thinks I'm good enough to play here."

That was not what she said at all, but it was the message Sadie had taken away. "If you're with your uncle Brock," she said quickly.

"Or we can try out the rainfall," Brock said.

"Can you take me to Ella and Penny?"

"They could come to you."

Sadie pressed her lips together. "No, I'm five. I'm older than them. I can do this."

Brock gave Sadie his patently careful gaze. "You are a brave birthday girl."

Sadie swept a wet streak of hair off her face and vaulted into Brock's arms.

"You coming?" he asked Natalia.

"No, I'd better set up the party room." But she watched as he swam the sidestroke along-

side a paddling Sadie, his free hand supporting her belly. Their niece would have a good
memory of the day she turned five, swimming into the deep end with her uncle Brock.
Natalia could already imagine Sadie's story
of her day to Rudy.

She was walking, dripping and chilled, to
the change room when she heard Sadie scream,
"Uncle Brock!"

Natalia whirled. Sadie splashing about and
no Brock. And then he erupted from below
the surface and had Sadie in his arms, and
she clung to him like a barnacle to a rock.
Her sobbing rose above all the noise, and the
pool quieted.

Natalia hurried over, her wet feet slipping
on the smooth tiles. "What happened?"

Sadie still clamped to him, Brock glided
over to the edge. "We were playing a game
before and Bridget's girls pulled on my legs.
I was only under for a second or two."

Bridget and Jack were in heavy consulta-
tion with their older girls, and they all swam
over together. At a nod from Jack, the girls
broke toward Sadie. "We didn't mean to scare
you."

It was hard to tell if Sadie had even heard

above her sobs. She hadn't cried like that since Daniel had died.

"Let's get her out of the pool," Brock said. "Now."

But when he moved to lift Sadie from the water, she clung even tighter, and so he used the stairs to leave the water and then he carried her away, straight to the family change room.

Natalia scrambled after them with towels. She tucked a thick one around Sadie's shivering, goose-pimply frame. "Everything's all right. You're safe. Everyone's—"

"How about you deal with the party room? I'll take it from here."

He was dismissing her and she didn't blame him. Sadie had said she was ready, but was that to please Natalia? Brock had warned her and she'd not listened.

She peeled out of her swimsuit and smoothed on her clothes, skipping the shower to focus on prepping the party room. She'd rescue Sadie's day from ruin.

But Sadie still hadn't emerged from the change room when a subdued bunch straggled into the party room.

Krista sidled up to Natalia. "Is there anything we can do?"

"I don't think so." The crying had stopped, at least.

"I asked Brock when we were all together in the change room, but he seemed to just want to be alone with her."

Everything was in place—cake, presents, friends. Only Sadie was missing, and without her, nothing could happen.

"I'll go check on them."

She could hear movements inside the stall when she entered the change room. Two pairs of bare feet, Brock's and Sadie's. Progress, then. "Hi," Natalia said. "Just checking to see how things are going."

"She's dressing," Brock said shortly. "And then we're heading home."

No. "But...there's cake and presents. Everyone's waiting."

"You'll have to tell them there's been a change in plans." The door opened and Sadie emerged fully clothed. Her hair was a mess, the ends of her braids like puff balls Brock must've towel dried it.

"I'm dressing and then we'll go," Brock said, closing the door.

Natalia drew Sadie into a hug. "You look pretty in your birthday dress."

Sadie nodded, not smiling, and pale. Brock

was probably right, but if Sadie left now, then so did any chance for a happy memory. She could bring the cake and presents home, but they would only remind her that the party had happened without her.

Like all the parties Natalia had never been invited to.

She had to try. "I saw Ella and Penny in their dresses, too. They are waiting for you in the party room."

From behind the door, Brock halted the progress of pulling on his jeans.

"I know you want to go home, but I think it would be polite if you stopped by and thanked them for coming."

And once in the room, hopefully the decorations and the people would work their magic.

"Lia." Brock's single word was a warning.

Sadie released a shaky sigh. "I'll say goodbye."

"All right," Natalia said quickly. "We'll go and let Uncle Brock dress."

She and Sadie left, amid the leather snap of Brock fastening his belt buckle. She crossed the hallway into the party room.

Ella and Penny sat at the table Natalia had heavily decorated for Sadie and her friends, their moms hovering nearby. "Yay! Sadie's here. We can have cake now."

Penny patted the chair beside her, the one with the five balloons. "This is your seat, Sadie. Come sit."

Sadie released Natalia's hand and took her seat between her friends. It was what Natalia had been counting on. Any thoughts of saying goodbye had fallen to the wayside.

Natalia quickly lit the candles and led off with "Happy Birthday," everyone joining in. As she set the cake in front of Sadie, Brock appeared at the doorway, his mouth twisted downward.

Natalia switched back to Sadie. "Make a wish and blow out the candles!"

Sadie sat, staring at the cake, a glazed look on her face. Natalia could feel Brock's eyes boring into her. "Do you want help with the candles, Sadie?"

Sadie kept staring at the cake as the five candles burned down. Natalia rushed on. "Let's all do this together."

She brought her cheek beside Sadie and whispered, "Blow." She looked at the girls. "Would you help us?"

It was Natalia and Sadie's friends who blew

out the candles. Sadie watched the thin trails of smoke lifting off the candles.

Natalia began cutting up the cake, and Brock knelt beside Sadie. "We can go now," he said.

That seemed to rouse Sadie. "I have to say goodbye."

She lifted up her hand and waved to her friends. "Goodbye."

"You don't leave yet," Penny said, her mouth rimmed in blue icing. "You eat cake and then you open your presents and then you give us party bags and then you go."

Sadie slumped in her seat.

Bridget set a hand on her daughter's shoulder. "Not every birthday needs to be how we do them, Penny. Sadie can go if she likes. It's her birthday."

Brock held out his hand. "Exactly. Let's go, Sadie."

Natalia stood with Sadie's cake in her hand, waiting. Sadie reached for it. Natalia set it in front of her but held on to the fork.

"Sadie, as much as I want you to stay with all your friends, you don't have to. You can go, if you like."

Sadie stared at her cake. At her friends eating away. "I'm five. I can do this."

She took the fork and loaded on a giant mouthful of the cake she'd picked out at the bakery with Natalia a week ago. Today, she took a mouthful, chewed and swallowed.

She gagged. Up came the cake. And it seemed a signal to the rest of her body to empty the contents of her stomach onto her plate. Ella and Penny sprang away like scared chickens, while gasps and groans broke from the rest of the kids.

Natalia reached for Sadie, but Brock swept her into his arms first and carried her away. She buried her face in Brock's neck, hiding from the shame that Natalia had not prevented.

ONCE WHEN BROCK was seventeen and Abby was fourteen, their parents flew off on one of their frequent weeklong trips to Las Vegas, leaving them at home. His dad had retired from the military, but the moving around continued. Home at that moment took the form of a rental house on the edge of town with a lawn more dandelions than grass and carpeting thin as a shirt. They'd left pickles and milk in the fridge, and forty bucks in fives, ones and change. They'd also left the second vehicle, an old red Honda that didn't know to stop working.

Brock's friends invited him to a party, tempting him with the promise of pizza and a girl he'd had his eyes on since moving there at the beginning of the school year a month ago. But there was the question of Abby. She insisted that she was happy to stay at home and listen to her music, but she observed his preparations to leave like an abandoned puppy. He persuaded her to come, that there'd be music and they wouldn't stay long, promise. They sang together on the drive over and Brock thought that maybe, just this once, Abby would have fun.

Except the girl arrived with another boy in an off-road Jeep—his parent's castoff, but still his. Brock got plastered and then crashed on the couch. When he came to early the next morning, Abby was sitting cross-legged on the floor beside him. He'd forgotten completely about her. She uncurled herself, her eyes still wide but now with dark circles. "Can we go home now?"

The shame he'd felt then was the same that burned through him now as he sat with Sadie watching *The Lion King*. He was supposed to have taken care of her and serve as backup for Lia. Instead, he'd given into the temptation to have fun on Sadie's special day, and when that imploded, he whisked her away.

And he had made it clear to Lia that the whole fiasco was her fault. Truth was, she had tried her best and he had made her feel bad for it.

His phone chimed another text from Lia. He'd already texted to say that they were watching a movie and he'd have Sadie call her afterward, but the text was for him.

I know I screwed up. I am deeply sorry. Is there anything, big or small, that I can do to save the day?

How many times had he apologized to Abby in his head, her silence mocking him? He couldn't do the same to Lia. He paused the movie, freeze-framing Timon and Pumbaa singing "Hakuna Matata."

"How about Auntie Lia watches the rest of the movie with us?"

Sadie frowned, pulled her T-shirt over her knees. "Okay. But only if she wants to."

A day where everyone sounded like him. "She'll want to."

Lia proved him right, pulling into the carport a short twenty minutes later, when the drive alone took fifteen minutes.

Sadie cracked the first smile since he'd swept her away from the party. "The balloons! You brought them."

Lia had also brought the presents and left-over pizza and ice cream. Mint chocolate chip, Sadie's favorite.

"I was thinking we could—" Lia broke off and bit her lip. She'd not looked at Brock since she'd come.

It was one thing to give people their space. It was another to cut them loose, and that was exactly what he'd done to the woman he ached to hold in his arms. Alone, she had sorted out the mess, had saved the day he'd run from.

He would never get forgiveness from his sister for neglecting her, but he could still give his own. "What's your plan?"

She gusted out a relieved sigh. "If Sadie wants, we could finish watching the movie. And then afterward we could have pizza and ice cream and open presents."

Sadie was trying to hug a purple balloon, the helium inside pushing it away. "Can we have ice cream while watching the movie?"

"Beats the eggs and toast we had for supper," Brock said. "Movie and ice cream. And then presents."

"If you want," Natalia said quickly.

Sadie released the balloon and it jerked straight. "I want."

They each had a dinner plate of birthday party leftovers as they watched Simba take his rightful place in his kingdom. Then they gathered around the dining table and Sadie tossed aside tissue paper and dug inside the brightly colored bags for treasures. A painting set, a Simba stuffie and a bead set for making jewelry. Five hundred tiny beads to go every which way.

"How about you keep that at Auntie Lia's place?" Brock suggested.

Natalia narrowed her eyes, knowing full well his reasoning. He grinned. She started, as if in surprise. Did she suppose he was tolerating her presence for the sake of Sadie?

Maybe his gift to Sadie would make Lia realize that he'd been thinking of her, too. "Your present from me is in a brown box out on the boot rack."

Sadie scampered off and then there was a gasp and a squeal, and she returned with a pair of cowboy boots, pink with tassels. And a pink riding helmet. "They're beautiful." She dropped to the floor to pull on the boots.

Brock leaned close to Natalia so only she would hear. "I know you bought her a perfectly good pair of boots and helmet. I just saw these and—"

"—and I'm the last person you need to rationalize your gift to," she said. "They're beautiful and practical."

"Reminds me of someone I know," he said. She did what he hoped and blushed.

"Thanks, Uncle Brock." Boots on, Sadie spun fast to get the tassels whirling, while at the same time trying to touch them.

"Feel them, Auntie Lia. They're so soft and new. I'm wearing them everywhere."

"Even to bed?" Brock teased.

"Can I?"

He refused to deny her anything today. "Your boots, your bed."

"Now for my present," Natalia said. "Here's my first clue." She touched her throat.

Sadie's hand flew to the ammolite necklace. "Your magic gem? You're giving it to me?"

"Yes," Natalia said.

"But you said that it's your most important, most valuable thing in the whole world." Exactly what Brock was thinking.

Natalia brushed her hand over Sadie's mussed hair. "Not as valuable to me as the person wearing it."

"You mean me?" Sadie whispered in a kind of awe.

"Of course," Natalia said and opened her arms. Sadie flung herself into them. "You're my magic," Natalia whispered into their niece's hair.

Bundled together, their bright hair enmeshed, it was the same sight as when they'd cuddled together in Sadie's room down the hall. He'd wondered then about the possibility of them all living together, and three months later, the possibility had hardened into resolve.

CHAPTER ELEVEN

NATALIA WAS SURPRISED that Brock followed her out to the carport. His anger with her seemed to have melted during the evening, but it could be an act for Sadie.

"Hey," he said, coming around the hood to where she stood at the vehicle door. "I wanted to thank you for coming out here. It made Sadie's day."

"You mean after I ruined it so badly?" She tried to smile but could only pull off a quivering of her lips.

His eyes settled on hers. "I ruined it, Lia. If I had been paying attention to her in the first place, instead of playing games like a big kid, nothing would've happened. And then I left you to pick up the pieces on your own, to depend on others. I am sorry, Lia."

Wow. It wasn't the first apology Natalia had received. Employees had apologized for tardiness, clients for unpaid invoices, men had even blamed themselves for breaking up with her. But nothing compared to Brock's. He actually looked as if her answer would determine his future happiness.

As if he ever had to doubt she'd endanger that. "Apology accepted." His shoulders visibly relaxed. Had he been holding his breath? "How about we say that mistakes were made but Sadie turned five anyway, and she fell asleep with boots and a full belly?"

"All right," he said. "I'll let it go."

Brock's default setting, but in this case she completely agreed. She beeped her vehicle open. "I should head back. The new manager and I are meeting first thing tomorrow."

He leaned against her vehicle as if they were about to start, not end, a conversation. "Manager? Aren't you running the place?"

"I am, but this was our first week of operation and there were the usual hiccups."

He winced. "I didn't even think to ask about your opening. You must've been run off your feet between the store and the party."

He cares about me. He felt responsible for her well-being, which means that—*No, don't overthink this.* "It has been busy, I admit. But Carolyn is working out and that's good. I can't always be there." And if Gina had her way, she'd already be two hours south of here.

"Will a manager free up your time?"

Carolyn would leave her with no excuse not to return to Calgary. With or without Sadie. Yet she still wavered, because of the man with his backside parked against her method of escape. "Sadie is the priority."

Brock smiled and his eyes softened. "Your magic, right?"

"Yeah." If today had taught her anything, it was how important Sadie was to her. It was more than auntie love now. Auntie love recognized that there was another being who was tied closer to her. "I realize that I love her like a parent. Or how I think a parent does. All fear and worry and an intense need to see to their future. I'm sorry. I'm not explaining myself well."

"You don't have to," Brock said. "I feel that way, too. Though I'm not sure my parents did. Abby and I were like pets. Left out food and water, provided access to the backyard, handed out gifts now and again, and then they came and went as they pleased. They were strange. And strange people do strange things."

Natalia had always thought herself the strange one, the damaged one. But if Brock admitted his parents were messed up, then hers more than qualified as dysfunctional.

"I admire you for getting out of the bush, away from your parents. I see where Sadie gets her bravery from."

His eyes were soft on her, like how they had been just before they kissed. But she'd mistaken his moment of weakness then for genuine feeling. He had moments, while she ran 24/7. She couldn't risk misreading again. Not when they had just admitted their deepening bond with Sadie. It might seem natural to extend her affection for Sadie to the other committed caregiver, but it wouldn't be reciprocated.

"I really should go."

He pushed off from her hood, but then took a step closer. "Thank you for the day, Lia. It made remembering Abby a lot easier."

She widened her eyes. "How is that possible?"

"I've always felt I'd failed her when she was young. She grew smaller and smaller, like a dimming light. I saw it but was too selfish to do anything about it. Today, I scooped Sadie away because all I could see was how I'd failed Abby once and I wasn't going to do it again. I guess I thought that in rescuing Sadie, I had finally done right by her mother."

"I helped by screwing things up so you could come to the rescue?"

"Except I didn't need to rescue Sadie from anything. She chose to stay, and so what if it didn't work out the way we'd hoped? Same with Abby. She found her own way with Daniel. She didn't need me to figure things out for her."

Natalia ached to hug him. But that would only take them down the same path of pulling away and apologies. "I think Abby would be proud of the parent-uncle you've become."

"And Daniel would be proud of his parent-aunt."

Oh no, he looked as if he might kiss her again. Unless she was mistaken. She could outright ask, but her heart wasn't ready for his refusal.

"I miss our talks, Lia. You sort out my world and sometimes I think I do the same for you. Do I?"

Sorted it out and shredded it at the same time. Love makes a home out of anywhere... and then blows it to smithereens. Only instead of love, it was Brock. Or were they one and the same?

Heat, hotter than ever before, scorched her cheeks. Without looking his way, she knew his smile had deepened. Natalia wrenched open her door. "I'd better go. Long day. Catch you later."

Back at her place, Natalia saw Brock had sent her a text while she'd driven in. It was a sticker of two puppies chatting through a line strung between two cans. So yes?

She turned off her phone. Her head would explode if she had to process any more drama today.

Carolyn was a godsend. She dusted, balanced books and could tally up inventory costs in her head before Natalia had pulled up her calculator app.

And she was a marvel with customers, if only because she didn't seem to care if they ever bought anything. "Hello, hello, hello," she said from where she was artfully messing up a crockery pot of yarn dish scrubbers, to three teenage girls when they walked in with their supersize pops and bare midriffs. "How's the beach today?"

"We haven't been there yet," the middle one said. "We just drove here." She twirled car keys on her lanyard. Natalia judged she'd come straight from the licensing office. Was she the only one who thought sixteen was too young for kids to drive without supervision?

Carolyn kept up the patter. "Drive? What do you drive?"

The middle one's friend poked her in the shoulder. "Her boyfriend's car."

And the other friend poked her in the other shoulder. "Her boyfriend's dad's car."

Eleven years, Natalia thought. That was all that stood between Sadie becoming any one of these girls. With a boyfriend. She was with Brock right now out on the farm. Wearing her pink boots and her pink helmet, which she'd barely taken off in the three days since her birthday. Right now that was all it took to keep her safe.

"Welcome to the store," Carolyn said. "Take a look around. Make yourself a wish list."

The girls moved as one along the shelves and Natalia noted their interests. They sniffed candles. The cranberry candle smelled like old socks and the pumpkin spice made them want to eat it. The rocker induced sleepiness and the paintings triggered memories of the places they'd traveled to.

Then they stopped at Grace's quilts.

Grace had shipped up half a dozen of varying bed sizes. It was the two baby quilts that the girls were running their fingers along now.

"Can we unfold them?" said one with legs that a giraffe would envy.

"Certainly," Carolyn said and shook both of the small quilts free. The giraffe girl held one and Carolyn the other, and all four exclaimed over how clever and bright they were, and wouldn't, the boyfriend girl said to the third, quiet girl, it make the perfect baby shower gift for your sister?

Sister? How old could her sister possibly be? Was she single or married to a boy she'd fallen in love with, or were they forced together because of the baby?

"How much?" asked the third girl, holding up the pale green one with a pattern of ladybugs and strawberries. Carolyn broke the news. The girl shook her head, her loose hair shielding her face, and muttered something about a baby sale at Walmart.

"We can chip in," said the boyfriend girl. The giraffe girl stared hard at the price tag as if willing it to reduce its amount, but agreed.

The third girl ran a finger down the quilt over the bump of the strawberries. Natalia herself had done the same thing, marveling at how Grace had bothered to give texture to the fruit. "It's still too much."

Carolyn seemed to agree, for she hung back. The third girl was wisely choosing to be practical. Yet Natalia had sent Sadie reams of useless gifts, and three days ago, another gift of jewelry to keep, to show Sadie in real terms that she deserved the very best from her aunt.

Natalia left the stove counter. "The quilts come from a family friend. She's a lawyer in Calgary, and in her spare time she makes these quilts. She would be thrilled if one of her creations played a part in the start of another family. And all proceeds go to a charity." It was her automatic selling line, but now she wished she'd kept her mouth shut.

"Which charity?"

Natalia aimed for nonchalance. "The pregnancy center here in town, I believe."

The sister flushed and Natalia felt heat in her own cheeks in sympathy. The other girls didn't seem at all embarrassed. The boyfriend girl said, "That's perfect. She goes there, right?"

"See?" the boyfriend girl said. "We could give her something really unique. She won't get much that is."

Ah, so there was that. The new baby would have an oddball family with this young trio as the new mom's loose support system. Just like an orphan might have an aunt and uncle, not married to each other, stand in as her parents and a man who considered the uncle like a son function as a grandfather. Unconventional but together. "Could you swing half the price?" Natalia said.

They could.

"Good call," Carolyn said after they left in a tight trio of swinging hair and bare legs. "Raising a child is hard. Nothing wrong with a bit of brightness to lighten the load. And it's all going to a good cause." She set to neatly folding a stack of napkins instead of throwing them into an artistic disarray. "This whole store is a good cause."

For Carolyn, Sadie and her. So also was a farmhouse about a quarter hour out of town with a man who was also Sadie's family. A man who had clearly signaled he wanted Natalia in his home, to stay indefinitely. A man who might change the course of her life again, if she let him.

"WHAT DO YOU want me to do with all the boxes from your brother's place?"

Natalia peered at her computer screen as Gina pivoted her own to show a bank of boxes in the Calgary warehouse.

"I don't know yet. I'll deal with them when I'm down next."

"They've been sitting here for more than three months. They need to be cleared out for Christmas stock."

This was no less than the fourth time Natalia had heard about it. "I get it. I promise I'll deal with them as soon as I move back."

"And when exactly is that?"

Carolyn had rendered Natalia redundant in the Spirit Lake store, at least on a daily basis. The collective marketing among the local crafters and her own efforts had generated brisk sales. The soft opening was going to allow for a strong grand opening at Thanksgiving six weeks from now. So far, her retail model had proved successful. Time to expand.

Time to return to Calgary.

"I'm not sure. Carolyn's great out front, but there's lots to get ready for the grand opening, and then there's Christmas right after."

"Will you hire more staff?"

"I'm already looking into that." She had put the word out through Bridget and had taken in résumés from walk-ins. "Hiring more people isn't the problem. It's getting someone to replace me."

"Isn't that what Carolyn's for?"

"She is. Only—"

Only Natalia didn't want to return to Calgary. Not yet. Not until things were settled with Sadie. And yes, with Brock. "Only she is one person. I'll need to hire Christmas staff and I can't until closer to the date."

"That's what we pay Carolyn for, right? To hire staff?"

Natalia reverted to the standard response. "Let's stick with our original deal. I'm here until Thanksgiving and that's still six weeks away."

Natalia's partner—and best friend—leaned closer, until her rosy cheeks touched the borders of the screen. "It is, but I need you back here with me. There's Carolyn's old location to finish, and I found another one that has all the shelving and fixtures in place. Matter of moving in Christmas stock and opening the doors."

It was never that simple. "That's a tight deadline, Gina."

"It is. That's why I need you down here like

yesterday. This retail project was your idea. It needs you."

"Taking over Carolyn's location was your idea. One you didn't even bother to consult me about."

Brock, for all his orneriness, had always made a point of reaching out to her. She was the one who had let a full twelve days pass and had still not answered his question. *So yes?*

Gina dropped her gaze. "I'm sorry. It was just that—" She shook her head. "Look, how about you come here for a couple of days a week and then you can be here full time after Thanksgiving. How does that sound?"

It sounded the exact opposite of what she had hoped for. "To be honest, things are still undecided in my personal life."

"You mean with your niece? You said that she was adjusting to her uncle's ranch."

"She is, but I'm still part of her life."

Gina pulled back, her face receding so that items on the shelf came into view. The trophy from the city for the most community-minded business. That was awarded the year after Natalia joined the company. A plaque recognizing their contribution to a children's fund. "Huh. You're not worried about leaving the store. You're worried about leaving your niece behind."

"Carolyn needs me, but I believe Sadie needs me more."

"I think you need Sadie more than the store."

She had never needed anybody more than she needed her work. Work brought value to her life like no one else ever had. Until Sadie. Until Brock.

But she had legal claim to Sadie only.

So yes?

Brock inviting his own claim on her. Or the other way around.

"I'm…at a crossroads, Gina. I don't know if I can come back to work with you if Sadie isn't with me, too."

Gina released a snorty sigh. "Can't you and her uncle come up with an arrangement? Some sort of joint deal where the niece stays up there and you have her for holidays or something like that?"

Or something like that. Up until Sadie, she would've agreed with childless, career-driven Gina. Now, she couldn't picture her life with Sadie pinched into a few stressed days throughout the year.

"It's not what I want," Natalia said softly.

"You want to stay there with Sadie and take care of the store, is that it?"

And maybe, maybe explore what lay behind Brock's soft eyes on her under a carport light. "I suppose that's it."

"That's a waste of talent, and you know that, Natalia. A year from now, months, you'll be bored, and then you'll be no good to anyone. It's one thing to choose family over career, but when the career is more of a calling, then you're not doing Sadie or the world any favor, Natalia."

Least of all the two people she longed to be with. "You are persuasive."

Gina sighed again, this one softer. "Yes, I want you to come back to Calgary. And I know that when women reach your age, the ache to start a family is strong. I never felt that, and I figured that given your upbringing and your history with men, you wouldn't want it, either."

"My history with men?" Natalia had avoided discussing her relationships with Gina. Talking only meant reliving the shame.

"Your relationships never lasted longer than meat in the sun. I figured you weren't much into them."

"I'm very much into relationships. It's just that men aren't very much into me."

Gina's face suddenly filled the screen again. "It's the uncle, isn't it?"

"Yes. Only nothing has happened. We haven't dated or anything."

"You're willing to give up your whole life for a man who hasn't even asked you out?"

"It's complicated. There's Sadie to consider."

"Sadie is even more of a reason for him to keep you close without committing."

Like inside his arms beside a rushing creek. "It's important to him that he not push others into decisions."

"Bully for him. But tell me, has he shown interest?"

Did a kiss count? Eyes that lingered on her like a slow hand? *So yes?*

"There are…signs. I guess I need more time, Gina. After Thanksgiving, okay?"

"You promised me you'd come back for Thanksgiving."

She had put off telling Gina about Thanksgiving for so long that she'd forgotten all about her promise. She bit her lip.

Gina's face filled the screen again. "Don't tell me you're having Thanksgiving with them."

"It's my niece. She's just lost her father. I can't refuse her. Come have it with us, Gina."

"I don't want to be where I don't know a soul." Before Natalia could protest, Gina said, "We'll stick to our original deal, but the day after Thanksgiving Monday, in six weeks, I expect your final answer."

Gina would hold her to it. Six weeks to discover if she had a future with Sadie's uncle.

So yes?

After the video call ended, Natalia opened her phone screen and tapped on Brock's unanswered message. Before she could talk herself out of it, she sent a reply. Yes.

BROCK SAT AT the end of the dock at Natalia's lake house, purple fishing pole in hand, the best that the dollar store had to offer. Natalia and Sadie had a yellow and pink one. The late August sun hot on his bare back and his feet numbing nicely in the ice-cold water, and his two favorite females on either side of him. Life was good.

He turned to Natalia, her upper face hidden under a floppy sun hat. "Do we have a backup plan for supper in case we don't land a whopper?"

"We're releasing them," Sadie said. "We're doing this for fun only."

Brock could think of plenty of other ways to have fun with water, but then he caught Natalia's eye and he remembered why he'd agreed to this in the first place. He'd wanted time with her. To maybe catch a quiet moment with her to talk. Or sit close. Or to drum up a way to explain how he'd like more of her soft kisses. Follow up on her texted 'Yes.'

He had experience pursuing women, but before it hadn't mattered what the answer was. He'd hold on to a purple pole and his pride until he wound up the courage to make his move.

"If you had to choose," Sadie said to Brock, "between living here at Auntie Lia's place or at Knut's place, which would you choose?"

Sadie was as subtle as a jalapeño pepper. He expected Natalia to divert Sadie, but she peeked at him from under her hat.

Because she was thinking about staying. "That's a question I never really had reason to think about," Brock said. "I guess I'd have to see if I got an invitation to live here first." There, he would bat the ball back.

"But suppose Auntie Lia gave you the chance," Sadie persisted. "Would you take it?"

In other words, would he be okay if Sadie chose to live with Natalia? Movement on Sadie's part, to even consider a more urban environment. But she still hadn't given up on her dream of Natalia and him living under the same roof. And no separate quarters here. Living space would shrink from a thousand acres to a quarter acre. And lake access.

"I've always liked water," he said.

Sadie peered over the edge. "I like it, too. It's so interesting." *Interesting* had become her latest favorite expression. Natalia reported that Bridget had used it to describe the girls' paintings. "I would rather watch it than be in it."

"For now," Natalia said softly. "Maybe Uncle Brock could help you get used to the water around here."

"I could do that," he said. Anything to show up at her place regularly.

"You have the key," she said. "You and Sadie can come anytime."

Not that. "I'd feel more comfortable if you were here. It is your place."

"Which you are welcome to visit whenever you'd like."

The same invitation he'd made to her. Was it with the same intent that he'd made his?

He tried to read her expression, but she ducked her head, straw hat hiding all but the tip of her nose from him.

"Uncle Brock! You still haven't answered my question," Sadie said. "Would you stay here if you could?"

"I suppose I could always commute between here and the ranch," Brock said. "I guess your auntie Lia did it the other way."

"And you could have your own room," Sadie said. "There's a bedroom and a bathroom downstairs that we don't even use, and you could choose your own paint color and everything."

Sadie had thought of everything, except for one serious flaw. "All true, but your auntie Lia only has this place for a little while."

Natalia's hat lifted. "That's not quite true. The Realtor called today to say that the owners are putting it up for sale. She wondered if I wanted to buy it."

"Buy it! Buy it!" Sadie said, "And then we can all live here forever." She'd taken Brock's not negative reply for an affirmative.

"That is a big decision," Brock said. There was a jerk on his pole and it nearly slipped from his grasp. A trout no more than a good six inches had latched on and was reeling out the spool of line.

"I got one!" he said and began to reel it in. Every second, he expected the cheap plastic to snap or the fish to break off the line lighter than dental floss, but by some small miracle, he brought the fish right up to the dock, where Sadie flopped on her belly and watched it splash frantically in the water.

"Let it go, let it go," Sadie pleaded. "You're scaring it."

"It's not wrong for us to eat it," Brock said. "Every time we eat meat, we're eating something that once lived."

"Yes," Sadie said. "But I looked in its eyes."

He released it. Having seen the upshot of fishing, Sadie pulled up her pole and asked to play a game on Lia's phone. She usually had a tight restriction on phone usage during after-hours, but she handed over the phone and Sadie, walking carefully, took it over to a wooden deck chair.

Finally, time alone with Natalia. She turned to him, her voice low and directed away from Sadie. "I appreciate you…humoring Sadie," she said. "And you are welcome here. Only…"

"You don't plan on buying."

"The plan is for me to go back to Calgary

soon. Gina wants me to finish setting up two locations in Calgary based on the model here."

"Send Carolyn, then. She's from Calgary."

"But her family is here."

"So is yours."

"Sadie."

"And me. We're in this together with Sadie."

She faced him, her eyes intense. "What do you mean? We're in this together?"

He'd sworn he'd not make her feel she had to run away. And not make her feel trapped, either. "We could have some kind of joint custody. If divorced couples do it, I guess two… friends could come up with an arrangement. The courts would be open to it."

She jiggled her pole, the bug hook skittering about. "I'm not opposed to that, Brock. But… I need to be where I matter. Where I feel I'm making a difference, where I… belong."

"You belong with Sadie."

"And I want to belong with Sadie. But she's in school ten months out of twelve, and what will I do with myself? I need to work."

"Plenty of work on the ranch." He looked out to the lake, to Sadie swinging her legs as she jumped e-frogs from log to log. "Persephone needs your help. There's the crop to take off soon. Mateo will help out, but still."

Natalia gazed across the lake, her face hidden, probably formulating a polite refusal.

"Knut is giving me two of his quarters."

That drew her attention back to him. "A while back, he told me. I didn't tell you because I only agreed to it in order to make myself look good financially for the courts. But if we settle on Calgary for Sadie, then I have no need for land."

"Are you asking me my opinion?"

Brock's turn to contemplate the lake. "I guess I'm letting you know that I have a stake in the ranch now—or I could have if there was a reason to. And that might give you reason to have a stake in me, too."

She jerked on her pole. "You really think my decision is based on your net worth?"

"No, but it's important to me that you know that I got a place of my own, and that you've got a place with us. With me."

She jerked on the pole a few more times, the bug hopping about. "I wish you hadn't told me about the land. Because it's about—" She reeled in the line, the spool grinding and clacking. "It's about you and me. That's it."

She had agreed to them together. She was

taking a big step, and he needed to reciprocate. "Just to be clear. If we need to make adjustments, I could see myself living in this house here…if that option ever came up between us."

He let the weight of his words settle, let himself enjoy the sight of her lips, and he thought it was more than the heat of the day that caused pinkness in her cheeks.

"I'll keep that in mind," she said.

Her words weren't a kiss, but his heart rate picked up, anyway.

CHAPTER TWELVE

"How does she feel?"

What exactly was Brock asking about Persephone? Natalia was riding the mare around the edge of the corral—a major breakthrough accomplished a few days ago—while Brock, standing in the center, functioned as the pressure point. They were working on the mare's shyness around men. Natalia could relate. In the week since their discussion at the lake, she'd searched for ways to get close to Brock.

"She seems...tight."

"Yeah, her head's up. Whatever's bothering her gets better when she lowers her head. If the nose goes down, a horse automatically relaxes."

That made sense. With Brock on the ground, Natalia's head stayed bent to him all the time. And she was feeling just fine. "How do we do that?"

"Next time her head comes up high, get

up in the bit and release as soon as she lowers her head."

Not as simple as he made it sound. He had to coach her from the middle of the corral, his voice quiet and steady in the cool evening air, as she worked through the possible meanings of "a little more" and "wait for her to go soft."

"This has to be frustrating for you," she said as Persephone lowered her head only to throw it back up when Canuck Luck let out a whinny from the stables.

Brock shrugged a shoulder. "I don't mind. We're making more progress than if I was on her."

"If she'd let you be."

"I wasn't a bronc rider for nothing."

She patted Persephone's neck. "I actually think she takes care I won't fall off."

"She is fond of you," Brock said slowly. "Let's try something. Get her going on a slow walk and then lean hard to the side, like you might fall off."

She did and Persephone stopped on her own. Natalia righted herself.

"Try the other side."

Natalia did, with the same results.

"Huh," Brock concluded. He regarded them

and then said, "Let's run another little experiment."

It started with Brock walking beside them, reins in his hands, getting Persephone comfortable with the arrangement, then he handed the reins back to Natalia. "Now, we're going to do the same thing with me walking alongside. Except this time when you lean, take your feet right out of the stirrups and actually fall."

"Uh—"

"Don't worry, I'll catch you. I did before, remember?" He gave her one of his warm, stomach-squishy looks. Yeah, she did know that. "All right, then. Let's do this."

On his word, she drew out her foot and let herself slip sideways. Persephone stopped and still she fell. Brock caught her, his hand low on her hip, her hand on his shoulder. He righted her, and Natalia fought against the giveaway heat rising to her cheeks. "What exactly are you trying to accomplish here?"

"I want Persephone to partner with me to keep you in the saddle. Make her think that we got the same interests in mind."

"Like you and me with Sadie."

"Yeah, like that." He paused. "Should we try it again?"

"We could, but I don't know how much she thinks we're faking this."

Persephone let them fake it three more times, three more times Natalia fell into his arms, and each time she swore his hands lingered longer than strictly necessary.

"How about we change this up?" he said. "How about we switch places?"

"You are going to get on her?"

"I haven't before, but I think she'll let me, so long as you have the reins."

"That's a big step," Natalia said and rubbed Persephone's neck. "You ready for this?"

"The question is if you're ready for it, Lia. You're the one in control on this one. If she senses you trust me, then she'll let me ride her."

"Of course I trust you," Natalia said. And not just with Persephone.

"Convince her," he said softly.

Natalia dismounted and held the reins, while Brock adjusted the stirrups. "Let her see what I'm up to," he said. "The more she understands, the less she has to worry."

Brock could have mounted her straight from the ground but instructed Natalia to lead her over to the mounting block. "It's what she's used to, and I don't want her to experience too much of a change." Exactly the way he treated Natalia. Except she wanted change. She wanted to fall into his arms and him to keep her there forever. She wanted to say "I love you" to him and see how that shook them up.

"So now as soon as my butt hits the saddle, you start leading her, so her mind switches to you, and then have her change direction, keep her attention on you. And most important, keep it natural."

Persephone threw her head at Brock's weight, but that was all. "Come on, girl," Natalia said, "I know you got that load of dynamite on your back, but let's pretend he's not there."

Brock didn't say a thing as they wandered about the corral, not pushing either of them to act a certain way. She could understand how some women might find his laid-back approach attractive.

"And since he's not there," Natalia said, "I suppose I can tell you a thing or two about him. You don't need to be the least bit scared of him. He's not scary, though he may pretend to do things that'll spook you.

"But that's his job. In his downtime, he won't do anything to scare anyone. And…" She turned so she was walking backward, and she raised her eyes to his, let him see the lava-hot scorch of her cheeks. "I sometimes wish he would scare me."

He frowned. "Not sure I follow, Lia."

She stopped and so did Persephone. Let the mare feel Brock on her back, let her figure out that there was nothing to fear. Not from Brock, anyway. How to express herself? "I hardly know myself, except that I came here because I didn't want Sadie to feel alone and trapped. And here she has friends and things to do and new experiences… I don't have to worry she will grow up the way I did. And now I want… I want what she has. I guess I'm asking you to help me see myself the way you see me. As someone who doesn't need changing, just new experiences. Are you up for it?"

She held her breath. He tipped back his hat. "What did you have in mind?"

She had lots of things in mind. Asking him out on a real date, sharing a meal, having a relationship with him that lasted longer than eleven weeks to date.

"Could you teach me how not to freak out every time I step into a bush?"

BROCK'S ANSWER BROUGHT them two evenings later on a second trail ride to the creek. He halted their progress down the slope to point out side trails that circled back up onto the ridge.

"Don't you dare tell me how I can back out of this."

Music to his ears, because, he hadn't wanted her scared. And yeah, it pumped up his ego to see the lengths she'd gone to be alone with him.

This time when they reached the creek bank, Natalia dismounted easily.

"You don't look as cross-eyed as you did last time."

She slung the reins over the pommel. "This was better, but I admit I'll be happier when we reach open ground again."

"We can head back, if you like. I still have to gas up the grain truck and clean out the augers."

"I thought you were combining tomorrow."

"We are. Trucks are for hauling the grain and the augers get the grain from the trucks into the silos."

"Oh. Well, in that case." She turned to Crocus, but nothing more. Reluctant to leave, he chose to believe. And so was he.

"We don't need to run off," he said, swinging down himself. "Quarter of an hour one way or another won't matter."

He led them to where he'd hoped to take her on their first outing. Three dead trees formed a crosshatch pattern for butts to fit in and backs to lean against. There was even a nest of branches to set their feet on. "I meant to show you this spot last time."

Natalia hopped onto a trunk long enough to seat two, and he settled into the open spot beside her. He had to tuck his shoulder behind hers to fit in, her elbow tucked into the bend of his. Perfect.

Above them, a hint of yellow had edged into the green leaves. Autumn shoving its way in already. "Knut says a wind came through here," Brock said, "back when the girls were young. He came down here with his wife, and they sort of made it their spot. When the girls grew older, they made it theirs, too. Then when I started coming here, I came across it and made mine. None of us told the other about it."

"You come here alone?"

Quarter of an hour wasn't long enough to lay out his feelings, but it was a start. "Until today."

She fixed her eyes on the point where her elbow nestled in the crook of his. "I have a confession to make. I wasn't exactly unconscious last time. I did get woozy and fade away for a while, but I recovered. And then I stayed there because—" she raised her eyes to his "—because I really liked being held by you."

He reached out, found her hand, wrapped it tight in his. "And I confess I suspected you were wider awake than you were letting on."

"Why didn't you call me on it?"

"I guess I was having too much of a good time, even if sitting on an anthill would've been more comfortable. I didn't mind you were pretending if it meant we stayed together longer. I like holding you, Lia."

"I didn't cross a line?"

She'd mentioned lines after the first kiss. He didn't understand what she was talking about then, and he didn't now. "You can cross as many lines as you like, Lia, so long as it's over to my side."

Her soft lips parted and he lowered his head.

From her back pocket her phone chirped out the Batman theme song. Lia's lips, nearly on his, thinned into a grimace. "That's Carolyn at the store. I better take it."

He liked Lia's manager, but her timing sucked. As did the entire thrust of her conversation from what he heard. He'd already guessed what Lia confirmed after getting off the phone. "Carolyn's brother-in-law got called up for surgery and he was going to drive the grain truck. She'll have to do it now, which means—"

"You're needed at the store."

"Yeah, I mean, I'll still help out here, but I'll have to take on more. This is Labour Day weekend, last chance with the summer crowd …and then setting up for Thanksgiving… I'm sorry."

"That's fine." Even if it wasn't, what could he say? Maybe just that. "I wish we had more time together."

She took his hand in both of hers. "We will do this again."

"And for longer than a quarter hour."

He might've tried again for a kiss, but no. He could wait for the perfect moment. For now, he had trapped her within his arms, and she'd liked it. Neither of them pretending.

RAIN ROLLED IN two days later, halting work in the fields, and overstayed its unwelcome for three more days. The next morning, the rain stopped, but moisture hung in the air. Another down day for Brock, but at least he could show up with Lia for Sadie's drop-off on her first full day of kindergarten.

Parents and caregivers were invited to see their kids to the teacher's door, most looking tearier and more nervous than the kids. Sadie sailed up to Ms. Whitby. "Do you remember me?"

"I do, Sadie. How was your summer?"

"Fine. I fished. I swam. I have four friends. How was your summer?"

"Wonderful, thank you." Ms. Whitby looked askance at Brock. He moved forward to introduce himself, but Sadie stepped up. "This is my uncle Brock. And you've already met my auntie Lia."

The adults acted on Sadie's cue and greeted each other.

"We have to go to my new class now," Sadie said. "Bye, Ms. Whitby."

Sadie's impeccable manners had him and Lia grinning as they exited the school. "She'll do fine," Brock said, acutely aware that he was alone with Lia and had nowhere to go.

"I admit I was worried despite her progress, but definitely a positive start. I can't wait to tell Mara."

They were walking toward their vehicles, and if he didn't do something, they'd soon go their separate ways. "How about we grab a coffee? Or a second breakfast?"

"I wish I could, but I'm meeting Mara in ten minutes."

"Aren't I better therapy?"

That earned him color in her cheeks, and she reached up to straighten his jacket collar. "You are in some ways, and in some ways I need a different perspective."

"Lunch, then?"

Her face scrunched in regret. "I stay open during the lunch hour. It's my busy time… I could meet afterward, but it would only be for fifteen minutes or so. Hardly worth a drive in."

The quarter hour alone he longed for. But no, he'd have to compete with a ticking clock, and in the end he'd lose.

"I get it. Another time." But as he sat behind her vehicle, her indicator signaling right while his clicked to the left, he wondered how often their paths would diverge. Lia was a traveler, an entrepreneur, a creator. And he was a retired cowboy who had lucked into some land. She liked him, yes, but for how long if she didn't come to like ranch life?

The questions still plagued him when he stepped into the horse barn to indulge water-loving Crocus with a ride in the spitting rain. Persephone immediately whinnied her request. What he wouldn't have given a month ago to have the mare show interest in him.

He'd not ridden her without Lia about, but today Persephone seemed to think that she was up for the challenge. He saddled her up and mounted her from the ground. She stayed soft along her flanks.

Pride surged through him. He brought out his phone and nudged Persephone forward, taking a video of the events. "Look who's out for a walk this morning. I think we'll take the road to Mateo and Haley's. I want to show her off. Talk to you later."

He sent the video, then recorded another one. "I forgot to add that I wish you were here." If he was to compete with the store, he might as well lay it out there.

"There's only one place Mateo will be on a rainy day, providing he's not at a horse sale," Brock commented to Persephone as they came up the Pavlic lane, letting his voice ground her, and looking about every bit as alertly as the horse for possible spook triggers. Nothing. He took her straight up to the open double-wide side doors of the arena.

Mateo must have seen them approach because he came out before Brock could dismount. "Is that the same scared horse we brought up nearly three months ago?"

"Sure is."

"Look at that, calm as can be. What'll happen if I go up to her?"

"Find out." Brock had no idea, either. "I brought her over to see how she'd do with others of her kind."

Mateo drew alongside but didn't reach out his hand, letting Persephone size him up. "She came up the road well enough?"

"Yeah, but we didn't meet any traffic. Otherwise, we would have taken to the ditch."

"And she's okay around Sadie?"

"She knows there has to be a fence between them or I have to be around—or Lia—but Perse doesn't even blink now. And the same with Pike. She stamps and he gives her a wide circle. She's starting to control her world a little more."

Mateo stretched out his hand, keeping it low. Persephone shook her mane, rippled flies off her flanks and lowered her head.

Mateo set his hand on her neck. "Would you look at that? You looked at her wrong when we first brought her up, and she'd rear up. I haven't seen better, and that's a fact."

"I didn't do it alone. Lia helped. She bridged Persephone's issues with men."

"Oh, yeah? Perse saw how much Lia liked you and decided to trust you, too?"

Brock couldn't suppress a grin. "Something like that."

"Good to see you two working it out. Doesn't always happen that way. Part of what I was going to talk to you about. You know Hawk Blackstone, right?"

Mateo's former boss and owner of a good line of cutting horses. "I do."

"He's selling his stock."

"All his horses?"

"Not all, but the best. I'll buy them, but I don't feel good about it, to be honest. His ex-wife wants a house in Calgary and he wants to help her with the down payment. He feels guilty about bringing her out to the ranch to live. He told me he knew she hated the country life but talked her into it, anyway."

Switch names, and it could be Lia and him. "They…couldn't work it out?"

"When the twins came, I was there for that, she couldn't seem to handle it and left. Anyway, I could do with your help getting them ready to train. Two of them are just colts. You interested?"

"I am." Mateo had provided the perfect opportunity to shift the conversation away from Hawk's break-up, but he couldn't shake off the prickles of dread. "Too bad about the way you're getting them. I guess it's different for every couple. Will and Krista are making a go of it."

"Krista's also got her family all around. Hawk's wife was here on her own. Added to her isolation."

Same with Lia. *Stop comparing. You're undermining all the good you two have built.* His phone chirped an incoming message. Lia with a "Yay!" emoji. Not the most personal, but who knows what she was busy doing.

He would send her a better video. "Hey, Mateo, I was wondering if you'd ride her."

"You sure?"

"Seems like the next step."

Brock let Mateo lead Persephone into the pen inside the arena, where there was less stimuli. And the sand made for a softer landing. Mateo led her around the pen an entire loop before he mounted her in one easy swing and got her moving right away. If anyone knew horses better than him, it was Mateo.

Brock set his phone to recording. So it was that he was looking at the screen as Mateo loped Persephone around the perimeter when two cats got into it, howling, and then tore across the pen, a ginger after a gray, leaping and falling in the sand.

There were no cats on the Jansson ranch.

Persephone twisted and reared, and Mateo held fast.

"Turn her," Brock called. "Get her up in the bit."

Mateo did just that, and Persephone fought, but eventually her head came down and she relaxed. But Brock could see her flanks heaving and the old scared look in her eyes.

He deleted the video. Mateo rode up and dismounted. "Not to worry," he said and handed Brock the reins. "Just a matter of time."

And place. Persephone struggled in new environments, but she had tried, trusting Brock. Lia was doing the same for the sake of their relationship and she seemed to want to do it. But he couldn't shake the gnawing inside him that he wanted what wouldn't make her happy.

BROCK HOLLOWAY WANTED HER. For the past week since their ride to the creek, Natalia sipped on that knowledge, refreshing herself as she ran nonstop from the shop to her place to Sadie and out to the ranch, where she caught only short snatches with Brock, never more than a quarter hour alone. Harvesting was in full swing on the ranch and Home & Holidays was preparing for its own.

And what an excellent harvest it would be. After which, she already had her answer prepared for Gina.

She popped her head inside the back office, where Sadie and Sophie, Bridget's seven-year-old daughter, were coloring paper jack-o-lanterns. They were part of a kit the store sold, and Natalia planned to display the girls' work as a sample of the craft. "How's it going here?"

"We're almost finished," Sadie reported.

"Two more to go," Sophie said. The girls were good friends, despite their age difference. Not that Sadie had shunned three-year-old Penny. She just reacted to whoever was around, like magnet to metal.

"Good. I'll be out front. Come get me when you're done. And remember Uncle Brock's coming to pick you up in an hour." One hour until she could sidle close to him, maybe hold his hand on the sly.

She reached the woodstove counter at

the same time that a girl entered. Two other women sat at the dining table, talking about how many pottery mugs they should buy. Otherwise, the store was quiet.

"Hello," Natalia said.

"Hi." The teenager was young and wore a T-shirt stretched tight over her pregnant middle. She looked familiar, and when she brought the bag with the Home & Holidays logo to the counter, it fell into place. The three girls had bought the baby quilt for her.

"Um, my sister gave me this as a gift. But I was wondering if I could return it."

Natalia peeked inside. Sure enough, Grace's stitching peeked out from the tissue wrap.

The door swung open. And there was Brock an hour early. Her heart skipped.

"Switching fields. I thought I'd pick Sadie up now."

"She's just in the back with Sophie. They're doing a little project. You can go there."

He looked from her to the girl and then to the back. "I can wait here a bit."

Looking for alone time with her? Natalia returned to the girl, eager to hurry her along.

"We only do returns with a receipt. Otherwise, it's an exchange only."

"It was a gift. I didn't get a receipt."

Natalia distinctly remembered enclosing a gift receipt. Either the girl was lying or her friends had forgotten to enclose it. "I'm sorry. That's all I can do. Was there a problem with it?"

"No, no. It's fine. It's just not..." What could the girl say? That it was the wrong color? That it didn't fit? "It's too much."

Ah. As the sister had suggested, and hadn't Natalia persuaded them otherwise? She withdrew the soft roll of material and spread it out on the counter. It was a wonderful piece, full of cheer and promise amid the symmetry.

The girl stared at the quilt, looking half-mesmerized herself. Then she shook herself free. "You can't make an exception?" She spoke softly, so the chatting women couldn't hear.

Natalia dropped her voice. "It's a choice between the quilt and money, right?"

The girl nodded. "I need diapers more."

At a shelf beside the stove counter, Brock was trying out a battery-powered lantern with a vanilla-scented candle. If he could hear their conversation, he wasn't letting on.

The women approached the woodstove checkout with six mugs and a vase of watery blues made by a local potter. Natalia packaged up their purchases, fielded questions about the store and its contents, and passed out business cards of the various crafters, all the while her mind on the quilt problem. The women left and quiet settled in again. She could hear Brock's boots tread on the wood floor as he moved through the kitchen section of the store with its bags of flour and jars of preserves and herbs grown and produced locally. From the back rose the singsong chatter of the girls.

One solution would help the girl and buy her a chain of quarter hours with Brock going forward. "What if you didn't have to choose?"

"What do you mean?"

"I'm short-staffed for the next month or so. What is your availability like?"

The girl spoke fast as if Natalia might retract her offer. "I go to school, but we get lots of Fridays off and I can come right after school. Tuesday and Thursday I have a spare in the morning, so I could come in early. But I can't go much beyond Thanksgiving." She indicated her baby bump.

"Perfect," Natalia said. "Can you start tomorrow?"

"But…but you don't even know my name."

Yes, hiring an unknown on the spot smacked

of recklessness. No, of seizing opportunity and promise. "Fair enough. What's your name?"

"Rebecca. Becca." She grinned. "And yes, I can start tomorrow. I'll be here right after school. And I can do the register. I've done that, and I'm really good at math. And I love this store."

"And I love that you can free up time for me." She looked over at Brock to telegraph who she intended to shower her extra time on.

He was watching her. It wasn't his usual soft and smiling gaze. It was sad. And regretful.

What had she done?

CHAPTER THIRTEEN

BROCK DIDN'T LOSE time bringing Sadie and Sophie over from the store to Penny's, the restaurant where Bridget was. He expected to see Sophie safely back and then head home with Sadie.

Bridget had different ideas. "Pull up a chair, fill your plate." She shooed the girls off to wash their hands and led Brock to a booth beside the plate glass window. He sat under the first *N* in *Penny's* stenciled across the glass.

"Start you off with a drink? Beer? Coffee?"

He craved a beer, but there'd be no alcohol content in his blood if Sadie was in the vehicle. "Root beer." He opened the menu. "What would you recommend?"

"I recommend you order the house special, because then you eat for free."

"I can't accept—"

"Of course, you will. It's the deal Natalia and I have. She provides childcare now and again, and I provide a meal."

"I'm not Natalia, and all I did was pick them up and walk them fifty yards."

The girls came skipping from the washroom and clambered into the booth opposite. "Are you having supper with us, Uncle Brock?"

"He sure is," Bridget said. "And if your auntie Lia comes along, she's also having roast beef supper."

And that was that. He texted Knut to say that he was eating in town. To which Knut replied, "Tell Lia to bring home the scraps."

He was assuming they were eating together, and an hour ago, coming into town, Brock had wanted that, too. A little quiet time with her, even if it was with two kids who chattered like irate squirrels.

But then he'd seen her operate in her store. Other times he'd come in, she was closing up or gathering up her stuff, or he swept in for Sadie and was out minutes later. Watching her in her element, he'd suddenly identified the gnawing inside him since the ride with Persephone. Guilt.

Bridget returned with drinks, slid the root beer to him and set water in front of the girls.

"Can we have milk instead?" Sadie asked.

"Eat your supper first."

Neither girl protested. A routine question with a routine answer. Natalia had built a support system that didn't require him.

"Scooch over," Bridget ordered, and the girls made room so she sat across from him. "I'm surprised you're not in the field."

"It's downtime while Mateo and Will move and clean equipment. I'm just running Sadie home and then I'll be back at it."

"Uncle and Auntie are very busy right now," Sadie explained to Bridget. "But once Thanksgiving is over, Auntie said there'll be changes."

What exactly had Sadie picked up on?

Bridget winked at Brock. "Oh?"

"Yes," Sadie said, knocking her ice cubes about with her straw. "First, Auntie Lia plans to stay here forever and not live in Calgary."

Bridget raised an eyebrow. "Is she now?" She glanced at Brock for confirmation.

Lia had said nothing to him, but she'd hired a girl on the spot to free her from the store to be with him, he was sure. A big mistake. "She'd be the one to talk to about that."

"It would be good news if it was true," Bridget said, rising. "Spirit Lake needs more enterprising people like her. I'll be back with your plates shortly."

Sadie leaned over the table, her knees on the booth cushions. "Auntie Lia told me today."

The choice he'd hoped for since the day she'd moved in, but that now depressed him. He had watched the way she interacted with the girl. Lia looked so much at peace, with a small, understanding smile for the girl that had broadened when the women came along with their purchases. She came alive in her store, in her creation. And he was expecting her if not to give it up, then make it a low priority.

And it wasn't just the store, he would be taking from Lia. She would give up her world traveling, confine herself to local jobs, play second fiddle to his dream of a horse therapy business. He told her there was nothing wrong with her and then he stood by while she upended her world to fit into his life.

And what could he offer her in exchange for her sacrifice? Half shares in a new horse operation. Land someone else gave him. Friends she could find anywhere. He could give her all the love she wanted, but not the life she needed.

"You know, Sadie, you don't need to be scared of Calgary. Lots of kids live there."

"But why go there when Auntie Lia wants to stay here?"

"I've been to Calgary," Sophie said. "It has a zoo."

"I don't need to live in Calgary to visit the zoo," Sadie said. "Right, Uncle Brock?"

"That's right, but you don't need to live at the ranch, either, to come visit it. You could live in Calgary and come up here whenever you want."

Sadie's eyes flicked back and forth. "But… but that's not the deal. You two are supposed to stay together."

If it wasn't so close to what Brock had envisioned himself and what he had just now rejected, he might not have answered so sharply. "Sadie, don't control other people's lives."

Her eyes widened and she slumped back into her seat, just as Bridget pulled up with the full plates. She gave both girls the mom's eye as she set down Sadie's plate.

"Eat, Sadie," Brock said. "Everything's going to be all right."

She didn't move but stared at him accusingly. "That's what you said after Dad died."

Bridget sorted out napkins and cutlery, keeping her mouth shut. That didn't mean she would later. A short line from Bridget to Krista to Will to the whole district.

"And everything did turn out."

"Not," Sadie said, "if I have to go live in the city. Even if it has a zoo."

She would get used to it, if need be. Just as he would have to. He wasn't about to let Lia give up who she was to satisfy the wants of Sadie or himself.

THE RANCH HOUSE was dark when Natalia slipped in, a half hour past Sadie's bedtime. Knut had nodded off in his chair, a sit-com blasting its laugh track, a photo album spread on his lap.

She tiptoed down the hallway, pausing outside Sadie's door at the sound of voices. For a hopeful second, she thought it was Brock. Instead, Sadie's tearful voice came drifting through.

"He said that I have to go to Calgary with Auntie Lia, and I don't want to go."

Rudy's staticky voice hemmed on the other end. "Well, you know, that seems odd. Your uncle doesn't strike me as a fellow to change his mind like that."

He didn't. Sadie had clearly misunderstood.

"But I heard him. Tonight, in the restaurant. I swear I'm telling the truth, Rudy."

"Oh, well now, let's see what tomorrow brings. Have you any plans?"

But Sadie was not to be deterred. "I'm going to be sad. Forever."

Natalia pushed open the door. Sadie had on her headphones, a death grip on the ammolite. "Hey, Sadie. Time for bed. Say goodnight to Rudy."

Sadie signed off, having her own agenda to pursue. "Auntie Lia, we're not going to Calgary, are we?"

Natalia lifted up the quilt for Sadie to slip under. "I have no plans whatsoever to take you to Calgary."

Sadie released a breath and her frown eased away. "But Uncle Brock said we had to go."

"Look, this sounds like some misunderstanding. How about I talk to him and we figure out what's going on?"

Natalia still didn't think there was a problem, when Brock returned with a full grain truck. She met him at the granaries, just as he switched on the auger to transfer the grain from the truck into the silo. It was pitch dark, except for the long headlight beams from the truck and a large halogen lamp overhead that cast a bluish light over the back end of the truck and Brock in his plaid jacket.

The auger roared like a turbine. Brock was bent over, watching, she supposed, the flow of grain from the trailer into the bin underneath before it blew into the auger. He started when she called his name and spun around. His face smoothed at the sight of her, though tension still hardened his jaw.

"Hello," she shouted.

He pointed to the front of the truck, where the din wasn't so intense.

Once there, she asked, "How's it going?"

"Good." He rubbed a hand down his face. "How can I help?"

That was…abrupt. As if she were a customer. "Uh, I settled Sadie down for bed."

Brock held up a finger, his ear cocked to the thunder of grain. He seemed reassured and turned back to her.

"She seems to think that I'm taking her to live in Calgary. Something you said?"

The headlights caught his features in a blinding glare. "Now's not a good time."

Okay, grain gushing out amid a decibel level that rivaled a rock concert had its drawbacks. But there hadn't been any good time in the past two weeks, and Sadie's worry mattered. The new relationship between her aunt and uncle mattered.

She'd wait for the unloading to finish. It only took minutes for the flow to slow and the auger to rattle the last grain into the towering metal storage bins. The silence after the noise was profound. She waited until Brock swung the bin out from underneath the truck before she advanced again. "I promised Sadie I'd ask."

Brock climbed a ladder attached to the truck box that rose above her like a building. From there, he said, "I told her she could move with you back to Calgary, if she wanted."

"But I'm not moving back to Calgary."

He climbed back down, his face hidden under his ball cap and the shadows of the night. "Why not?"

Because they were trying to build a life together.

"I don't understand. We agreed that Sadie would live here permanently, and I'm looking into ways to make that work."

"That's the problem," he muttered and edged past her to the truck cab. "I got to keep going. I have another load waiting."

He seemed to think their discussion was settled. "I'm coming."

Before he could stop her, she skirted around the hood, cutting through the glare of the headlights, and executed a near trapeze act to swing inside the cab. She'd never been so high up in a vehicle. Brock pulled the truck into gear and it rumbled forward. Natalia reached behind her shoulder for the seat belt.

"It's a lap belt," Brock said. "You'll have to dig it out. I don't think it's ever been used." He wasn't using his, but they were only crossing a field in the direction of some other field.

Brock drove as if he wore night vision goggles, the headlights pointing out tracks across a pasture of green-brown grass. The same one they had taken with the horses. The creek might be to their left, grain field straight ahead. The cab was warm and the light from the dashboard cast a soft glow. She might've relaxed into their cocoon, if it wasn't for the fact that they were teetering on an argument. They'd not disagreed, not really, since the day she'd come and misunderstood what he was about. She hoped that she was wrong again.

"What do you mean by 'That's the problem'? What's wrong with me trying something new?"

Brock hitched in his seat. "I saw you in the store today." He fell silent, and when she'd about resolved that he had nothing more to say, he abruptly added, "You've made something special there."

Carolyn had said much the same. "Thank you," she said cautiously.

"I see what you did there, and I see what you did with Knut's house and it's all good."

He paused again and she waited. "You're finished with the store. You can bring in new stuff for one holiday after another, but putting together the store itself, that making something from nothing, you're finished with that."

"That's why I'm looking for something new. That's why I'm out here with you."

"And then what?" he said. "You know how many times I've taken this path to the grain field? You know I've been hauling grain for Knut since I was eighteen? That's fifteen years. A different truck, but the wheels still turn and the path's not changed."

"I hadn't pictured myself driving a grain truck, to be honest."

"I know. You like new things, Lia. You have traveled to more countries than you can count. I guess what I'm saying is that you would get bored with life on the ranch, with small-town life. You live in Calgary, but I bet you go on trips three, four times a year."

He and Gina sounded alike. "Things change here. You get different horses, the seasons themselves mean new chores, new priorities."

"It sounds to me as if you're looking for a bright side among all the negatives." The truck strained at an uphill and Brock switched gears, the engine dipping into a steady grind. "I know you're trying, Lia. And…and if it was up to me, I'd… I'd have you here for always." She barely caught his words above the chugging motor, but she clung to them like Sadie to her necklace.

"Then…have a little faith. In me."

"I do, Lia. More than you know. I don't want you to become somebody you're not. And you're having to try hard, aren't you? You can get over your fears of bush and tight spots, but that doesn't mean you want to be around them."

"I want to be around you." She had a blazing insight. "This isn't about you not believing in us. It's about you not believing in yourself."

"Your turn to have faith in me. I do believe in myself. I know who I am and how I want to spend my days. And I think I know you. If you were given the choice, you wouldn't stay here. Am I right?"

He was trying to corner her. "I have a choice to be with you and Sadie or not. That's the choice I'm making."

"But it has to be a realistic one. Couples too far apart at the start don't just come together because they want to."

"Look at Will and Krista. They did."

"Look at—Others have bad endings. And what happens then to Sadie, when we don't make it?"

When, not if. He couldn't mean this. Not the Brock who'd stood at his sister's wedding and spoken words that had changed her own life. "That's not the way it works, remember? You said it yourself at Abby and Daniel's wedding."

He turned to her, frowning.

Of course. She'd never told him the impact of his speech. "At the wedding. You stood there and said to them, 'Love makes a home out of anywhere.' Those words, they changed my life right then and there, Brock."

An open gate appeared ahead and the truck bumped across the cattle gate pipes.

"I gave up my job and approached Gina. She

was my landlady then and she ran Home & Holidays out of her garage. I told her I could make it into a million-dollar business and I would do it under the slogan of Love Makes a Home Out of Anywhere. And I did, Brock. I did. Because I believed what you said.

"And now, now when it comes down to you and me, you're not following what you believe in. Make it come true for you and me."

Far off, the lights from two combines came into view as they rolled across the field. Brock steered the truck toward them.

"I'm sorry," he said. "I didn't know... When I saw that saying in the store, it sounded familiar, but I didn't make the connection. The thing is, I'm terrible with speeches. I remember watching YouTube and searching stuff up online."

He finally met her eyes. "Lia, that was just a saying I found somewhere."

She'd built her whole existence, the whole meaning of her life, on empty words. She looked away, out across the dark field and the bright lights on the massive machines ahead. She sat in the truck seat as the box filled with the harvest while Brock got out and talked with Mateo. Probably to avoid her. The return trip was silent, and when they arrived back in the yard and Brock had backed the truck up to the grain bin and shifted into Park, she reached across and set her hand on his arm. Hadn't he always said that she could cross the line over to him anytime?

"I love you, Brock."

He regarded her hand on his arm and then gently set it back on her lap. "I'm your trap, Lia. Run." He opened the truck door, swung down and slammed it shut, startling Natalia.

She shoved open her door and stumbled back to the house, back to her vehicle and back to her silent, dark home in town.

THE LAST DAY of combining fell on September twenty-first, and the following afternoon Brock and Mateo returned to their first love, horses.

Brock drove over to Mateo's the following afternoon in time to help him unload a bay colt into a pen near the arena. His first buy from Hawk.

He wished Lia were here so she could see for herself the fallout from a relationship broken by people too different for each other. Their communication since their own breakup ten days ago consisted of texts about who did what when with Sadie. It was inevitable, and he could only hope that they would recover. Or that she would. He'd go around with a life-long hole.

The colt shook himself out and scanned his new property. He locked onto the mares in the pasture and whinnied. Risky B raised her head from her grazing, observed the new-comer and returned to the grass.

"You got him for Risky B later on?"

"Tempting, but Haley would serve me divorce papers if I finally got our horse pregnant now that she's pulling in competition money. Besides, it's enough work to have Haley pregnant."

He remembered Haley from her first pregnancy. How he'd been all kinds of thankful that Mateo had turned up when he did, and had eventually become a father to Jonah, despite not sharing DNA. "She was pretty... intense for the first few months."

"I swear it's like she's possessed." Mateo straightened. "Speaking of which."

Haley was coming across the yard, carrying Jonah. Mateo moved to greet them. Jonah tilted into Mateo's arms automatically, and hands-free, Haley rubbed her rounding middle. When was she due? She gave him a sly grin. "You're scared of my bump again."

"I've got reason. You're growing a monster in there."

"Making a monster out of me."

She caught Brock sliding a look of recognition to Mateo. She swiveled to her husband. "For the love of Pete, you complained to him?"

"Not really. I don't mind what you're going through."

"Because you're not going through it!"

"Exactly."

Brock was prepared for Haley to completely lose it at her husband's callous remark, but then Mateo pulled up the hood of Jonah's jacket against the sharp fall breeze, and Haley gave a quiet smile of defeat. She turned to Brock. "Anyway, can you tell Natalia that I've got the pictures she wanted for Thanksgiving ready? I went to text her but I must have lost her phone contact. I'd call Dad for it, but it's just as easy to tell you."

He pulled out his phone. "Here, I'll give you her number."

"I don't have my phone with me. Can't you just tell her?"

"I'll text you her number."

"Suit yourself." She squinted at the bay. "So that's where the kids' college fund went."

"And how it'll get refilled," Mateo said. "This one has futurity potential."

Brock didn't know enough about the big equine leagues, but the colt was a beautiful animal.

"I'm hoping that Brock can fine-tune him a bit before I train him up. What do you think, Brock?"

This he could make a ruling on. "It won't take long before he knows who's boss."

Mateo grinned. "And if you can't show him, Natalia will. Right?"

He'd better nip this in the bud. "I'll be flying solo on this one. Lia's heading back to Calgary after Thanksgiving. For good."

Husband and wife exchanged looks. Mateo set Jonah on the ground and he beetled for the back of the open horse trailer.

"Crap," Mateo said, and it was a fact, given four hours of transport for the colt. Mateo handed Jonah a broom, took up a shovel and went to work. Haley set her hands on her hips, her middle thrust at Brock like a cannonball.

"What did you say to her?"

"Nothing."

"I can believe that. You have a habit of avoiding confrontation."

Brock wasn't sure how to answer that, so

he didn't. She shook her hands at him as if a bunch of spiders were crawling on them. "See what I mean?"

"I'm not avoiding anything. I just think that it's between her and me what was said or not said."

"Not when family is involved."

That was from left field. "Come on," she said, "if Knut figures you're his son, then that makes me your sister."

"Jonah's my nephew?" There, that should make her rethink the familial connection.

Haley didn't blink. "Sure, you're his uncle Brock. You excel in that role. So, what's the story? Because Natalia told Dad a couple of weeks back that she's planning to stay."

Brock wished she hadn't. Knut would be disappointed in him when he discovered the truth. If he hadn't already figured it out by her irregular absences.

"She'll be there for Sadie, and that's the important thing." They'd not yet had the difficult conversation about custody.

"But not for Dad or you."

"Look, we're from two different worlds. Did you know she'd been to no less than forty countries? And she and her partner plan to launch a couple of stores in Calgary and then

Vancouver, Toronto. That's her. She's not built like us. She was trying too hard for me. I couldn't let her do that."

"Wouldn't that be her choice?" Haley said. Lia's argument.

"No. I have to live with myself."

"More like by yourself."

"So be it."

"She'll always be in your life, because of Sadie."

"I can't give her the life she deserves. She made something out of her life. I'm basically a glorified hired hand with a few rodeo runner-up trophies who's got a little sideline fixing problem horses. I don't have your guys' ambition." He didn't mention Knut's offer of the two quarters, unsure if Knut had spoken to her about it. "And I'm okay with that."

"You're more than all that," Haley said quietly. "Maybe you got something you don't know about."

"What exactly would that be?"

"Listen, I just said you're family and you didn't include that in your little bio. You figure out you, bro." She turned to the trailer, where thumps and Jonah's high voice mixed with Mateo's low-pitched instructions.

"Here's a hint, unfolding right in front of you. Crap happens. But you don't have to shovel it alone."

CHAPTER FOURTEEN

NATALIA READIED HERSELF to leave town. She declined to place an offer on the lake house and gave her notice to vacate by the end of October. She informed a delighted Gina that she'd report for duty the Tuesday after the Thanksgiving long weekend. She'd also confirmed that she wouldn't be in Calgary for Thanksgiving. Gina had taken half a day to reply to that text and then it was with "Fair enough."

She hadn't told Sadie, other than saying that her work in Calgary would take her away for longer. It wasn't a lie, and she didn't have the strength for the full truth. Brock apparently hadn't said anything, either. Then again, he would avoid it.

He was working on a new horse at Mateo's, Sadie reported. The horse had just come today and he'd taken Sadie over to see it before dropping her off at Natalia's. On the nights before her days at school, Sadie now slept in the spare room of the lake house, and it was on one of those nights in late September that Natalia stepped onto the deck and drew her sweater coat tight against the chill of the air as it came across the dark lake. The waters swilled and slopped against the dock and rocks, set in motion by a trio of paddlers, their night lights and soft voices drifting over to her. A peaceful scene.

Would Daniel's last experience with water have been the same?

She shivered and stepped back inside, but a glance at the coffee table showed that Daniel was still with her. Sadie adhered to the weekly exchange of the urn, and this week it was Natalia's turn.

She dropped to the sofa. "I'm sorry, Daniel. It's been a crazy week. Sadie's adjusting to kindergarten just fine. No special friends, yet. But she comes back with all kinds of crafts and stories. She'll do fine, wherever she ends up."

Natalia drew breath. "But I'm going to have to deliver her some bad news. I'm... I'm going back to Calgary. Things...didn't work out between Brock and me." Natalia tried to laugh. "No surprise there, given my track record."

She pulled her knees up to her chin and set her forehead on them, bone pressed to bone. Her nose buried in the folds of her clothing, she drew in the woodsy scents of the store. Brock had joked that he could smell her a mile away.

"Besides, Gina has this great opportunity for me to open up more stores across the country. A career changer. Maybe Sadie could come with me from time to time. See a bit of the world. But I know that's not what you would want for her."

Natalia unfolded herself and touched the burnished edges of the urn caught under the warm glow of the lamplight. The urn was cold. As death itself.

She stood abruptly. There was no comfort to be found in what was no more than an object. Sadie could keep it. Time to move on. Throw a beautiful Thanksgiving for Sadie and her new family, and then clear out.

That reminded her… She moved to the ham radio. Rudy came on almost immediately.

"I don't have Sadie with me," Natalia rushed to explain. "It's just me."

"Just you is fine with me."

Her shoulders softened under Rudy's quiet, modulated tones coming through with the usual scratchiness over the air waves, just like when she visited with him as a child. "I'm throwing a bit of a Thanksgiving dinner this year, and I would love if you could come."

There was a long pause. "I'm not sure… That's usually reserved for family."

Natalia had somehow assumed that Rudy didn't have family close by. "I'm sorry. It is. You have family, then?"

There was another pause, this one not quite as long. "Not the Thanksgiving sort of family."

Rudy was intensely private, despite the years of connection. He had avoided talk of his family and had never volunteered where he lived. It had been an unspoken line never crossed. "Oh, well, the invitation is open. I mean, all these years and I don't even know where you live, so it might not be possible. But I'd be happy to pick you up at the airport."

"Thank you. I'll think about it."

"Sure, let me know. Only I'm keeping the possibility of your arrival as a surprise for Sadie."

"Not a word out of me."

"Okay, thanks." She hesitated. She had

nothing further to talk about with Rudy, but it seemed impolite to cut him off so quickly.

He came to the rescue. "Busy this time of year?"

"Yes." She described her dawn-to-dusk round of activities, skirting around any references to Brock.

"You sound exactly like the girl Daniel talked about," Rudy said.

Natalia had taken their conversation standing, since she anticipated it wouldn't last long. She sat on a chair.

"Daniel talked about me?"

"All the time," Rudy said. "You were like a news item with us. Sort of 'Today Natalia has arrived in Copenhagen or Moscow or what-have-you to take in the sights before moving on to her next destination.'"

"I didn't...know. We talked about where I was going and where I had been, but I thought it was just something to talk about."

"He kept a log of all the places you'd been and when. Did you find it among his stuff?"

He had cheered her when she escaped to a new life, and then recorded it, when she couldn't be bothered. "I didn't. Neighbors packed it up and had it shipped." She remembered the stack of boxes at the company warehouse. No more than a couple dozen.

"I got the sense he traveled along with you. He'd look up the places and shoot off facts about the rail system you used or the food they ate there. I kind of think he was doing it to psyche himself up for moving out of the cabin."

She was glad she was sitting. "Moving out?"

"He didn't talk to you about it?"

"No. Tell me."

"There was nothing written in stone, but he talked to me about leaving the cabin, coming into town so Sadie could have more... experiences. He worried Sadie could turn out like—" Rudy didn't finish.

"Me," Natalia said for him. "He worried that Sadie would turn out warped like me."

Rudy cleared his throat. "He thought Sadie was like you. Outgoing. He didn't want to make the same mistake as your parents and end up with his daughter running away."

The receiver shook in her hand. "I wouldn't want that, either."

"He was tired of trying to persuade you to come to him. He didn't blame you. Like volunteering to go to prison for you, he thought. So he decided to make the move."

Daniel had seen through all her delays and excuses and had planned to come to her instead. But that cruel river hadn't let him, had taken him forever into its clutches.

"I hate that piece of the world," Natalia said, her entire body shaking now. "I know he loved it, but I will forever hate it for taking him from me."

Rudy fell silent.

"I'm sorry. I came on strong."

"That's okay," he said softly. "I'm none too fond of that river myself right now, either."

She hitched out a laugh. "You're saying that Daniel wouldn't mind if Sadie traveled the world with me?"

"I think," Rudy said, "he already planned for that to happen."

BROCK EASED OUT of Sadie's room, leaving his phone open to Natalia's number on her bedside table. Although Lia no longer slept at the ranch, Sadie had not wanted to return to Brock's quarters, preferring the comforts of her own room. She had struck a deal with her aunt that she could call her anytime if she woke in the night.

The phone was the only way Natalia could speak to Sadie tonight, anyway. She was spending the weekend in Calgary. Sadie said she was "run off her feet" getting Thanksgiving ready for the Spirit Lake store and another one in Calgary. To him, Natalia had only said that she would pick Sadie up Monday at six thirty.

In the kitchen, the coffeepot dribbled out its contents. Knut sat in the living room, Pike dozing at his feet. A while back, Knut had hauled the photo albums from his bedroom out to the living room. He'd set up a table in the corner and taken over the computer to upload pictures. The area with its one-of-a-kind memorabilia was strictly off-limits to Sadie.

Brock filled two cups and brought them to Knut on the couch. He sat beside him. "How goes the battle?"

"Oh, I start off every day with big plans and then get bogged down. Miranda kept saying she needed to organize them, but, well... now it's on me." Knut fell back against the cushions. "It wouldn't be so hard if I didn't have to look at them."

"Brings back memories?"

"Right. The ordinary ones hit the hardest. Like this one."

Miranda in the garden, digging up potatoes in an old jacket shirt and rubber boots. She looked peeved. He spotted another figure in the far background, carrying away a metal pail. "Hey, that's me. I think I remember that day. The crops were under water and the garden was mud."

"That's right. Felt like lifting a concrete block with every step." Knut paused. "You think the grandkids want to hear about that?"

"Sadie would listen." Brock caught himself. He'd included Sadie as Knut's grandkid, all but admitting that Knut was like a father to him. He didn't seem to notice as he pivoted his phone screen to Brock. It was a pic of Sadie planting marigolds.

"See there? I remember, Sadie had come up with a plan to get you and Natalia together."

"I know… I overheard."

"Did you now?"

"I was coming around the side of the house…and, well, I told Natalia. We…played along. For a while. And then for a time, we weren't playing. For a while it seemed real enough."

"I take it something has changed again."

"It has, I guess. We get along, but, well… there's nothing between us now."

Brock expected Knut to give him the gears the way Haley had. After all, Knut had been co-matchmaker. Instead, he picked up a picture. "Another one of Miranda," he muttered. "You know, I took all these pictures because if she was in the picture, my life was explained. I knew what was happening, where."

He sat back, his hands wrapped around the steaming mug. "There's not a day that goes by I don't miss her. Sometimes it's just a twinge, like arthritis. Lately with all these pictures, it gets so I can hardly move."

Brock thought of Lia gone. Not in Calgary, not on the other side of the world. Gone. "I'm sorry to hear that."

Knut shrugged. "Is what it is. At least these pictures prove I've done all the important things. Had a family, built something to pass on to them. I could die tomorrow and it wouldn't matter."

"It would matter."

"It shouldn't. Not if I've done it right."

Brock wasn't prepared for a world without his second father. He gestured to the muddle of albums and boxes. "Clean up this mess first."

Knut grinned. "I guess I'm not going anywhere soon." He squinted at another picture, and sighed. "But this is the start, what I'm doing here. Letting go…of things, people, feelings. Grudges, disappointments…those are the hardest, let me tell you. Let it all go until you've shrunk down to nothing."

"That's kinda depressing, Knut."

"No, all in good time. Depressing is when it happens before it should."

Brock bowed his head. Miranda's sudden death had hit home for him, too. You couldn't meet her without feeling thankful for having known her. "I miss her, too."

Knut frowned. "I wasn't talking about her. I meant you, Brock."

He took up the picture of Miranda in the potato patch. "We all come to nothing in the end. But think that at your time in life and it'll make for thin memories."

"Is this about Lia and me?" Brock said.

Knut lifted his cup of coffee. "It always was, my boy."

"THERE'S ONE!" Sadie pointed here and there to keep up with the fitful aerial acrobatics of a blue morpho butterfly. Natalia had combined a delivery run from the Calgary warehouse with a side trip to the city zoo. If she intended to take Daniel at his word, then she might as well get started.

Sophie's suggestion of the Butterfly Gardens to Sadie had proved a good one. The temperature outside hovered at freezing, but inside the Gardens, temperatures and humidity approximated the tropics. "And there's another one!" Sadie said. "Wait! There are birds! What's that one called?"

Natalia consulted the nearby display, but Sadie flitted to the next thing. "Take my picture and send it to Uncle Brock, okay?"

"You need to stand still for that to happen." She captured Sadie leaning against the railing, an ibis and a camouflaged turtle in the background.

She typed in the caption, Sadie at the zoo. Wasn't that obvious? She backspaced and entered, Find the turtle. Before she could question her ploy to engage him, she sent the message and hurried after Sadie as she ricocheted from one railing to another, following the erratic paths of the butterflies and birds.

They thwacked through the soft plastic panels to emerge from the tropical biome, and cool air enveloped them. "Where to now?"

"Where else is there to go?"

Natalia consulted the map. "The Canadian exhibit. Animals from Canada. Like the owl, moose, bison."

"I've seen all those in the wild." Right. She'd had these as backyard animals. Sadie had not left Alberta but was better traveled than many.

"Would you like to give it a skip, then?"

She didn't, but as they passed from one pen to the other, her step slowed. At the exhibit of the three bison, Sadie wrapped her fingers around the square wire fencing. "I saw more than that where I lived with Dad."

"You might have seen the same ones I saw when I lived there."

Natalia meant it as a joke, but Sadie nodded. "They looked old. And they just stood there, but they weren't trapped, like these ones."

"Maybe they don't want to move."

"But if you're not moving and you're a human, you're—" Sadie thumbed a smooth wire "—dead."

Natalia wasn't sure how to navigate this weighty question about what constituted life. "Some people like the zoo animals have a small range. Others have a much larger one. Your mom…she had a small one. Your dad had a small one, too, though he thought about making it larger. And me, I've always had a really large one. Humans can pick their ranges."

Sadie gave a slow, thinking nod.

"What size of range would you pick, Sadie?"

"When I'm with you, it's big. And with Uncle Brock, it's small. And when you're together, it doesn't matter."

The last option wouldn't happen. It was two weeks to the day that Brock broke what had barely started. Neither of them had mustered the courage to tell Sadie. Natalia had hoped that her niece's dream would simply fade away. But it was unfair to let Sadie keep believing the impossible. Mara had counseled her to pull the bandage off quickly, but gently. Was that possible?

She dropped into a squat beside Sadie. "You want Uncle Brock and me to marry, the way your parents did. Am I right?"

Sadie thumbed the wire and nodded. "Knut, too."

"Well, your uncle Brock and I tried to be together, but in the end we couldn't make it happen."

Natalia let that soak in for Sadie, readying

for her teary blast. Instead, she blinked and nodded. "Okay."

"We both care for you and we'll work together to make sure that you have everything you want."

"Okay."

This quiet defeat wasn't Sadie, not the little butterfly from just a half hour ago. "Do you have any questions?"

"Who am I going to live with?"

"We thought it should be your uncle Brock. I'm moving back to Calgary to open up new stores, and Carolyn will take over the Spirit Lake store. Is that okay?"

"But…how will you be able to take care of me, if you're not around?"

"I'll be around. I'm only two hours away. Remember when you called me all those months ago and I came right up. That'll stay the same."

She nodded and thumbed the wire over and over.

How to restore her bubbly Sadie? "I was talking with Rudy the other night and he told me a secret I can share with you. He said that your dad was thinking of moving nearer to me, so you could see things like the zoo. And me. You here today, that's like a wish come true for him." Sadie just stared through the wire at the old, tired bison.

"I was thinking that we could keep the dream alive. You and I could do some traveling together. There are lots of parks and fun places for kids in the world."

Sadie whispered, "Sophie said that there's a big mall in Edmonton that has lots of slides."

Slides, rushing water, watery dunks. Sadie's swimming lessons were paying off. "There is. We could stay in a hotel room together. They have theme rooms. Space or an igloo or an old-time stagecoach or others. We can go online and make a plan."

"But… Uncle Brock won't be with us."

For his niece, he might, but that wasn't the safe bet. "No guarantees."

Sadie finally pulled her gaze away from the bison and turned to Natalia. She fumbled at the back of her neck. Before Natalia fully understood, she had lifted the ammolite necklace over her head and held it out. "Here, you can have it back."

Natalia's once favorite possession sat in a small silver pool in Sadie's palm. "But it's yours. What about the magic?"

Sadie took Natalia's hand and laid the necklace on it. "Auntie Lia, it doesn't work any-more." She started down the path. "Can we go home now?"

CHAPTER FIFTEEN

ONCE AGAIN, Brock held a check, feeling as if he didn't deserve it.

"I'd like to split this with you," Brock said to Natalia at his quiet place at the back of the barn. He'd told her that Persephone was leaving today, and she'd shown up. Rested her cheek against the mare's neck and whispered that she didn't need to be afraid of anything anymore. He ached to wrap Natalia in his arms and tell her the same.

She didn't even read the amount it was for. "I thought you asked me here to talk about Sadie. You know I won't take a cent. It was never about the money. At least, for me."

"It's about you, Lia. I couldn't have done it without you, and splitting the money is my way of acknowledging that."

"You would've found someone else. Keep the money. I don't want it."

Or need it. He folded the check and slipped it into his pocket. "Sadie said you had fun at the zoo." He hadn't gotten much more than a mention of butterflies and bison, but he didn't press her.

"I told her that we weren't ever getting together."

That would explain the silence. "I guess I could've told her." He paused. "Thanks. It couldn't have been easy."

"It wasn't." She picked up a large corn broom and began sweeping as if determined to wear a hole through the floor. Pike stretched and joined her, pawing at straw and dirt. "Did the social worker call you?"

"No." He pulled out his phone. "There's a missed call from the government."

"That's probably her. She wants to confirm the meeting for later in October where we present our plan."

"Joint custody, right?"

"Yes. I told her that was the general plan, but then she asked if we'd worked out specific arrangements. Who gets Sadie when, child support, medical and educational support, emergency planning if something should happen to either one of us."

He'd not given it a thought. "I doubt even biological parents have all that worked out. Abby and Daniel probably didn't."

"Abby, no, but Daniel—Daniel, it turned out, had roughed out some plans."

She spoke with determined brightness. "I spoke to Rudy last week, and apparently Daniel was thinking about selling the property and coming to live closer to me."

It made sense. "But...when did he tell Rudy this?"

"Sometime during the winter, I think. It sounded as if he was planning to tell me when I arrived back from Amsterdam."

"He didn't mind that you traveled a lot?"

"That seemed to be part of the plan. He was worried that Sadie might end up...stuck. He could see that she was like me...more extroverted."

It took a couple of breaths to steady himself, but he finally got it out. "You think it best if you get full custody, then?"

Natalia stopped sweeping. "How did you make that leap?"

"If that's what Daniel wanted, then I guess we should honor his wishes."

"You would let Sadie go based on hearsay about what Daniel wanted?"

"Not let her go, exactly—"

"Then what, Brock? You've made it clear

you don't want me in your life, but Sadie? You giving up your claim on her, too?"

How close they'd once been to not having this conversation. To filling a quarter hour with kisses. "I'm trying to do the right thing here."

"Then be in her life. I don't want to raise her alone, even if we're doing it from two different places."

The same triumph and relief coursed through him as if he'd planted a landing off a bucking horse. "All right, then."

She resumed her brisk sweeping. "I'm bringing this up because I was wondering if this agreement we'd take to the judge could include her traveling with me now and again."

"I'm fine with that."

"Say, if I were to take her to Vancouver?"

That was a short one-hour-plus flight there. "Sounds okay."

"Texas?"

"Some pretty country down there. I have some contacts from when I lived there years ago."

He could go along with them, too. Make it a family holiday of sorts. But he didn't trust himself not to angle for something more. Having her in this barn had him fighting the urge. With a sinking heart, he realized that he probably always would want more. He would always have to fight his heart with her.

"St. Petersburg?"

"Uh…that's unexpected."

She tapped the broom to shed the clingy bits. "Not right away. In a few years from now. My family's ancestors come from there."

"All right," he said. Nothing to worry about. His head was already spinning.

"Only…"

"Only what?" She was scanning the barn, and he knew for what. He reversed the wheelbarrow out of the back stall, loaded on a shovel and rolled it over to her, the loose shovel rattling against the metal bottom of the barrow. He waited until he'd parked it alongside her before continuing.

"Only…if it's as you say that we have to decide for Sadie, then I don't want her traveling so much she gets to hate change, like Abby did."

There, he'd said it. She cracked a small smile. "That's what you're for. To bring her balance. To be her anchor. I'd like to show her the world, but your home will always be her home."

"Well, my home thanks to Knut."

She stripped off her gloves. "You would think that people are nice to you out of the goodness of their hearts. Did you ever think that maybe, just maybe, people are willing to twist themselves into pretzels for the chance to have you in their lives?"

He loaded his shovel. "I'd say that they don't know me well enough."

She leaned her broom on the wheelbarrow and slapped dust off her jeans. "I don't think you know you well enough."

She exited, her boots rapping on the floor. Haley had also accused him of not knowing himself. But the fact of the matter was he knew himself only too well. He was only as good as the people around him believed him to be.

THANKSGIVING SATURDAY AND the store was a zoo. Natalia had scheduled for all hands on deck, including Becca. And then a half hour after opening, she'd emerged from the washroom with a stunned expression to say that she thought she might be going into labor. Carolyn called in a friend to function as a warm body. It didn't help that Natalia had decided last week to change the grand opening into a grand sale.

Everything was at least 50 percent off or more. Carolyn had cautiously questioned her about the markdown, but stock needed clearing in order to make room for Christmas items. Also, the faster the evidence of Thanksgiving, with all her ruined hopes, vanished, the better.

She still had to survive a full-scale Thanksgiving Day in the presence of the one who had rejected her love.

"All this," Carolyn said, setting a shawl, a baby quilt and jars of jam on the woodstove counter, "is for my lovely friend." A very useful friend who had used her Facebook page to let her few hundred friends know about the sale. A few hundred avid shoppers.

And they all seemed to have descended at once. Natalia eyed a woman holding place mats and glancing about in search of assistance.

"How about I leave you to ring this through," Natalia said to Carolyn, "and I'll see how I can be of help?"

Natalia glided into the thick of people. A quick head count revealed that they were only three under maximum capacity. She touched the elbow of the woman with place mats. "How may I help you?"

"Oh, do you have a matching runner?"

On her office desk. She'd set it aside for Thanksgiving dinner, along with place mats, the second the loom weaver had brought in the goods more than a month ago, during those brief days when Brock seemed to want her.

"I'm sorry, no."

The woman groaned. "I guess I've left it too late. I'm trying to impress my mother-in-law. I've been married six months and the wedding didn't go off exactly the way she wanted, and so I'm trying again with Thanksgiving. She suggested that I couldn't pull it off, and now I'm proving her right."

As if a runner would make or break an event. Why, then, was she hoarding what essentially amounted to a strip of cloth? What did it matter, when the entire Thanksgiving dinner was a staged event for someone else's family and her niece, who was already disappointed in her? "You know, let me check overstock."

"And place mats. I need one more."

Right. She retrieved the items from her office and hurried back to happy gasps and effusive thanks from the newlywed as she headed to the counter with her purchases.

Natalia did another head count. At capacity. She eyed someone with full arms. "Is there anything I can help you with?"

"Could you set these aside for me? I'd like to take a closer look at the shawls."

"Of course." She weaved her way to the front and set three candles, a lantern and a goblet inside the oven. "We're at capacity for the fire code," she whispered to Carolyn.

"That's good, isn't it?" Carolyn said.

So long as no one did a live demonstration of the candles. Then in walked Brock with Sadie, Haley with Jonah and a tall, blonde woman whose focus immediately went to the wall display of Grace's quilt. Natalia realized that the quilt maker was viewing her creation. To draw interest in the store and to provide emotional support to Becca, Natalia had arranged with Grace to raffle off an autumn-themed quilt with all proceeds going to the pregnancy centre.

Obligation required her to greet Grace, but Haley had joined her sister, and together they gazed at the quilt like two ordinary shoppers. Let them be. She would not look at Brock.

"What do you think?" The woman she was helping had tried on the largest shawl, the one

Sadie and Sophie often tucked themselves under when crafting.

"The colors look great on you," Natalia said, and the woman beamed. Another satisfied customer. And another memory of her time here slipped into a bag and carried away.

It was all being carried away. The little candles Sadie had learned to count by, the milk stools Sadie had rocked on, the pillows she'd napped on. Natalia would be so thankful when Thanksgiving was over.

A tap on her waist. Sadie. "It's all squishy in here today."

"I know. It's the grand opening and there's a sale on. How are you?"

"I'm okay." Okay was the only feeling that Sadie admitted to since the day at the zoo two weeks ago. Even when she looked ready to cry.

Brock, his broad shoulders and his gender out of place in her store, wove around a clutch of moms and teenage daughters to stand close. Because of the crush of shoppers, of course. "I...uh, came by to see if you needed any help."

"Do you know how to work Square?"

"I don't even understand what you just said."

"Then I'm good."

His eyes rested on hers, began to soften. He blinked. "Okay."

"We're going to Penny's for lunch," Sadie said. "We can save you a seat."

"I wish I could, but we are short-staffed, as it is." And it would mean sitting at the same table as Brock. Dinner tomorrow would be awkward enough.

From across the store, Haley waved and pointed to the door. *Thank you, Haley.*

Sadie took Brock's hand automatically and crossed to rejoin Haley and Jonah. Grace waved them on, not budging from her spot before the quilt.

Even as Natalia and Carolyn served another half-dozen customers, Grace stayed fixedly before the Thanksgiving quilt of a giant maple leaf, stitched in reds, yellows, browns with flashes of purples and greens. During a break, Natalia eased beside Grace. "We're on target to sell out today."

Grace's eyes widened. "That's a thousand tickets. At twenty bucks a pop."

"You've made new moms, new families very thankful."

"It wasn't me. It was you."

Natalia shrugged. "Let's say it was both of us."

They both gazed at Grace's creation. The millions of stitches, the sharp corners, the scraps of cloth pressed and folded into a large work of unique art. "Someone will have a very memorable Thanksgiving," Natalia offered.

"I've worked on that quilt every Thanksgiving since Mom died," Grace said. "Can you believe I actually thought I could get it done in time for the first Thanksgiving? I got the points on the leaf completed. That was it. Each year, I did a little more, and finally ten years later, you gave me the push to get it over the finish line."

"I'm glad I was of help."

Grace gave a wry smile. "Now there's nothing for me to do except show up for Thanksgiving dinner."

"You've made your dad happy."

"Yeah, but…" She turned to Natalia. "I hate Thanksgiving."

Perhaps because Grace's words reflected so much of what Natalia felt, her response came quick. "Me, too."

The two women stared at each other. Grace mirrored Natalia's own sad, bitter memories

suppressed under the pall of forced grateful-
ness. Then as one, they burst into laughter.

"Thanksgiving," Grace said through a broad
smile, "was the first holiday after Mom died.
Haley burned the turkey and undercooked the
potatoes. The only edible thing was the can
of cranberry jelly."

"Thanksgiving," Natalia said, tears of laughter clouding her vision, "was the first holiday
after I left home at seventeen. I spent it alone
in my room while my supposed best friend
went with his mom and dad to his grandpar-
ents. I ate a chocolate bar from the conve-
nience store."

Grace wagged her finger. "Oh man, you
had it worse, girl."

"I win!" Natalia said. "My prize is to organize Thanksgiving for the Jansson family."

"And you have to eat with us. At least Haley's
not cooking."

They giggled and snorted together like
old friends. Grace sighed. "Man, that felt
good." She gazed around, her eyes coming
to rest on a stack of signs. The one item that
wasn't selling. "'Love makes a home out of
anywhere.'" She turned to Natalia and side-
mouthed, "People actually buy that crap?"

Natalia flushed. Yes, she had bought that

crap. Built a life around it. All the laughter inside her was sucked away.

Grace didn't seem to notice that Natalia had frozen up. "Love has got nothing to do with it." She poked Natalia in the shoulder. "It's you. You make a home out of anywhere."

She lifted her arms. "Look at this place. Look at Dad's house."

She dropped her arms. "It's all you, girl." She waggled her fingers. "See you later."

Natalia watched her pass by the front window display on the way to lunch with her sister and nephew, and Sadie and Brock, a small smile playing on her lips. She couldn't know that she'd completely upended Natalia's life.

Fire.

THE SINGLE WORD texted by Mateo had Brock pushing his chair back from his breakfast and breaking for the door. "Fire over at Mateo and Haley's," he said to Knut. "You got Sadie."

Knut went wide-eyed, then nodded.

Brock tore up the Pavlic driveway and sighted smoke coming from the arena. Inside, Mateo stood in front of a stack of bales, holding a fire extinguisher, at the straw smoking away, white foam over the mess.

"I think I got it under control," Mateo said.

The half-dozen horses in the stalls didn't seem to believe him, but snorted and stamped. "They're all riled up."

"We'll get them sorted," Brock said. "Maybe we should take the bales out, split them apart in case of hot spots."

Mateo gave a shaky breath. "Yeah, you're right." Yet he stood there. Brock had never seen his neighbor this rattled. Check, he'd never seen him rattled at all.

"I'll get the tractor. The front-end loader still on it?"

"Uh…yeah." Mateo pointed the extinguisher at the bales, as if the stack might make a sudden move.

Once the smoldering hay was dumped near a horse trough, they scattered the hay, stamping out anything that glowed or smoked.

The quiet teamwork seemed to loosen Mateo's tension. He stole a sheepish look at Brock. "I suppose I could've handled it myself, in the end. But, you know…fire."

"I don't blame you," Brock said. "We all want to remember this Thanksgiving as a happy one."

Mateo threw a shovelful of dirt on a smoking pile. "You're right there. Wasn't thinking about that. I saw fire and I immediately called you like a kid calling for his mom."

"Not Haley?"

"Didn't even cross my mind. I don't want her near fire." He gave another sheepish grin. "Also, I was too scared she'd tear a strip off me." He sobered. "She's my wife and I love her to bits, but in times like this when you can barely think straight, then you need someone like you."

Brock kicked at a lump of straw. Sparks flew and immediately blinked out. "Someone always around, not going anywhere."

"No. Not that. I mean, a year ago we didn't know each other. But Knut liked you and Haley treated you like a permanent fixture at the ranch. And Will thought well of you. I figured I might as well get to know you myself. But I had a hard go with that."

"I dunno, I'm pretty much an open book."

Mateo laughed. "Right. Like whatever's going on between you and Natalia. Haley and Grace were up half the night trying to figure that one out."

"I told her. We're not compatible."

"No, there's something going on there that the girls can't figure out. Neither can Will nor me."

"My ears should've burned right off my head with all the gossip, I guess." Brock felt a spark of annoyance, as sharp as the ones at his feet. Today was going to be hard enough without undergoing the constant scrutiny of folks disappointed he'd broken things off with Natalia, even though they hadn't dated. Except they had lived together and cared for a child together and supported each other through thick and thin.

Except that he couldn't stop thinking about her. *No, face it.* He couldn't stop loving her.

Mateo scooped a bucket of water from the trough and poured it on the straw. "I feel kind of bad. I might have given you the impression that you're just an employee. And maybe in the beginning you were one, but I've come to count on you for more than that, and I never made that clear. And I should have."

The man must be still in shock to lay on such an unnecessary apology. "I haven't brought much to the operation. You and Will have put in the capital and the vision and taken all the risk. I show up just like you say, to work."

Mateo set down his bucket. "Then why didn't I call Will today? His horses are in there, too. He's just as close."

The patch of burnt and steaming hay at their feet hissed and gurgled. "I don't know."

"Because yeah, Will and I built all this and we got the ideas and we got the money and the contacts to make it happen, but you're... well, you're Haley's brother, which makes you more than an employee to me. I'm not going to embarrass us with a bro show here. All I know is when I felt it all falling apart, I turned to you to put it back together."

"You would have found someone else." He stopped. Weren't those the exact same words that Natalia had told him when he thanked her for her work with Persephone? He denied it then, told her she was special, but he hadn't convinced her. And why should she believe him when he hadn't tried to find a place for her here with him?

"The point is," Mateo said, "I didn't have to. You were there for me. That's got to count for something."

Exactly what he should have told Natalia. She'd transformed her life based on his kitschy saying, but she had believed in what he said and then, over the summer, in him. And he'd chased her off.

"I mean it," Mateo said. "I mean it so much I'd like to offer you a partnership."

"Okay, you need to cool it, Mateo. You talked to Haley about this? Will?"

"Back during harvest, when you ran the truck for both of us, we all talked about it. I'm floating the idea with you now."

A partnership, even a minority one, would give him additional financial stability to provide a comfortable life for Sadie. But it would also chain him to the ranch. Even more now that he had accepted Knut's offer of the two quarters. He didn't want any more ties, unless it was on a long-term basis to a certain bright-haired dream maker.

"I'm not sure I'm your man," Brock said. Mateo grimaced, but before he could protest, Brock added, "I'll talk to Natalia first."

CHAPTER SIXTEEN

NATALIA OPENED THE door to Home & Holidays at the Lake at quarter to seven on Thanksgiving Monday morning. It was cold and dark inside and out. She had come to fill the shelves and tidy the store before Carolyn arrived at ten to run the show. Carolyn's friend had offered to help with customers, now that Becca was a weary but proud mama of a baby girl. She'd sent Natalia a picture of the newborn wrapped in the ladybug quilt.

She flipped on lights to a store nearly as empty as when she started so many months ago. She had better get busy with restocking. As she removed her wrap, it caught on the corner of the wood plaque. *Love makes a home out of anywhere.* Not according to Grace.

Her casual confidence in Natalia had rattled around in her head as she had padded around the lake house last night, packing.

Grace had made it feel as if Natalia held the

power to bring it all together. That she could wield her own magic over Brock's heart and make him love her so much that he'd join her to build a home together.

She didn't. Wishful thinking.

Anyway, it wasn't as if she had made a home. She'd renovated a couple of bedrooms, cooked a few meals. Her greatest accomplishment had been helping Sadie feel at home. Yes, then, partly true.

But she'd also taken the magic out of Sadie's life. The necklace remained in the side pocket of Natalia's purse. She couldn't bring herself to wear it, nor could she bear not to have it with her.

Natalia righted the board on top of the stack, adjusted the sale sign. For the next hour, she emptied boxes from the overstock, but the dresser in the bedroom section remained empty. Wait, didn't Carolyn mention that Gina had sent up Christmas stock? Never too early to showcase the next major holiday.

She discovered more than Christmas stock. Behind the boxes was a stack from a moving company. Daniel's belongings. They must've been sent up by mistake, or Gina got tired of looking at them. Natalia lifted away a few, like dismantling a wall, to uncover a total of a dozen boxes.

They couldn't stay here. She'd ask Knut for storage space, until she had time to sort through them.

One box caught her eye, much smaller than the others, with bold packing stripes of orange, purple and yellow. She tipped the box to read the top. On a rectangle of red construction paper, her first name was printed in block letters. The last three letters were oversized, Daniel's trademark styling for all his correspondence to her. He must have planned to send this box, but then the river had stolen him.

She carried it to her desk and slit it open. A stack of scrapbooks, lined notebooks with stuffed pockets. A note on a lined sheet rested on top.

Hi Lia,
I thought you might like a record of all the places you've gone to date. I apologize if I got a little bit too much of me in there. I guess it's my way of making sure you don't forget me when you're thousands of miles away.

See you soon.
Love,
Daniel

The records of her travels that Rudy had mentioned. She opened the first book. A binder with soft rings and inserts and loose-leaf papers. *Amsterdam* stretched across the front and underneath a glued picture of one of the canals. A little project of Sadie's. And then a note on March 27 *Natalia departs for Amsterdam. Plans to visit tulip gardens, the Rijksmuseum, Stedelijk Museum and a flea market?*

She had been haggling for an antique music box for Sadie at a Dutch market when the Canadian embassy in Amsterdam had called.

Natalia flipped the page to an insert. Sadie had painted a woman with an owlish face with trees in the background. Also, a figure in pink, drawn like an X with a dot on top. Beside the pink, a large X in blue, and another in green with a floating brown hat. Natalia had seen enough of Sadie's drawings over the months to recognize herself, Daniel and Brock. On the backside, Daniel had written: *Family portrait as interpreted by Sadie Garin.*

Natalia closed that scrapbook and opened more. Had he kept logs of her every trip?

She peered at the first picture. Her, waving in front of the Greyhound bound for Edmonton. Daniel had taken it on his new smartphone. She'd not had one then.

There was his wedding photo, different from the side-by-side one he'd sent to her. This one was closer, from the waist up, their foreheads together in an intimate heart shape.

Underneath was his printing on a lined sheet.

Wedding day. I told Abby about the way you looked at Brock. The same way I catch her looking at me. Funny, she said. She'd caught Brock looking at you the same way. We joked about setting you and Brock up for a blind date.

But then we decided that if you two were meant to be together, it'll be some force greater than us that'll make it happen.

Yeah, their deaths. No, Sadie.

Natalia scanned the page again, locking onto the one line. *Funny... Brock looking at you the same way.*

Brock had fastened his dark, melting-heart eyes on her right from the start.

He'd not pursued her then and had pushed her away now. He said there was nothing wrong with her but then called her love for him a mistake. The two didn't sync. If she was whole and good, then her love for him wasn't wrong, either. And neither was he, if only he'd believe himself good enough for it.

Time to make the next biggest move of her life.

She piled Daniel's books back into the box and taped it shut, the screech of the packing tape dispenser harsh and decisive in the quiet.

Thanksgiving would have to wait. She had more important things to do right now.

"WHERE'S AUNTIE LIA?"

Sadie fired her question from where she sat on the front porch stairs. Grace had directed Brock there when he came in from morning chores. "I can't budge her," she said. "She's keeping vigil."

"I guess, she'll be along shortly." He'd checked the time on his phone so often that he already knew that Natalia was running twenty minutes behind schedule. She always phoned if she was delayed, so Sadie didn't freak.

"Can I call her?"

"I'm sure she's busy."

"She always takes my calls."

True. Natalia's lateness didn't sit right with him, either. Something was wrong. He handed over the phone.

He could hear the rings, each buzz stinging his nerves. The sixth ring was cut off with Natalia's soft greeting.

"Auntie Lia. Are you okay?"

From the way Sadie's eyebrows eased back into straight lines, Natalia was. And apologizing, too, based on Sadie's muttered "It's okay."

"When are you going to be here?"

The straightforward question produced a long answer from Natalia that had Sadie's face flicking through a half-dozen expressions, ending on dismay. "But you'll miss Thanksgiving."

What? Sadie listened as Natalia continued. She thrust the phone up at Brock. "She wants to talk to you. Make her come home, okay?"

Come home, which meant she was heading in the opposite direction. "Hey there."

"I've upset Sadie." He could hear the hollowness of her words on hands-free. She was on the road.

"Everything's okay," he said, mostly because he wanted it to be.

"Everything will be okay," she modified. "I'm heading to Calgary. An emergency has come up, but I still plan to be back in time for dinner."

"What happened?" In another life, he wouldn't have considered it his business, but things had changed since this morning.

She paused. "I'll tell you about it later today. Maybe after dinner."

"But aren't you in charge of making it?"

"I am, but I already called Mateo, and he'll handle the turkey. You can see that I got the store dining table delivered already. As for the rest, there are enough of you to make it work. Just keep Haley out of it."

He turned from Sadie to look through the front window. Knut and Grace were staring bleakly at a mound of potatoes. "Dinner is planned for two. And the district hayride happens right after, at four thirty."

"I'll be back. And if I'm not, I'll let you know, and you guys can start without me."

"That's not going to go down well. For Sadie." He stared down at his sock feet. "Or me."

"Can I talk to Sadie again?"

Whatever Lia said to reassure Sadie didn't seem to work because she sat hunched after the call.

"We were going to make dinner together," she whispered. "We had the whole day planned. Setting the table, cooking, decorating. It was supposed to be a beautiful day."

Sadie turned red, a sign of crying ahead. This time about a disaster that hadn't happened and therefore could be prevented.

"I've set tables before," he assured her. "How hard can it be?"

"But it was with special plates with leaves on them, and heavy silver forks, and we made a centerpiece with pictures of all of us and everything."

"I'm sure we can figure that out."

"But everything's at Auntie Lia's place."

He withdrew his keys and separated out a bright yellow house key. "Again, that's not a problem."

"YOU CAN'T QUIT on me now."

Gina spoke as if they were meeting in the warehouse office, and not in Gina's kitchen, the smell of homemade apple pie infusing the air.

Natalia clattered dirty baking implements

into the sink. "I'm not quitting, and I'm certainly not quitting on you, Gina."

"Saying you're not going to Vancouver or Toronto or anywhere unless Sadie and that man come with you sounds as if you're quitting, because you know as well as me that mountains will crumble before he steps off that farm."

Natalia had expected Gina's resistance, but not her hurt. Gina wore no makeup and was wearing a gray T-shirt and black leggings, the complete opposite of their usual festive attire. Their traditional outfits combined Thanksgiving and upcoming Halloween in garish shades of fall.

"You don't know him," Natalia said. "He's flexible. He does things for other people. Maybe too much, but that's him."

"Then it's hardly fair to drag him around the country to suit yourself." She slipped a wine bottle off the rack on the kitchen counter. "You want a glass?"

"No. I'll be back on the road soon."

Gina applied the corkscrew to the bottle. An expensive red, the same kind they drank every Thanksgiving, just the two of them. Two unmarried female CEOs with nowhere to go. "Right. Back to the traditional dinner with all the folks at home."

"Come," Natalia said. "Ride with me or follow me up."

Gina glugged wine in her glass and took a big gulp. "I can't drink and drive."

A deliberate rejection of Natalia's invitation. "Gina, you're creating your own misery."

"And you're not helping. You plan to leave me high and dry."

Natalia had expected to talk to the rational Gina. Instead, amid wine and apple pie, her boss sounded distraught.

"Remember you came to me with absolutely nothing? I took a chance on you."

Natalia pointed out the kitchen window to where the garage still stood, home now to Gina's high five-figure, fully loaded vehicle. "Remember how we operated out of that garage and used my commissions to pay your mortgage? We took a chance on each other."

Gina took another gulp of wine. "Fine. We needed each other. And now apparently, you don't need me. You're moving on to your new family."

New family. If Gina had been Sadie, Natalia wouldn't have hesitated to cross over and gather her partner in her arms. But Gina in her hurt held herself like a pole. "I didn't know you thought of us as family," Natalia said.

"What of living under the same roof and working together and sharing holidays doesn't make us family? Do we have to call each other sisters or mother and daughter to make it real?"

"I didn't know."

"You could've brought your niece here, for all I cared. The place could've done with a little noise. Instead, you moved in with that man."

"His name is Brock Holloway. And you know that I didn't move in with him in the usual way. The house belongs to Knut."

Gina set down her wineglass and picked up a pastry brush. "And you made yourself at home."

"Because—" Natalia stopped. She had not risked missing Thanksgiving at the ranch to fight with Gina. "I guess I didn't think I had the right to call you family. I spent years before then drifting from place to place, sometimes from couch to couch. I have always felt indebted to you. Daniel was my brother, but we hadn't stood in the same room since his wedding almost eight years ago. I guess I felt so grateful to you for what you had given me that I didn't think it could be anything more."

Gina opened the oven door to twin apple pies, bubbling away. "But that's not how it works." She brushed buttery milk onto the goldening crusts.

"Why are you baking pies?" Natalia said.

"Because that's what I do on Thanksgiving."

"But you'll eat them alone."

"Not if you stay."

"And not," Natalia said, "if you brought them with you." She paused and then said what clearly needed to be said. "I'd like my families to meet."

Gina straightened from her work at the hot oven. Her cheeks were red, maybe from the heat or the wine or from the unshed tears. "I'm family now?"

"Sister or mother. Which would you like to be?"

"Sister, since I don't have one of those. Also, we can get into scraps as a matter of course." She stripped off her apron and tossed it to Natalia. "Take the pies out of the oven in twenty minutes. I'm slipping into something so bright it'll blind everyone."

"But what about my idea?"

"We'll discuss it over dinner. All of us."

CHAPTER SEVENTEEN

SHORTLY BEFORE ONE in the afternoon, Brock caught Sadie at the table, a silver fork suspended in her hand, her gaze once again drifting to the front windows.

"Here, how about you let me finish up here?"

Sadie relinquished the fine cutlery and draped herself over the back of the couch to keep watch for Lia.

"You have to fold the napkins like envelopes before slipping in the cutlery," Grace said over the whine of the hand blender as she made mashed potatoes.

Brock wished he could be shoveling out stalls right now. Grace had already given him the gears about not having a runner, which, she had to explain to him, was a long decorative cloth that ran down the table. "But we're going to pull them open and wipe grease off with them."

Beside her sister, Haley wrinkled her face.

"Remind me not to look at you while I'm eating. It's hard enough to keep food down."

"You're six months pregnant, and still puking," Grace said. "What's your problem?"

Brock had learned on day one with the Janssons that constant squabbling defined the sisters' relationship. He kept his head down and concerned himself with the intricacies of napkin folding.

"Gee, I guess I'm having a baby with your attitude," Haley said. "And must you drink wine right in front of me? You're supposed to be sensitive to my needs."

"Get used to it," Grace said, deliberately swilling her wine under Haley's nose. "Mateo has his way, you'll turn into a milk-feeding, baby-making machine until you hit menopause."

As he tossed salad at the counter, Mateo looked pointedly down at where his wife stood. "Bare feet and in the kitchen, too. Got her right where I want."

Grace narrowed her eyes at him, and Mateo grinned right back. He had once confided to Brock that Grace appreciated a little toe-to-toe exchange. Brock preferred to dodge the elder sister. Haley was chili powder; Grace was the entire jalapeño pepper.

The jalapeño turned to him. "Here, let me help you." She came over and slipped the napkin from his hand. "There's not a piece of cloth I can't bend to my will."

Fingers that had constructed a couple dozen quilts flew over the napkin as she glanced over at Sadie, her little head angled to see as far as possible up the road. "Is Natalia coming or not?" Grace whispered.

"She's coming. She'll text otherwise."

"You don't think she bailed?"

"No. She won't disappoint Sadie. She won't."

"She doesn't show, Sadie won't be the only one disappointed."

"You mean me?"

"I mean everyone under this roof. None of us wants to see our big brother stood up, even if it's by someone I like. Did I tell you she and I both hate Thanksgiving?"

"She doesn't hate Thanksgiving," Brock said automatically. "She planned all this."

"The things we do for the people we love," Grace said, "make liars of us all."

Liars. Natalia hadn't lied to him ever. But she had organized a family dinner around a holiday she secretly detested. For Sadie's sake.

And for him. She'd been willing to give up her life to be with him. He'd given in to his old, baseless feelings of worthlessness and rejected her gift of love. He stood to lose his chance at happiness for himself and those he loved, if he didn't set things right with Natalia.

"Somebody's here!"

Sadie's announcement had all heads turning to the front window. The newcomer, carrying a liquor bottle in a brown bag, approached the door.

"Do you know this guy?" Haley said.

"He's bringing alcohol," Grace said, heading for the front door. "Let's welcome him with open arms."

Sadie identified the well-dressed senior when he answered Grace's greeting in a quiet, rumbly voice. "Rudy!"

She bounced off the couch and straight for Rudy. Grace rescued the bottle before Sadie wrapped her arms around her old friend. He lifted Sadie right into his arms, though Brock knew from personal experience that she was a fair weight now. "There's my girl. I had a picture in my mind of how you looked, but you're even prettier."

"It's because I look like Auntie Lia. She's the prettiest of them all."

Rudy looked at everyone in the living room

and open kitchen. "Where is your aunt? She's the one who invited me."

Brock didn't allow even the slightest hesitation among the group. "We're expecting her at any moment."

Then, as if he and Natalia had orchestrated the entire entry, she drove up and parked in her spot in the carport.

She was here for Thanksgiving. It was on him to make it one to celebrate.

BETWEEN THE RUSH of introductions of Rudy and Gina, and the last-minute flurry of setting extra plates, filling bowls and glasses, Brock didn't get a chance to talk to Natalia.

Natalia solved the problem of the missing runner. "We'll use this." She brought out the long board with the familiar *Love Makes a Home Out of Anywhere*. Brock cringed at the reminder of how he'd mishandled her confession of the impact those careless words had made on her life.

But the saying was now different. *Love* had been crossed out, the lines new and harsh across the four letters, and replaced with a fully capitalized *WE*. *Makes* had been modified to *made*. And there were slash marks through the beginning letters of the last word, leaving only *here*.

"'We made a home out of here,'" Haley read. She shrugged. "Works for me. Let's set the veggies on it."

Natalia had her eyes on him. A tentative smile touched her lips. She was offering up a testimony to the good thing that had happened between them during this past season or two.

"Couldn't have said it—" he began but was interrupted by Grace drumming a bottle opener on the roaster lid.

"All right, everyone to your places."

That was much like pushing a dozen head of cattle down a chute. The group rushed, hesitated, shuffled or, in the case of Knut and Gina, parked themselves and waited for the dust to settle. Brock confined Pike to the mudroom and rushed back, only to have Grace snag the seat next to Natalia at the foot of the table and he was obliged to sit to Grace's left, straight across from Lia.

"Finally," Haley said, "let's eat." She reached for the mashed potatoes but was cut short by Knut.

"Not yet," he said. "Remember we go around the table and say what we're thankful for. And then when we're all done, Sadie will say grace and then we eat."

Haley turned to Jonah on his booster seat between his parents. "Tell your granddad how you will scream nonstop if subjected to this torture."

"It's not torture. It's self-discipline," Grace said. "I'll start. I'm grateful to Rudy for bringing wine. And to Natalia for showing up. You have no idea how grateful I am." She patted Natalia's arm. "Your turn."

Natalia opened her mouth, but Knut interrupted again. "It has to go in the other direction. Clockwise. Otherwise, we're unwinding time, bad luck."

"Natalia is clockwise."

"My clockwise."

"That's superstitious," Haley said.

"It's also," her father said, "Brock's turn."

It was a weird kind of muscle memory that had him on his feet holding his wineglass, as if making a toast. The last toast he'd made was at Abby's wedding when he'd brought up the "love and home" line. But somehow, here in this home with these people and this woman, the occasion deserved to have him standing.

"I am grateful for everyone here at this

table that I've known for almost half my life or—" he nodded to Gina "—almost a half hour. I am grateful for the opportunities given to me by Knut and Mateo, two men that are like father and brother."

"Hallelujah," Haley said. "He's finally admitted it."

Brock let it flow. "And to my sisters, then, Haley and Grace, who scare me to death. I owe them my continued existence."

Mateo laughed, in complete comprehension.

"But the woman I am most grateful for is Lia." She blushed, ducked her head. He turned to Sadie kneeling on her seat beside Lia, her face bright with excitement. To her, he continued, "I met your aunt at your parents' wedding. It was a tiny wedding, not many more people there than are here today. So, she was hard not to notice. But I think that if there had been as many as say were at the zoo, I would have still spotted her."

"Because of the hair," Sadie explained.

"No, it was because I was meant for her."

Natalia raised her head, set her light brown eyes on him, and he didn't hold back. "I didn't know it then. I only saw a beautiful woman who traveled, took risks and came out on top.

It never occurred to me that she would ever be part of my life. I was just a cowboy with an old truck. We had nothing in common.

"And then…there was your dad's accident."

Everyone's head dipped at the table, except for Natalia, who turned to Sadie and rubbed her back. Sadie gave her a brave smile and turned back to Brock.

"Suddenly you were what we had in common. She and I had different ideas about how to raise you, but I like to think that we got that sorted, and along the way, I got to know your aunt well enough to know that, well… we still had nothing else in common."

"Horses. You both like horses," Sadie said.

"Horses, yeah."

"And fixing up bedrooms."

"There's that."

"And fishing."

"Yeah," Brock said, "maybe there are a few things. The point is, she's still the same beautiful, successful woman I can't keep my eyes off. It's me that's changed. It's me that's figured out that I might not deserve her, but I deserve the right to become that man. I have no idea how that's going to work, but we all know that I'm not the planner of the two. All

I'm grateful for, Sadie, is that I've got the chance and this time I'm not letting it go."

He stopped. Sadie shook Natalia's arm. "Tell him. Tell Uncle Brock you'll marry him."

Natalia pushed back her chair to stand.

"Sit," Knut said. "The both of you. We're not changing direction."

His daughters squawked, but Knut didn't cave. There was a sparkle in his eye. The old matchmaker was drawing out the drama. Brock sat.

Beside him, Haley said, "I'm grateful for food and family. Mateo?"

"You forgot Jonah," Knut said.

"He's eighteen months."

"He can talk."

"Fine. Jonah, who are you grateful for? Mom—" Haley held out an orange slice "—or Dad?"

Jonah swept the orange slice from Haley's hand. "Dad."

"He was merely repeating the last word spoken," Haley protested amid laughter, but the answer was good enough for Mateo to take his turn. He made a show of standing like Brock as if to make a speech.

"Don't you dare," Haley and Grace said together. Haley snatched up the open wine bottle. "I'll feed our unborn baby the entire bottle, I swear."

Mateo smiled softly at her. "No, you won't."

Haley took a firmer grip on the bottle. "Watch me."

Mateo kissed his wife on the lips, and Brock thought, *I want that for Lia and me.* He stole a look at Natalia, but she was playing with Daniel's bracelet. "I'm grateful to my wife," Mateo said, "for delivering me a healthy family now and to come."

Grace reached past Brock, her hair nearly up his nose, to poke Haley in the arm. "I told you from now to menopause."

"Well, I'm not standing, but I am going to make a little speech," Knut said. "As you know, I decided to sort through old photos this past summer. Some of them ended on the table here." All heads turned to the centerpiece Brock had taken from Natalia's earlier that day. Among autumnal garlands of leaves and grain stalks she had planted framed pictures—Brock on Persephone, Sadie and Pike rolling together, Haley and Grace in a rare pose of linked arms, Miranda and Knut laughing together, and Natalia smiling from a selfie. "Most of the sorting I did was with myself. My memories, my mistakes, my successes. My two greatest ones are sitting at this table." He raised his glass to his girls seated on either side of Brock. "Somehow with their mother's hard work, God's intervention and my dumb luck, I got two beautiful, intelligent, good-hearted, honest daughters I'm proud to share with the world."

Haley and Grace squirmed and twitched, their earlier high spirits subdued under their dad's declaration.

"This is where," Brock said to them, "you say 'thank you.'"

Unbelievably, they did. "And between them is the man who just gave me the great gift of calling me 'like a father.' Circumstances being what they are, he and I will always be 'like father and son.' Not the real thing, but that never matters where it counts. Right, Mateo?"

Knut's son-in-law stroked Jonah's hair. "Right, Pops."

The group turned to the simple live picture of Jonah clamping his hands over Mateo's and pulling it down to the food tray, the better to wrestle with. "I'll finish up here," Knut said. "I'm grateful now and to the end of my days for the people at this table." He dipped his head to Gina and Rudy. "May we all find love and happiness."

"I already have," Haley said, setting her hand over the big and little ones on the tray.

Brock spoke quickly before he could stop himself. "Me, too."

He looked across to Lia and she gave him a quiet, mysterious smile he had no idea how to interpret. Neither, it seemed, did Sadie, who turned to Gina. "Your turn. Hurry, please."

"I'm grateful to Natalia. I'm not telling you all the reasons, I don't know any of you, and it's none of your business. But I'm grateful she gave me the chance to share the best apple pie you'll ever eat."

"Your turn, Rudy," Sadie said. "And then it's mine."

"I better not keep you waiting, then," the ham operator said. "I'm grateful to Natalia, too, for inviting me here to be with you, and to my host, Knut, for welcoming me, and to Sadie. For keeping me company when I was lonely."

It had been just as much the opposite, and Sadie must've known it because she reached her arms up to Rudy and said, "Me, too."

Sadie settled herself back in her seat. "And now it's Auntie Lia's turn."

"Yours first," Natalia said.

"But I just did with Rudy—Oh, never mind. I'm grateful to everybody and everything. Okay, now it's your turn."

Yes! And because whatever Lia said would decide his future, it was his turn again.

NATALIA WAS ACCUSTOMED to a room of people focused on her. She had given sales pitches at trade shows, employee pep talks and presentations to loan officers. Once in a Tokyo hair salon, she'd become the centerpiece for the hairstylists as they cooed and debated over her red and wavy hair.

Both nothing compared to this small gathering of people she loved and who loved her back. It was this last realization—the force of their love—that scared her.

And gave her the strength to rise to her feet, and face the man who had declared his rightful place in her life, no matter what.

"I don't think we've had the chance to say 'hello' today…so, hello."

"Hello," he said, his eyes the same dizzying, stomach-flipping, warm lights as always. "Glad you are here."

"Me, too," she whispered and then gathered herself to speak louder. "You should know that I don't have a plan for us. Like Knut and his pictures, I had memories to sort through. Of Daniel, of choices and places. And of you. I made an impression on you at our siblings' wedding, but you—you changed the course of my life with your words. And then you told me that they were someone else's words, that they meant nothing to you. That crushed me. I felt as if everything I had believed in was nothing, because you didn't believe in it, too."

Natalia braced for the rush of pain that always rose when she thought of what happened in the dusty and dark cab of the grain truck. This time though, there was just quiet ease and the abiding hold of his eyes on her.

"But you know, I discovered that sometimes we speak the truth even when we don't believe it, because we want it to be true. How many times did we tell Sadie that everything was okay when we were pretty sure it wasn't?" He winced, nodded.

"The thing is, Brock, in wanting it to be true, we made it true. We believed in making a home for Sadie. That was an easy enough truth to say. But we also wanted a home for you and me. And we got that, too. Here, if Knut will have us."

"I will," Knut affirmed.

"Or wherever else we are. I made the mistake of thinking I needed to find a way to fit in on the ranch to be with you, the way we fixed Persephone. Except, well, you're right. I don't need fixing. Neither does Sadie. Nor you. You don't have to become 'that man' for me. You already are. And I would be most grateful now and forever if you would accept me for yourself as 'that woman.'"

She stopped, drew breath, waited.

For the first time since she started speaking, Brock looked away from her. He turned to Grace. "Get out of my seat, sis."

THE SPACE ON the bale beside Natalia stayed empty, even as people piled on and arranged themselves on the stacks, toddlers and babies dropped into a straw-padded play area in the center walled off by bales.

Even Sadie avoided the space occupied by Natalia's plaid scarf. She clambered about, trying this spot or the other. Rudy and Gina opened a space between them to accommodate Sadie. Gina had a glow about her in the final hours of daylight that Natalia had never seen before.

"Is this seat taken?" Brock spoke from the ground, gesturing to the plaid scarf.

She set the scarf about her shoulders. "Yes, by you."

He handed a squirming Pike up to her, and then in an easy lift and swing, he sat down beside her, filling the empty space and her heart. He glanced about. "Where's Sadie? Oh…there."

He bent his head to hers. "Did you see the way Rudy and Gina have been looking at each other?"

"You noticed, too?"

She and Brock had become their siblings when they'd talked about them on their wedding day. She hadn't time to tell him about Daniel's logs or what had gone on today. They hadn't had any time alone, even for a kiss.

"I hope they don't take eight years to act on it," she added.

Brock drew his gaze back to her face. Her lips. "Speaking of which—"

"Brock, here?"

He kissed her, not long but long enough to fill her with the urge to pull him off the hay wagon and take them to a private spot. To maybe exchange more than words of love.

"I'm not waiting for a quarter hour with you ever again," he said.

Will flicked the reins over the horse team,

and the wagon rolled slowly forward. They grabbed for Pike's scruff at the same time.

"I might walk alongside. Safer for the dog, I think," Brock said. "Want to join me?" After a quick glance at Sadie still sandwiched between Gina and Rudy, she nodded. Brock hopped off with Pike and she followed, Brock steadying her. He settled his arm around her shoulders and she wrapped her arm around his waist, solid and warm.

"Perfect fit," he said softly.

They walked together in the stubble from the grain harvest, Pike sniffing in all directions. Shouts and chatter rose up from the wagon and the low talk of the adults walking beside them. But for the moment it was just the two of them.

No time like the present. "Brock, I lied."

"Oh?"

"I do have a plan."

"Different from the ones talked about at dinner?" True to her word, Gina had launched into a discussion about what Natalia and therefore Brock could do together. Mateo had pitched his hope that Brock would become a partner, and Gina had countered with hers of travel. As the levels in the bowls lowered and plates and glasses were emptied and refilled, proposals were presented, hashed over, countered. Natalia and Brock had quietly eaten, with their feet, hidden from the others, entwined.

"Yes, or maybe, it's all of them."

"All ears."

"There's another frontier of retail that Home & Holidays hasn't launched. Online. We have a platform for distributors but nothing for ordinary customers."

"For that shopper in India who wants a Grace Jansson quilt?"

"Or that shopper in Calgary who wants a sari from a weaver in India."

Brock's arm tightened its hold. "That involves traveling."

"Eventually, but it can all start from any place with internet."

"Like the ranch?"

Natalia rested her head on his shoulder. "Like the ranch."

"Will you have any time to help out with any sad horses that come my way?"

"All the time in the world."

They crunched on the straw stubble, steps matching. Pike fell into step beside them. "When is all this happening?" he asked.

"Not until the New Year. There's another project to complete first."

"Oh?"

"It involves a wedding, not a big one but soon, after the holidays, late January. It'll be out at the ranch."

"The barn," Brock said. "Right up the center aisle. Set up chairs and string decorations across, hang them from the stalls."

"That'll work. Sadie could be the ring bearer. And the bride could come down escorted by Gina."

"And if Haley and Grace are the bridesmaids, Mateo and Will could be the groomsmen."

"My thoughts exactly. And afterward, a catered lunch in the house."

"A lunch, not a dinner?"

"The bride and groom have a plane to catch."

"Great! Where to?"

"Wherever the bride and groom decide."

He pressed a hand between her shoulders to bring her around to face him. "And who are the bride and groom?"

Natalia said through her blush, "I haven't figured that out yet. Who would you suggest?"

"Huh." He pulled her into his arms, his face

close as if he was about to kiss her. "Lia, you know I love you more than horses and good company. Will you make us the bride and groom in our plan?"

She brought her lips to his and breathed the one true word that would bring them together as husband and wife on a frosty day in the New Year, date to be announced.

EPILOGUE

BROCK AND NATALIA married on a cold January Saturday in the Jansson barn with family and friends and six horses as witnesses. They departed for a two-week honeymoon in the Caribbean, returned to pick up Sadie, before heading to southeast Asia to source suppliers for the Home & Holidays online store. Photos and videos of them amid temples and crowded markets drifted back to Knut which he faithfully downloaded onto his computer.

One night, while he and Pike were dozing in the living room, there was a thump of vehicle doors, and then Sadie burst in. "Knut! Uncle Brock wants to know if you got the coffee on."

Around the dining table Knut asked, "Are you staying this time?"

Natalia wrapped Knut into a tight hug. "For as long as you need us."

"Don't promise that," he said gruffly, "or

you'll never get the chance to step foot off the property again."

She did, of course. And so did her husband and niece. Sometimes it was only for a few hours to attend a horse sale or take a calf to the vet or pick up product in Calgary.

Sometimes it lasted much longer, like when the newlyweds with Sadie in tow traveled to Peru in search of alpaca yarn, and for Brock and Natalia together to conduct a workshop on calming spooked horses.

On these longer trips, Daniel also came along. The urn made for interesting discussions at border crossings, and unusual decor in hotel rooms but his presence pleased Sadie and Natalia, and for that alone, Brock would have continued to haul around the ashes of his brother-in-law.

"When are you two settling down?" Mateo asked upon their return from a jaunt through Spain in July.

"Your days of picking up the slack around here are winding down," Brock said. "Lia wants to stay and redecorate her old room." He took his wife's hand. "Back into a nursery."

That September, the three of them made

one more, shorter trip with Daniel. Brock told Lia that they didn't have to do this.

"I know," she said. "But Daniel only wanted to leave for Sadie's sake. I think we should let him go home now. Home to Abby."

Brock squatted before Sadie, just as he had more than a year ago at the foster home. Except this time, she sat on the Jansson ranch couch and he had to lift his gaze a couple of inches to account for her growth. "You're okay with this?"

She nodded. "You're coming too, right?"

That was never in question. He stood beside Lia and Sadie on the bank of the Peace River at the spot where it was speculated Daniel had fallen in. The land and cabin had been sold, but the present owners had granted them access. He held Sadie's hand, and Lia held the urn in both hands, her attention fixed on the wide flowing river.

"You okay?" he asked her softly.

She looked up at him. He expected to see anger, grief, guilt. Instead, she smiled. "I'm okay."

She was, too. The trees were brilliant autumnal shades and The Peace flowed wide and blue. The scenery was stunning, as fine as any she had seen in the world. She could see it through Daniel's eyes now, and not through the lens of a bitter, lonely girl. Thanks to the man beside her.

"Do you remember," Natalia said to Sadie, "how I showed you this river on the map?"

Sadie wrapped her hand around the ammolite at her throat. "The Peace goes to the Slave River and then the Mackenzie River and ends up in the Arctic Ocean, and the Arctic circles around to the Pacific and Atlantic."

"Which means what?"

"Daddy will be joined to the world."

Yes, to the beach in Lima where they'd splashed about months ago or the Vancouver inlet where the new Home & Holiday shop would open for Thanksgiving.

She opened the urn and took out the tightly sealed plastic bag. "Would you like to help me, Sadie?"

Pressing herself against Brock's leg, Sadie shook her head.

Natalia untied the bag and poured the contents into a bowl lined with alpaca yarn, a pink cowboy boot tassel and horse hair and then set it onto last Thanksgiving's table runner. She had pulled it out of storage last week and while the chiseling had turned gray, the words were still clear: *We made a home out of here.*

She set the bowl on the board. "Brock and I will take good care of your daughter." She laid her hand on her swelling middle. "And your niece or nephew. See you somewhere else, Daniel."

She carried the precious load down to where the water had carved a curve in the bank and launched the little vessel. As if the river were waiting for Daniel, the current instantly swept it away.

"Goodbye, Daddy," Sadie called and waved.

Lia rejoined her family on the bank, and Brock drew her against him. They stood together, watching and dreaming, at peace.

* * * * *